Freefall

Genevieve Mckay

Chapter One

"Mama, look at the whales!"

I glanced up from my phone, pausing the horse archery video I'd been watching for the millionth time, to see a tiny, blonde-haired girl in pigtails throw herself at the ferry railing.

Her purple running shoes scrabbled against the metal grating as she shimmied upwards, not stopping until she'd laid her belly precariously over the top rail, hands stretching out toward the ocean.

"Callie, no!" Her mother appeared from nowhere, pale-faced, eyes wide with panic. She grabbed a handful of the girl's pink jacket by the scruff and jerked backward, giving her daughter a final shake like a cat might do a naughty kitten. "Get down right now."

"But I want to see the *whaaales*," the little girl said, clinging determinedly to the railing with the tips of all ten fingers.

Not releasing her own death-grip, the mother cautiously peered overboard at the dark, churning water below. Instantly, her face softened. "Orcas," she said, "a whole pod of them. They must be hunting salmon."

She deposited her daughter safely on the deck and turned, her gaze seeking out another girl, this one tall and dark-haired, maybe twelve or thirteen years old. "Come see them, Nor-Nor," she called, "they're beautiful."

The girl sat hunched a few feet away on the same cold metal bench as I was. It was actually a storage locker for lifeboats, but it also served as a sheltered place to sit huddled for protection against the constant wind. She sat with her back pressed against the cold metal hull of the ferry, her knees up near her chest, chin tucked into her jacket.

"I told you not to call me that, *mother*," she said scathingly, rolling her eyes but not looking up from her phone.

I stood up slowly and stretched to get the kinks out, stuffing my phone into my pocket and moving toward the rail. Growing up near the ocean, I'd seen hundreds of whales over the years, but the sight never got old; there was something magical and otherworldly about them.

The salty wind grabbed at my hair and I held the curls back off my face with difficulty, squinting into the setting sun glare on the water. It had taken Allan and me all day to make the long drive down to the Island from my aunt's ranch where I'd lived all winter, and we'd been lucky to make such an early ferry. At least now we'd get the horses safely to Hilary's farm before dark.

"There," said an older man with a beard, pointing off the starboard stern. And there they were, a lithe group of cetaceans gliding through the ocean, their knife-straight dorsal fins splitting up through the waves, glistening backs arching out of the water and then sliding back down again into the depths, only to rise up again a moment later.

"Ooh," someone said as a particularly big one poked its shiny black nose straight up in the air, rotating in place so its white underbelly was clearly visible. It fixed one rolling eye on the ferry briefly before sliding back down again.

It lasted only a few minutes. The ocean churned and boiled where the whales had been, and then gradually settled back down again, smoothing over like nothing had happened. The people who had gathered at the rail to watch sighed collectively and, when there was no reappearance, began drifting back to wherever they'd come from.

"Mama, when I grow up I want to live in the ocean, can I?"

"Um, sure," her mother said, laughing, "maybe you can invent the first underwater house to live in. Like a reverse aquarium. Instead of you watching the fish, they'll be swimming by watching you."

She looked up and caught me staring, and sent me an easy smile, rolling her eyes toward her younger daughter as if to say, *aren't kids ridiculous?*

I smiled politely before turning my gaze back to the water. I wondered if *my* mom and I had ever ridden the ferry together like this before she died. Did she have to chase around after me, too, curbing my enthusiasm for the world? There was no time before this last year that I remembered being a happy and spontaneous type of person. But I'd changed at the ranch and I felt more free and comfortable in my own skin than I ever had before. I just hoped it would last.

I frowned, looking down at the frothing white wake that bubbled up from under the ferry like uncorked champagne.

There was a rustle of movement beside me; the older

daughter had followed me to the rail and now stood a few feet away, glaring grimly out at the ocean as if it had somehow offended her.

She felt my gaze and turned, raising an eyebrow as she scanned me from top to bottom dismissively. When she reached my paddock boots she froze, eyes fluttering wide and her lip curling in what could have been a smile but was probably more of a sneer.

I looked down, hoping my boots weren't plastered with manure or anything but they were fine; just dusty, maybe.

"Oh, did you find another horse girl to hang out with, Nor-Nor?" her mother said, beaming as she strode over with the smaller girl in tow. "We can always spot horse people a mile away, can't we? I think we saw your horse trailer downstairs."

"*Seriously*," the girl said, her face tight with anger, "I told you that if you called me that ridiculous nickname *one more time—*"

"Almost ready, Astrid?" Allan, the transporter bringing the horses and me to the Island, appeared beside me, nodding at the little family. "We're getting close. I want to get downstairs to the truck before they announce that we're ready to dock. I'd like to beat the stampede."

I sent the mom an apologetic smile and followed Allan inside and down the stairs, through the cafeteria area and down more stairs to the dimly-lit car deck below. It stank like exhaust, diesel fuel, and ocean brine. Technically, they didn't want you down here before it was time to leave, but there was nobody to stop us, and we threaded our way past the empty parked cars to the big truck and trailer that held all my worldly possessions.

"Hi, everyone," I said, stepping up onto the running board to peer inside, "Did you have a nice rest?"

The only sound was contented chewing. The horses didn't know they were suspended in a tin can over six hundred feet of rolling ocean. They just knew they were in their comfy, familiar trailer with their friends and plenty of snacks. They trusted us to take care of everything else.

I reached inside to scratch Red gently behind his ear in the spot he liked best and then moved on to peek in at the others.

Possum was my favourite next to Red; she was a cream-coloured buckskin mare with cute, black-tipped ears and an alert, friendly expression. Rob was lucky he was getting to work with her.

I wasn't so sure about his other project, though. The solid black gelding, Maverick, was a four-year-old out of Aunt Lillian's stallion, Doc, but he was nothing like his easy-going dad or sweeter half-sister. It wasn't that he was spooky or mean; he just didn't seem to like being around people very much. He was grudgingly obedient, but he didn't like to be fussed over and he wrinkled his nose in disgust at every treat offered to him.

Hilary's project, Ellie, was a long-legged Palomino with a golden mane that hung about a foot down her shoulder. I thought she'd make a better western horse than a dressage horse, but Aunt Lillian thought otherwise, and Liza had agreed.

"She'll make a fantastic amateur horse," Liza had said, "people will be falling all over themselves to take her home by the time we're done with her."

I stared into the trailer, seeing in my mind the horses I'd left behind; the mares and all the foals I'd cared for at the ranch, but mostly Folly and my first horse Quarry.

I sighed, a pang of regret twisting in my belly. They were in the best of hands at Aunt Lillian's but, still, not being able to see Folly every day would be strange. I'd dedicated a year to caring for her, worrying about her, and finally earning her trust. In the end, I'd learned to love her as a friend.

She'd been a lot of work and she certainly hadn't always appreciated me, but how would she feel when somebody else showed up to feed her breakfast tomorrow morning? Would she be upset? Would she miss me at all?

The boat shuddered as it neared the shore; there was a loud chiming sound over the speakers followed by a crackly voice saying something I couldn't understand, but that probably meant we'd reached our destination.

Wow, I thought, *I can't believe I'm actually home.* A gust of salty wind blew down the car deck and I inhaled the smell of the ocean greedily, as if I'd been a parched desert wanderer suddenly offered water. I hadn't known until that moment how much I missed the coast. This landscape had become a part of me somehow; even the light was different here, softer and more translucent than that up at the ranch.

I pulled open the heavy truck door and climbed inside, leaning back against the soft leather seat to watch all the people flooding down the stairs to start the search for their cars. It was a big ferry and usually there were at least a few people stumbling around last minute from deck to deck scrambling to figure out where they'd parked.

"Well, kid," Allan said, "we're almost there. Excited?"

"Yes, I think so." I thought about our sterile condo and about what life with my dad and Marion could be like and a shiver ran through me. I wasn't sure if it was excitement or fear. Surely things would be different now.

I reached into the backpack at my feet and pulled out the bag of Aunt Lillian's homemade caramel chocolate cookies to calm the fluttering butterflies in my stomach. I offered the bag to Allan and then took two for myself, closing my eyes as the sweet-salty taste hit my tongue. They were supposed to be for Marion, and my dad, too, but Allan and I had gone through nearly the whole bag on the way home.

As soon as I ate, I felt better. *Things will be great this year*, I told myself, *I have Red, I'll get back into archery full-time, and I'll spend the whole summer with Rob and Hilary. Everything will be just fine.*

The ferry shuddered as it prepared to dock, engines rumbling and humming, and the walls vibrating around us like we were inside a giant beehive. Finally, the boat gave a lurch and then came to a full stop.

Car engines started on all sides. Allan turned the key and we were moving. I crunched nervously on another cookie.

Even with Allan driving slowly and carefully with our precious cargo, Hilary's new farm was less than an hour from the ferry terminal. The sky was now tinged with pink, but we still had enough light to see by, which was good because we nearly missed their driveway as it was.

There wasn't a fancy stone gate like there'd been at Hilary's last home; there wasn't even a sign. In fact, without the truck's navigation system guiding us, we probably wouldn't have found their driveway at all. It was just a rutted, overgrown laneway with fingers of grass poking up through the patchy gravel. Trees lined the driveway on both sides, leaning so low over us that their branches scraped sharply across the top of the truck and trailer, making high-pitched shrieking sounds.

"Oh, that's not good for the paint job," Allan muttered, peering through the windshield. "I hope there's a place to turn around up ahead. I'd hate to get stuck in here."

I nodded, not saying a word, biting the inside of my cheek and twisting my fingers nervously together on my lap. I kept my eyes glued to the trailer cam mounted over our heads. All the horses besides Red had stopped eating and were staring curiously out their windows to see what the noise was about, but they didn't look ready to panic yet. Red, of course, had his face stuffed in his hay net, eyes half-closed as he swayed back and forth with the motion of the trailer.

Before I could get too worried, the laneway opened, and we'd entered a huge pasture bordered by overgrown blackberry bushes and falling down fences. Cracked fence posts and broken boards lay stacked in a pile off to one side.

We were parked at the bottom edge of the field, but it dipped in the middle before it rose up steeply to join a slightly better-looking fence-line at the top of a hill.

"Huh," Allan said morosely, "this isn't quite what I expected."

"No, me neither. Hilary said that the barn was right off the driveway. She didn't say anything about driving through pastures."

"Is that her?" Allan pointed to a small figure at the top of the hill who was dancing up and down and frantically waving her arms to get our attention.

"I think so, probably." My phone chimed about eight times in a row and I quickly pulled it out of my pocket. "It's her. She said to wait here, she's on her way."

It was lucky we hadn't gone any further because, as Hilary came running down the hill in mud-splashed breeches and a pair of knee high rubber boots it became obvious that the whole lower part of the pasture where it dipped was a bog. Hilary sunk nearly to the top of her boots in places but finally, she squelched over to us, laughing breathlessly and waving her arms.

I opened the truck door and jumped out just in time for her to barrel into me and wrap me in a hug that practically squished the life out of my body.

"Astrid, I'm so glad you're home! I missed you so much!" She pulled back and then hugged me again, bouncing up and down at the same time so that I could hardly see straight.

"I missed you, too," I gasped when she'd calmed down, "but, Hilary, where are we?"

"I'm so sorry, this is the back entrance and it's so awful that we never use it. I should have warned you that the GPS always sends people this way. The real entrance is down the road and there's a sign and a real driveway and everything. I'm so sorry, Allan, I hope your trailer isn't stuck. We can always unload the horses and lead them up this way if that helps."

Allan sighed and shook his head, but I could tell he was irritated. He got out to the truck and walked in a big circle, studying the truck tires and then the ground.

I should have studied the directions better, I thought, chewing my lip nervously. *That was stupid of me. What if we're stuck in the mud or if the paint on his truck is all scratched up? I think that costs a lot to fix.*

"I should be able to turn around up here where it's dry," he said finally, rubbing the back of one hand across his eyes, "why don't you ride with us, Hilary, and you can point out the right driveway."

I held my breath while Allan slowly navigated a large u turn in the middle of the field. The tires bogged down a few times, but the trailer lurched along, moving steadily toward the exit.

Allan didn't say a word the whole time and my stomach churned with anxiety. In my experience, people who simmered with quiet rage were the most dangerous, likely to erupt without warning at any moment. The dread of the explosion was almost worse than the outburst itself.

"There," he said as we finally cleared the field and headed back up the narrow laneway. "We're on our way." He sent me a quick smile and I huffed out a breath of relief.

He wasn't about to fly into a rage at all, I thought in surprise. *He was just irritated. Nothing bad is going to happen.*

"Oh, I'm sorry about this," Hilary said, wincing as the tree branches scraped against the outside of the trailer for the second time. "I should have given better directions." She laughed and shook her head, not looking worried at all. "I'm so glad you're here, Astrid." Things have been so crazy." She stopped, glancing over at Allan. "There's still so much to finish here. We don't have any pasture because the fences are all rotten and we can't use the ring right now because the guys are working on the indoor. I hope you won't mind all the construction, Astrid."

"I'm sure it will all be fine," I said, only half paying attention. I was busy watching the horses on the camera. Maverick had pinned his ears back and tossed his head when a particularly large branch *thunked* against the trailer over his head. I held my breath, but he didn't blow up, he angrily wrenched out a wad of hay from his net and ate it sullenly.

We finally turned back onto the road and it wasn't more than a couple minutes before Hilary said, "there it is, turn here."

There was a small, hand-painted sign that said, "Harvest Farm–future home of Harvest Bistro."

"Harvest Bistro?" I asked.

"My dad's restaurant." Hilary laughed. "He's beyond excited. It won't be open until the fall, though, and that's if we're lucky. We have so much work to do on the rest of the place first. It's been nothing but renovations and construction since the day we moved in."

This driveway was much better, the gravel was smooth and the grass at the edges grew at a respectable length. The few trees that lined the driveway sat politely off to one side rather than crowding. White board fences, their paint flaking off in chunks to reveal the grey wood underneath, ran on either side. A few of them leaned precariously to one side and I was glad to see that there were no horses in the fields.

"It's a great place," Hilary said, quickly. "It just needs a lot of work."

"I can help you this summer," I said. "I like painting and building stuff."

It was true, after turning Aunt Lillian's dirty, spider-infested barn into our archery range this winter, I'd discovered that I liked transforming old, run-down things into something new. There was something about making abandoned things look loved again that made me happy. Plus, I knew Hilary was giving my dad and Marion a huge discount on Red's board. I was going to help her out as much as possible.

We pulled in to a wide gravel parking lot in front of a brand new red metal barn. It wasn't huge, but it was nice and neat, with white trim and a metal roof and big pots of flowers standing just outside the front door. It had a large rolling door that stood open to reveal a roomy concrete aisle way with stalls on both sides. Behind it, towering two stories high, was the massive, hulking skeleton of the yet-to-be-built arena. It didn't have a roof or walls yet, just the framework was in place, but it looked huge.

"Right now, we have room for eight horses," Hilary said proudly as we slid out of the truck. "Four stalls on each side and they have run-out paddocks just like at your Aunt Lillian's. There's a tack room, a bathroom, hay storage, and there's even room for a suite upstairs even though it's not finished yet."

She grabbed my hand and pulled me toward the barn. "There's just you and me, Pender, and Sadie for boarders right now. Ally won't move Severus from Mud Lark until our indoor is built, even if she has to put up with gross Cole until then. The only reason Pender and Sadie moved over now is that they went on vacation to Europe together, so they wouldn't be riding anyway. They're not going to be happy about the lack of pasture, though; I'm way behind on everything. You wouldn't believe how expensive it is to build stuff."

"Well, that arena looks massive."

"Actually, it's just a small one." Hilary frowned, her forehead wrinkling into three parallel lines. "Nobody from the old place would agree to come if we didn't have an indoor."

She sighed and lifted her gaze to the unfinished roof, "I had to put *something* up. I guess we all got pretty spoiled at Claudia's farm. My dad figured out a way to work it into the business plan, but I'll have to have the place full of boarders by the end of the summer to make it work. I had to cash way more of my investments than I wanted to."

Investments? I thought incredulously. Sometimes Hilary seemed so much older than me.

"I had a misunderstanding with the contractor about how much it would all cost," she said slowly, not looking at me. "But I think it's almost all sorted out. It might just take longer to get finished, that's all."

"I think it will be amazing."

"I hope so." Hilary shook her head and grinned at me in her usual way, but I couldn't help but notice how tired she looked. "It should be finished by next month, and it will pay itself off in a few years. I know I'll feel better about it when the rains hit and we're snug riding inside."

One of the horses in the trailer neighed and there was an explosion of sound and movement from inside the barn. Horses shot from their stalls into the outside paddocks, prancing and snorting dramatically at the sight of the trailer.

"Wow," Hilary said, rolling her eyes. "We've been parked for ages and they just noticed the trailer now; I have serious doubts about their survival skills if they ever had to fend for themselves in the wild."

A familiar big bay stood closest to us, his chest pressed up against the fence and eyes practically bugging out of his head as he stared at the trailer in fascination. Oversized ears swivelled around in all directions. He arched his neck and pranced in place, tossing his nose up and down at the new arrivals.

"Oh, Rabbit," Hilary said, shaking her head. "You'd think he'd be settled in by now, but I swear he gets crazier every day.

He gets the rest of them worked up, too. They've been like this ever since they arrived. I was hoping they'd settle down much sooner."

"Um, ladies?" Allan said behind us, "are you planning to unload these horses any time soon? I'd like to get my supper."

"Right, sorry," Hilary said. "We're on it."

We unloaded Red and Ellie easily and without any fuss. Even though Ellie had never set foot off my aunt's ranch, she sauntered off the trailer looking calm, cool, and collected. She surveyed her new home with mild interest and nudged Red as if to tell him to get going so she could check out her new stall.

They didn't even panic when the three horses, led by an overexcited Rabbit, crashed excitedly back into their stalls with a thunder of hooves, snorting and sounding like fire-breathing dragons as they leaned over their stall doors, straining their necks to get closer to the strange new horses.

Red's feet clopped steadily on the bare concrete as he followed Ellie inside, and he nickered low under his breath at Rabbit, Jerry, and Riverdance.

"That's his stall there," Hilary said, pointing across the aisle, "it's all ready for him."

I led Red to the end stall across from Ellie and slid the door open, glad to see that it was knee high with a fresh bed of shavings. He'd be able to relax properly after the long trip.

Red stood politely for me to unbuckle his halter and then dropped his head to sniff the thick pile of bedding, his breath puffing in and out, blowing up small poofs of wooden shavings, the smaller pieces sticking to his nose and chin. It was much different than the straw we'd used back at the ranch.

"He's probably never seen shavings before." I laughed. "You're such a silly horse, Red."

Ellie was doing much the same thing in her stall across the aisle and, before Hilary could back out the sliding door, the mare's legs buckled, and she dropped down with a satisfied groan. Then she flipped on her side and began to roll, legs flailing wildly in all directions.

"Ack," Hilary said, slipping out of the stall and shutting the door quickly behind her. "She nearly rolled on me."

"She's still a baby," I reminded her. "Aunt Lillian says that young horses are like baby humans; impulsive and not always in control of their bodies."

"Right," Hilary said, frowning. "Jerry was so clumsy when he was younger. It took him forever to grow into his legs."

"A-hem?" Allan stood behind us, hands on his hips. "Are you about done here? We need to get those other horses to their destination. Which one of you is going to show me the next farm?"

"Oh, there was a change of plans," Hilary said quickly, "we'll unload them here for tonight and Rob will pick them up tomorrow when it's light out. Darn it"—she looked at her watch—"I have to run to rehearsals in twenty minutes and I'm not even showered and changed. Are you okay unloading the other two by yourself, Astrid?"

"Um sure," I began, but she'd already turned and was jogging up the driveway in what I guessed was the direction of the house, her long blonde ponytail bobbing in all directions.

"Thank you!" she called over her shoulder. "See you tomorrow."

Allan grumbled something under his breath and I hurried to help him unload. I tentatively took the lead rope Allan handed me and walked a sullen Maverick to his new stall, hoping that he wouldn't bite me. He was kind of cranky. But he went into his stall obediently enough and stomped through the shavings as if he'd been bedded down in them all his life, barely giving his stall a second glance before marching outside to stand in the back of his paddock, glaring at the barn suspiciously.

Allan put Possum in the empty stall beside Maverick and shut the door, ushering me back to the trailer with an impatient wave of his arm.

We quickly unloaded all my stuff from the truck and, when we were done, I was surprised when Allan pulled me into a quick hug. "You take care of yourself, kid," he said gruffly, "and you call your aunt if you need anything at all. I mean it; I know she worries about you. Don't let them boss you around too much here; you make sure you're not overworked."

"Okay," I said, surprised by the worry on his face, "don't worry, I'll be okay."

"Right, take good care of those horses."

"I will," I said, more positively this time. If there was one thing I'd learned how to do well it was take care of horses.

I waved until the truck and trailer were gone, seeing my last link with life at the ranch disappear into the distance.

Feeling a little lost, I carried my saddle, bridle, and grooming stuff into the tack room. Hilary had already set up a hook for us with Red's name above it on plastic tag stuck to the wall. Our saddle rack was right beside it and I carefully put Red's saddle, which was Quarry's old saddle, into place and smoothed the cover. I draped the girth gently over top and looked around for a place to put my helmet and grooming stuff.

The far wall was lined with wooden lockers and I was touched to see there was one with a brass nameplate for me already. I went over and opened the narrow cupboard, glad to see that there were hooks to hang up clothes and shelves for my brushes and room for my boots. Marion hated when I brought my horsey things home to our condo, so it would be good to have a place to store all my barn clothes and anything that smelled like a horse. I packed my things away neatly and then took time to explore the rest of the room.

The barn was too small to have both a tack and feed room, so they'd been combined in one. A big counter with a sink ran along one wall and underneath were stacked neat rows of plastic tubs, each carefully labeled with masking tape. There was even an empty one for me to fill with Red's food. There was a small fridge for drinks and snacks and a tiny, two-piece bathroom.

Wow, Hilary, I thought, *you've thought of everything.*

There was a low whickering noise from the alleyway and I trailed back out into the barn.

"Do you need your dinner, boy?" I asked, seeing Red with nose stuck out into the aisle, looking hopefully toward the feed-room door. I'd like to think he was pining for me, but at that moment it was definitely food on his mind.

The other horses were outside in their paddocks, all three boys entranced with the beautiful palomino who had moved in next door.

Ellie squealed as she touched noses with Riverdance over the paddock fence, striking out with one front leg, her hoof clipping sharply against the bottom rail.

Riverdance squealed back and nipped her behind the ear. And that set Jerry and Rabbit off; they both started whirling around, rearing and bucking, pretending to kick one another in an effort to impress.

Rabbit spun on his haunches and came crashing back into his stall, slamming his big shoulder into the wall so hard that the whole building shook.

"Rabbit, stop that," I said sharply. "What is wrong with all of you, settle down. Why did you all wait until I'm alone to start causing trouble?"

There was more squealing and thumping of hooves, and then the rest of them piled inside, lining up at their stall doors to stare at me expectantly, ears pricked and very innocent expressions on their faces.

I looked at my watch and frowned. It was definitely dinnertime for the horses back at the ranch, surely all these horses needed to be fed, too. Hilary hadn't given me any instructions or said what time she expected to be home, but I didn't want them to go hungry.

Hilary, do you want me to feed everyone hay? I texted and was relieved when a response came back almost right away.

Oh my gosh, I completely forgot to do dinner. Just throw a big flake to everyone and I'll be back to do night feed. Sorry! Can you check waters, too? I'm not sure if I filled them.

Okay, I typed slowly. It wasn't like Hilary to forget something so important. She'd always been super conscientious back at Claudia's place.

I stood in the middle of the aisle, pivoting around slowly until I spotted the big sliding door near the back of the barn. That definitely looked like hay storage. I went and slid the door back and surveyed the neatly piled stacks of greenery. It all looked harmless, no alfalfa or anything exotic that I could see. I went to the closest open bale, grabbed a few flakes and went to Red's stall first, throwing them over the door into the nearby manger.

This set off a loud chorus of outraged nickers; apparently, I'd broken a horsey rule by feeding the newcomer first.

"Okay, okay, I'm coming," I said, grabbing a few flakes for each horse and tossing them inside one by one.

They settled down instantly. Even big, goofy Rabbit looked less anxious. He grabbed a mouthful of hay and dragged it back to his stall door, leaning over and chewing while watching Red's stall intently as if it were a television playing his favorite show.

"Rabbit, you're getting hay everywhere," I told him, but he ignored me.

I swept up the hay I'd spilled in the aisle and went back to Red who was eating contentedly as if he'd lived there all his life. I brought his brushes from the tack room and got to work on cleaning him up, working the tension out of his muscles and the travel dust out of his russet coat.

My phone pinged again, and I fished it out of my pocket.

Hey, did you arrive okay? Are the horses good?

Shoot, poor Rob must have been waiting forever to hear from us.

Hey, they're fine. Here, I'll send some pictures.

They didn't turn out great in the dusky light, but they were enough to reassure him that they were okay. Possum looked adorable, of course, and Maverick looked like a malevolent shadow in the corner of his stall. He refused to keep eating his hay when I pointed my phone at him and he wouldn't prick his ears for the camera.

Sorry, we had a family thing tonight, but I'll be there first thing tomorrow. Breakfast?

Yeah, that would be great, I typed, making an effort to sound casual but my heart jumped at the thought of seeing him again.

The light faded to near-night as I worked on Red's coat and the temperature dropped enough that I shivered in the spring air. Finally, I had to go and find the switch for the barn lights so I could see properly and pull a sweater out of the luggage I'd left piled next to the barn aisle. Where was Marion? I'd texted her before the ferry arrived, but I hadn't heard back. I checked my phone again but there weren't any missed messages.

Finally, I heard car tires rolling up the driveway, but it wasn't Marion's car, it was a strange black SUV. I hesitated in the doorway of the barn, acutely aware that I was all alone in a strange place with no one nearby to hear me scream.

"Astrid," Marion called, waving one hand elegantly as she stepped out of the strange vehicle. She hesitated, looking around uncertainly at the unfamiliar barnyard cast in evening shadow. She frowned at the falling down fences on the far side of the parking lot and at the skeleton of the newly started indoor arena rising up behind the barn. It was nothing like Claudia's perfectly manicured stables, and I knew anything that was untidy, run-down, or messy in any way sent her into a panic.

"It's okay, Marion," I called, "it's just a work in progress, come see Red."

She came toward me then, smiling tentatively, and I was so happy to see her kind, familiar face that I pulled her into tight hug.

She froze, sucking in a sharp breath, but the next moment she'd melted and wrapped her arms around me gently. "It's so good to see you, Astrid. You've grown since I saw you last...taller, I mean," she added quickly, stepping back. "And you look so mature; you're not a little girl anymore."

"Um, thanks," I said, deciding she'd probably meant it as a compliment.

Marion followed me to Red's stall, wisely skirting Rabbit who had stuck his head way out in the aisle, flapping his lips in the air in an effort to greet her. Red looked up calmly and moved to the door, his feet swishing through the deep shavings. He stood very still while Marion gingerly petted the end of his velvety nose with the tips of her fingers, not moving back to his hay until she dropped her hand back to her side, holding it out at a sharp angle so as not to touch her clothes.

"He looks great, Astrid. Much less fluffy than when I saw him last."

"He's shed his winter coat." I laughed. "At least most of it. I'll still have to clip his chin hair."

"Oh, I think it looks distinguished," she said, "like he's a wise professor. Are you ready to go, Astrid? We have the squash tournament to get to and your father's next game starts in an hour. I promised I'd have you back in time. I know he'd like it if we could sit up-front and center."

"What?" I asked. "What tournament?" I groaned inwardly, wanting nothing but dinner and bed after my exhausting full day of travel.

"Sorry, Astrid. I told you all about it last week. Our racquet club is hosting the big squash tournament this weekend. Your father has become very accomplished in his division. It's the finals so it's a very big deal and his second game is tonight. We won't have time for you to go home and change so see if you can find anything clean to put on. We want to look our best."

I briefly considered arguing, but in the end, it wasn't worth it. I was too tired, and she'd already turned and disappeared into the small bathroom next to the tack room to scrub her hands after her brief moment of contact with Red.

Okay, fine, I thought, rooting through my luggage until I'd found a pair of clean jeans and a sweater that wasn't covered in hay. She definitely had NOT told me about any tournament. Surely, I'd remember something like that. I had no idea what a person was supposed to wear to watch squash, but I figured this would have to do.

By the time I'd changed and cleaned up as best as I could, Marion had already ferried most of my stuff from the barn aisle to the back of the brand new black SUV.

"Where's your car, Marion? This looks like a mom-mobile."

"Oh, that," Marion laughed. "I sold it; this is just a lease for now, but it fits in with our new lifestyle better. Between your barn things and your father's exercise gear, my poor little car couldn't take it anymore. This vehicle is much more appropriate. Your father sold his vehicle as well."

"Oh," I said, glancing over at her quickly. My dad had loved his little sports car. Were they hurting so badly for money that they could only have one car? Would they still have money to pay Red's board? Hilary was giving me a big discount already in exchange for me helping out, but what if we couldn't even pay that?

I went from stall to stall one last time, peering in to make sure that the water buckets were full, and nobody would starve before Hilary got back from rehearsals. I'd already set out Red's grain in his bucket and soaked his beet pulp so all Hilary had to do was mix it up and serve it to him. Still, it was hard to walk away. I'd gotten so used to taking care of a barn full of horses back at the ranch, it felt weird to hand over the responsibility to someone else.

Finally, sensing Marion's impatience, I climbed reluctantly into the car.

"Hey, where's Caprice?" I asked. Marion usually always had her little poodle sidekick with her.

"Oh." She frowned. "She's at the boarding kennel. She hurt her knee and she's supposed to be resting. With all the chaos of the tournament this weekend, and you and the horse arriving, we felt that she'd heal better if she was kenneled."

"Oh no, how did she get hurt?"

"Well." Marion sighed. "Your father's therapist said he needed to develop his empathy skills."

I wonder whatever would give a therapist that impression, I thought, wisely keeping my mouth shut.

"It was felt that your father would benefit by spending time bonding with a pet. So, he started taking Caprice jogging every morning and actually, they had a great time for a while. The trainer had already told us that Caprice needed more exercise, so she'd stop being so anxious and reactive in the house.

"But then she started limping off and on. Even on her good days, she couldn't keep up with your dad anymore. The vet said she had torn or stretched ligaments in one of her hind knees and she couldn't be expected to jog that much in a day. She's supposed to be resting to see if we can avoid having surgery. We had to cut way back on her activity."

"Oh," I said, "that's awful. I hope she's okay."

"She'll be fine. It's the enforced bed rest that bothers her the most."

The drive to the racquet club wasn't long but I was so tired that I nearly fell asleep in the car about twenty times, only waking up enough to mumble vague answers to Marion's questions about the trip to the Island and to half-listen to her lesson on the rules of squash. A lesson that was completely wasted on me.

I sat up and rubbed my eyes when we pulled up in front of a fancy glass and concrete building. It looked very modern and intimidating; more like an art gallery or a museum than a gym.

A black and gold banner hung above the doorway that read 'Welcome to the International WorldCor Squash Tournament'. It was already dark outside, but huge floodlights lit up the brick-lined courtyard. It was a beautiful space, full of stone benches and a fountain, and to my surprise, it was also full of well-dressed, sporty-looking people milling around in small groups, talking animatedly to one another. I gulped and slid down in my seat.

When Marion had said, "squash tournament," I'd assumed that it would be full of old people my dad's age dressed in white pants and golf shirts. But all around me were ripped young guys in high-tech athletic wear plastered with sponsor ads, striding around confidently with Kool-Aid-coloured power drinks looking like they owned the place. There were lots of women, too, lithe figures dressed in those second-skin dresses that tennis players wear, their gazelle-like, bodies athletic and powerful in a way I couldn't ever aspire to. Even in the semi-darkness, everyone glowed with good health and good spirits; tanned skin, perfect white teeth, and jovial laughter surrounded me on all sides. It was like being encircled by genetically-altered super-people or aliens.

Maybe I'm the alien, I thought darkly, *I'm the one out of place here.*

I slid out of the car as unobtrusively as possible, ducking my head and hurrying after Marion, not making eye contact with anyone.

"Come on, Astrid. His division is coming up now. We're just in time."

We had to thread our way through an ever-thickening crowd of people to reach the spot that had been reserved for us. A small card with Marion's name on it sat in the middle of the front-row bleachers. I sat down and stared around with wide eyes.

It was like something out of a futuristic sci-fi movie; three large transparent glass cubes were set up side by side in front of the bleacher area, each big enough for the players, their rackets, and a wildly ricocheting ball. I'd never seen anything like it.

Only the middle cube, the one in front of us, had players in it. And I only had to watch for five seconds to realize that this was not a sport for the weak or timid. It was a like high-speed tennis without a net and the players could smash the ball off all four walls of the cube they were locked in at various crushing speeds.

I'd blocked out Marion's earlier description of what the rules were, but from the outside it looked like the players took turns bashing the ball in all directions and narrowly avoiding hitting one another in the face with their rackets.

This was apparently the seniors' division, but they didn't look like any old people I'd ever seen.

"There's your father," Marion said excitedly, pointing to a man I hardly recognized. Despite his insistence that everyone around him should strive for perfection, my father had always carried a few extra pounds around his waist and had looked stressed and unhealthy most of the time. But he'd clearly thrown himself fully into his new sport and he looked the part.

Seeing my own father dressed in skin-tight lycra was not exactly thrilling, but even I had to admit that he looked pretty fit, for an old person, I mean. There was a spring in his step and a competitive glint in his eye; if confidence was any indicator then he was going to win his match hands down.

"His therapist insisted that he play doubles," Marion whispered in my ear, "it was supposed to help him learn to be more of a team player and develop empathy."

"Uh-huh," I said, watching him smash a serve into the opposite corner of the glass cube he and three other players were stationed in, sending the ball ricocheting around so fast it nearly took out his opponent's eye. "How's that working?"

"Really well," she said earnestly, and I wasn't sure if she was kidding or not.

"Marion, does he actually have *sponsors*?" I asked in disbelief, noticing his shirt plastered with logos from about ten different businesses.

"Not personal ones, not yet. But the tournament itself has a number of sponsors, including WorldCor. It's a very popular sport," she said, sounding like she was reading straight from a squash publicity brochure. "It's been a long haul, but we're right on the cusp of pushing the sport into the Olympic arena." She paused, her eyes lit up as she fixed her gaze on the game. "Oh, did you see that shot? Your father's been working hard on his technique."

The rest of the match lasted nearly forty-five minutes, and the whole time the players were leaping and falling and smashing into the glass. As someone who hated high-impact sports with a passion, the whole thing looked like a nightmare to me; the players gasped for air, covered in sweat, and one guy was bleeding from a gash in his elbow. Everyone else in the audience was riveted to their seats, cheering whenever anyone made a good shot.

In the end, my dad's side won, as if there'd been any doubt in the outcome. He came out of the competition cube beaming and lifting his hands in the air victoriously, and a fit, blonde-haired woman ran up to him, her pony-tail bouncing up and down like it was a living thing.

To my shock, she practically threw herself up against him even though he was drenched with sweat, kissed his cheek, and then laughingly handed him a towel.

"Who is *that*?" I asked Marion, but she'd already stood up and was moving purposefully toward my father.

"Um, Marion?" I stood, undecided whether I should follow and was surprised when there was a light tap on my shoulder. I turned quickly to find a dark-eyed guy in his twenties or thirties standing behind me, a polite smile fixed on his face. He looked strangely familiar and I narrowed my eyes, studying his face intently, wondering where I'd seen him before.

"You must be Astrid," he said, in a smooth, sultry accent that made me think he must be from Greece or some other Mediterranean country. He had dark curly hair and huge brown eyes that looked deep into mine. Again, I had that impression that I knew him from somewhere. He took my hand and held it in both of his. "I'm Darius."

"Um, nice to meet you," I said, my voice coming out an embarrassed squeak. Heat crowded up my neck and cheeks before I could stop it.

"I wanted to let you know how much your father has done for us here. He turned this club into a top-notch facility, and he's been invaluable to our campaign to bid for inclusion at the Olympics."

"Oh," I said and carefully withdrew my hand from his grasp, hoping he had overlooked my sweaty palms. "It's a beautiful building; did he help with renovations or something?"

"No." Darius opened his eyes wide. "He built the whole thing. We tore down our old facility and made this a world-class building just for racket sports. Your dad found the funding and the architect, and was responsible for the majority of our sponsors. He's a hero."

"Wow, I had no idea." *And where did he come up with the money for it all? I thought his court case meant that we might be losing everything and that he was looking at jail time.*

"Um, I guess I'd better go," I said glancing over to where Marion was standing on the outskirts of the entourage surrounding my father. She couldn't even get close to him what with all the people congratulating him and slapping him on the back. And that blonde woman was in the thick of it, hanging off my dad's arm and looking up into his face as if he were her personal property. "Actually, wait, Darius, who is that blonde lady?"

He looked over to the group and frowned. "Who, Nancy? She's one of the coaches here. She's helping your dad."

Uh-huh, I'll bet, I thought.

"Okay, thanks, it was nice to meet you."

"Make sure you stick around long enough to watch my match. It will be…intense."

"Okay," I said, hurrying away from him. Darius himself was a bit intense, but he'd given me lots to think about. Apparently, my dad and Marion had been quite busy while I'd been away.

"Astrid," my dad said, looking out over the heads of his sea of admirers. He did look genuinely happy to see me. "I'm glad you're here. Everyone, this is my daughter, Astrid."

I said shy hellos to everyone and was glad when they made their excuses and melted back into the crowd. The blonde coach, Nancy, detached herself from my father and sent insincere toothy smiles to both me and Marion before drifting away to do whatever squash coaches did in their spare time.

As soon as she was gone my dad shifted closer to Marion and put his sweaty arm over her shoulder. She smiled up at him adoringly as if she hadn't just two seconds ago been completely snubbed.

"I saw you met Darius. I thought you two might have something in common, since you both play with horses. Of course, he doesn't have time for that now; our club helped sponsor him to come to Canada and he's our star player. We're using him to leverage our Olympic bid. What do you think of our building and our new courts?"

"It's beautiful, Dad," I said honestly. I didn't have time to think about what he'd said about Darius and horses because he was already talking again.

"WorldCor needed some write-offs," he confessed, dropping his voice a few notches, "and they needed some good publicity what with all that nonsense from last year, so they sponsored most of the building and the home team, and I pulled a few strings with the city to get our permits fast-tracked."

"So, everything is okay then, with um, work?" I said lamely, not wanting to talk about the court case here.

"Sure, it's fine, our lawyers did good work. It's all settled; just water under the bridge. I'm on sabbatical for this year, but this will pass and soon everything will be back to normal. Now, what did you think of that game. We crushed them, didn't we?"

"Definitely," I said, although I hadn't actually been able to tell by watching, who'd won and who had lost.

"Well, you two go have a seat and I'll hit the showers and debrief with Nancy. You don't want to miss Darius's match."

Debrief with Nancy, I thought, *yuck.*

I followed Marion back to our spot on the bleachers, yawning and rubbing my eyes. We'd started the drive from my aunt's ranch before the sun had even come up and driven hard the whole way. And then there'd been the ferry and getting Red settled into his new home. I was ready to fall into bed and never wake up.

"Just a few more hours, honey, and then we can go home."

I half-dozed my way through the rest of the seniors division, but woke up in time to see Darius play. He was in a singles match against another lithe, muscled athlete who looked like he'd been playing since birth.

"Holy cow!" I sat up and paid attention, amazed at the acrobatics these guys were going through to smash that ball. It was like watching two people caught in an intense whirl-wind, or lightning-quick martial arts like in the movies. They never let up the pressure until it was finally over, and Darius held up his hands in victory.

I wiped my palms on my jeans and sagged back on my bench, surprised at how caught up I'd been. It was exhausting just watching them and I felt like I'd run a marathon. I yawned, hoping against hope that it was over and I could go to bed.

"Marion," I said, remembering something, "what was that about Darius and horses?"

"Oh, his family bred horses back in his own country, I think. He doesn't talk about it much, though. Come on, sweetheart. Time for the reception; you must be starving."

"Okay." My last real meal had been lunch on the ferry and my stomach grumbled at the prospect of food.

I fell asleep again a few times on the way to the reception. My dad had ridden with the rest of the team and Marion had been content to let me nap.

The same smartly-dressed people buzzed around the hotel lobby, carrying glasses of alcohol and chattering loudly in bright, high-pitched voices. As soon as Marion went to mingle, I found the table with the appetizers and cheese and made myself at home.

"Are you finding everything to your liking?" Darius stood beside me, smiling politely, his wide brown eyes staring directly into mine.

"Sure," I said, blushing under his gaze. He sure was intense; did the man never blink? "Um...." I searched desperately for something, *anything*, to say. "Where are you from, Darius? My dad said you rode horses?"

All the warmth drained from his eyes and he pulled himself upright. "*This* is my home now," he said almost fiercely. "I do not talk about my past."

Wow, I took a step back in alarm and instantly, that smooth smile was back on his face, although dimmer than before.

"Forgive me for being rude," he said quietly, "I do not like to talk about my life before I moved to this beautiful country. This is my home now and that's all that matters. Besides, it is not a nice story."

"Sorry," I said in a small voice and turned back to the cheese.

He cleared his throat as if he were about to say something further. The silence stretched out, and when I finally looked up, he had disappeared into the crowd without another word.

What on earth was that? I took a deep breath wondering what I'd said to offend him. That strange sense of having seen him somewhere before was back stronger than ever, too. Had he been a famous rider or something? I would have to Google him later and see what I could find out.

Finally, it was over, and when we made it back to the condo, I didn't even bother to look around and see if things had changed in the year I'd been away. I just mumbled a quick goodnight and stumbled to my room where I thankfully, blissfully fell into dreamless sleep.

Chapter Two

The morning came far too soon. I'd accidentally left my phone alarm set to wake me up to do early morning feed at the ranch, so it went off just around the same time the sun came up. I groaned and burrowed my hand under the pillow where I'd stuffed my phone, swiping randomly at the screen with one eye open until it shut up and allowed me to drift peacefully back into oblivion.

"Astrid," Marion called softly from the doorway just as I was nice and cozy, "I heard your alarm. Are you up? Come on, breakfast is ready. We have a big day ahead of us."

No, I ducked my head into my pillow to shut out the daylight now streaming in from the hallway through the open door.

"Come on, sleepyhead," she said, laughing, "your father's already out jogging. I want to talk to you privately before he gets back."

That got my attention. I yawned, dragged myself wearily out of bed and shuffled out into the hallway and then down to the kitchen. Marion was standing by the counter, dressed in her designer yoga gear, looking rail-thin and radiant as usual.

"Good morning, darling," she said, pushing a bowl of yogurt and granola toward me. "Here, I made your favourite. I even added a few blueberries as a treat."

"Um, thanks," I said, thinking longingly of the heaping plate of bacon, eggs, and hash browns I'd eaten only yesterday morning with Aunt Lillian. That already seemed like a lifetime ago.

"So, sweetheart, you know your father always has your best interests at heart, right?"

"Hmm," I mumbled noncommittally.

"Well, he is very excited that you've returned home and he wants to share his new love of fitness with you. He has created a very strict fitness regime for himself and me, and I know that he'd love to include you in some of our activities."

I looked up in alarm, now completely wide awake. My dad was the most competitive, bossy, sarcastic person I knew. Sharing any fitness routine with him would be a complete disaster.

"But," she said, staring pointedly over the rim of her coffee mug at me, "I warned him that you'd probably already set up a schedule for yourself, one that would perfectly compliment your chosen sports of archery and horse riding. I told him that you'd need to help Hilary out at the barn and that Red needs to be exercised *every single day*."

She raised her eyebrows meaningfully and it dawned on me that she was tossing me a life-ring here.

"Yes," I said, catching on at last. "I need to help Hilary at the barn and ride Red every day."

"That's what I thought. Have you spoken with Earl about when you'll return to the range?"

"No, not yet." I hesitated, not sure how much to tell her. I'd been avoiding even thinking about how sore my arm still was. The doctors felt that it had healed well and it was fine for everyday things, but when it came to archery it was still weak and I barely had a full range of motion. "My arm's still not very strong yet," I said, telling half the truth. "I need Earl to see me shoot so we can come up with a plan."

"Hmm," Marion said thoughtfully. "We should go there this morning, then. If your arm's not strong enough for archery then that probably rules out playing Squash as well. I know your father was very interested in introducing you to the game."

"Oh, no." I looked up in alarm. "I'm definitely not ready for that."

"That's what I expected. But, Astrid, I do think that it would be nice for you to find one activity that the two of you can do together. Something that's not too competitive, but where you can enjoy spending time with each other. Can you think of anything?"

"I'm not sure," I said hesitantly. "Until yesterday I didn't even know that he liked anything at all except work and making money."

"Astrid," she said, frowning, "that's not fair. He worked so hard to make a better life for this family, you can't blame him for that."

I shut my mouth, not willing to argue with her when she was trying to help me. Marion had an inexplicable blind spot when it came to my dad; she pretty much thought he could do no wrong.

"Fine," I said, "what does he like besides running, squash,

working, and making money?"

"Well, we've turned the guest room into a weight lifting room; he works out there every day. And he cycles, and plays tennis and, well, besides the squash, I think that's about it."

"Wait, like a bicycle? I could do that, I think. Even if it was only a couple days a week."

"Astrid." Marion beamed at me. "That's an excellent idea. I'm so glad you said that. Come on out into the landing."

I followed her through the kitchen and living room, and out the front door to the private landing where our elevator was. I'd been so tired the night before that I hadn't noticed the changes that had occurred since I'd lived here last.

Since this whole top floor was ours, nobody but our family could come up here unless invited. You needed a special key to access this part of the building from the elevator. The space by the window used to have a bench and some fake plants, but now one whole end had been given over to a giant locker with a padlock on it and a bike rack with three bikes attached to it.

"You already got me a bike?" I said in surprise. She'd expected all along that I'd agree to this.

"Well, they were on sale," Marion said quickly, "and the store gave us a good deal for buying three at once. Don't worry, darling, you'll love it. We've been driving to all sorts of parks and wilderness areas to cycle. I've actually been enjoying it myself. We can go in the evening a few days a week if that works for everyone's schedule. Now, eat up your breakfast so we can start our yoga and then we'll drop by the range before I take you to the barn. It will be just like old times."

"Okay," I said, already feeling overwhelmed. Back at the

ranch I'd been pretty much in charge of my own life and my own schedule. As long as the chores got done and I went to school, Aunt Lillian didn't care what I did or in what order. Here, it felt like every second of my life would be scheduled down to the last millisecond. I didn't know when I'd have time to even *think* on my own or read a book or just be myself.

It *was* fun doing yoga again, though. I hadn't bothered up at Aunt Lillian's. At first, my arm had been broken, and then I'd been healing or just too busy to add another thing into my life.

Marion led me to her office, half of which had been taken over by a big-screen TV and a wall full of rolled up yoga mats of varying thicknesses, foam blocks, Pilates balls, and other pastel-coloured exercise gear that I couldn't begin to recognize.

Marion put on an easy yoga video and, after struggling to coordinate my body for the first fifteen minutes, I actually found that it was all coming back to me. By the end I felt energized and happy again.

"Well, well, what's this?" my dad said, appearing in the doorway, still dressed in his running clothes. "My girls are up early, too."

"Hey, Dad," I said shyly, thrown off by his genuine, open smile. He hadn't look like that very often in the old days. Maybe the therapy was working.

"Bruce, Astrid is quite excited to start cycling with us. Maybe we could head out tonight to that park we both liked so much, after your tournament."

"Marion, don't be ridiculous," he said coldly, his smile falling away like a light switch in his head had been flicked. He shook his head in exasperation. "You know I have to focus on my matches today."

"Yes, dear, but I thought that afterward—"

"Use your head," he said abruptly. "This is not a good weekend. We'll put cycling on the schedule for Monday afternoon. Write it on the fridge planner. I have to go shower and get ready."

"Oh…of course," Marion said quietly. "I'm just going to drive Astrid to see Earl at the range and then drop her off at the barn. We can head to the club after that."

"Fine." And like that he was gone. I raised my eyebrows and looked over at Marion, but she was already rolling up her yoga mat, her shoulders hunched and her face completely devoid of all emotion.

"Go get dressed, Astrid," she said finally, her voice overly bright, "we should leave soon."

The ride to the range was mostly silent. Marion was lost in her own thoughts and my stomach churned with butterflies at the thought of seeing the range and Earl again. On the one hand, I was finally going to get to shoot like I'd wanted to, but I was anxious about what Earl would say about my arm. I only hoped that I hadn't waited too long and wrecked everything. I also wondered if my old frenemy Miranda would be there.

My phone pinged, breaking the silence, and I fished it out of my pocket. *Hey, we're just leaving now to pick up the horses. Are you still up for breakfast?*

Oh, no, I'd forgotten to text Rob this morning. How could that have possibly slipped my mind?

I'm so sorry, I have to go to the range first. Lunch instead?

There was a long delay before he answered back. *Got to get the horses home and settled in. Another time.*

Darn it. I tucked my phone away with a sigh just as we pulled up in front of the range. A thrill of expectation ran through me when I saw the familiar old building again. After the accident at the lake, before I'd discovered Claudia and the horses, I'd spent every waking moment wanting to be back here. And the fact that I was allowed to just walk in here any time I liked was a bit of a miracle.

"Do you want me to come with you, sweetheart?" Marion said, turning off the car and pulling her tablet out of the big leather bag she toted around with her.

"Oh, no, it's okay," I said, "not if you don't mind waiting."

"Of course not, take your time. I have lots of work to catch up on."

Marion had her own travel agency that she'd built up from scratch, but she hardly had much to do with it anymore. She checked in with them now and then, and made sure the accounting was right, but she let her manager, Trudy, do most of the day-to-day work.

I was so excited I almost skipped up to the glass doors and pushed my way inside, inhaling the gymnasium smell like a weirdo even though it was nothing compared to the smell of barn, hay, and horses. It still reminded me of some of the best moments of my life.

"Astrid!" Earl wrapped me in a tight bear hug before I could even say hello, and then twirled me around in a big circle like I was five years old, making me burst into breathless laughter. He broke away and stood back surveying me with satisfaction. "You have been away too long, kiddo. Are you back for good?"

"I'm back," I said, still laughing, "I'm ready to shoot."

"Yeah? How long until you hit the Olympics?"

"Five years," I said, feigning confidence, "six, tops."

"Ah, I like the spirit, Astrid. Let's see it then."

Feeling excited, I strung my bow swiftly, ignoring the subtle twinge that always zipped through my shoulder at times like this.

Earl didn't waste any time; he had me shoot at a few different distances, standing back and watching critically with his arms crossed over his chest. It didn't bother me to have him scrutinize me so closely, though; Earl had been my coach for most of my career and any criticism he'd ever given me had always been both kind and fair.

My first few shots were good, but by the tenth one, my initial exhilaration had worn off and my arm had begun to shake as I drew back; the dull ache in my upper arm and shoulder had begun.

"Okay, hold up," Earl said, frowning. "Is that all you can shoot without maxing out?"

"No," I said defensively. "I can totally keep going." I fired off a few more shots just to prove my point. Each one hit the bulls-eye dead center. I hadn't lost my touch at all.

"Astrid," he said quietly, "on a scale of one to ten, how bad does it hurt?"

"It's fine," I said quickly, resisting the urge to rub the aching throb in my shoulder. "I can push past it."

"Pain is a message, Astrid," Earl said seriously, "it's not something you should ignore. Sure, you can push through it in the short-term, but long-term you're going to do some permanent damage. Did you go to physio when you were away?"

"Yes, I did," I said slowly. "Most of the time it feels okay, but

I can't move it as much as I did before and it doesn't have very much strength. It still gets tired and aches sometimes. I just need to practice more, that's all."

"Hmm," he said thoughtfully. "Maybe. What weight are you pulling right now?"

"Forty pounds," I said cautiously, wondering where he was going with this.

"Astrid. You're not going to like what I have to say."

Yeah, I guessed that, I thought hollowly, my heart picking up its pace.

"Okay, first of all, you're not ready to start practicing seriously yet. Wait," he said, holding up a hand to stop me from arguing. "Just listen; you're tiring much too quickly. You need to build your strength up before you can start pulling those weights again. That's a lot for healing muscles and bones to deal with."

"Earl," I protested, "I know I can push through this. I've dreamt about coming back and starting training again. It's all I want."

"Look," he said patiently, "this is just temporary; you need to build yourself back up slowly. Don't think of it as a demotion. Think of it as cross-training; your path to getting better and stronger."

I looked down at the ground, mortified to find that my eyes were prickling with tears. This was the whole reason I'd come home, wasn't it? I could have cross-trained anywhere. I could have stayed at the ranch. Why had I thought that Earl would be able to magically solve everything?

"Hey, don't cry," he said, his forehead wrinkling with

concern. "I'm not saying you have to give everything up; just take it easy for a while."

"But I don't *want* to take it easy," I said stubbornly, knowing I sounded like a child. "I'm ready to start training."

Earl sighed and laid a hand on my shoulder. "I know, I get it, believe me. But, Astrid, part of being a true athlete is knowing when to push and when to back off. Right now, your body is telling you that you need to gain strength and stamina; if you listen to it, then you'll come back next year stronger than ever."

I shrugged, not knowing what to say.

"Hey, I have an idea. What about those horse archery videos you sent me? Why don't you focus on something like that this summer? It would be fun and something different to keep your mind occupied while you heal. You can get a lighter bow just for that."

I looked up to find him staring at me, his eyes full of concern.

"Yeah, I suppose," I said, mostly to make him stop looking so upset.

"Look, I'd say anything that improves strength and stamina is going to help at this point. You know you're welcome at the range any time, but there's not much use of you coming here every day to practice if you can only last a few minutes."

"Yep, I guess so," I said in a small voice, seeing my dreams of an archery-filled summer go swirling down the drain.

"Hey, in the meantime, why don't you help with a couple of the camps here this summer? You were always great at teaching."

"Um, okay, I guess I could do that." The thought didn't raise my spirits, though. I didn't mind helping Earl, but I'd spent the entire last year teaching other people. This summer I was supposed to be focusing on *me* and my career. That was the main reason I'd moved back here.

"Great, and don't look so sad, Astrid. This is just a bump in the road; by the end of the summer, I'm betting you'll be back here full time. For now, go to physio, teach at the camps, and build your strength; in the meantime, get a lighter bow and do your horse thing at home. Come on, you're a kid; you're supposed to be enjoying yourself. Archery is a lifetime passion; you've got plenty of time to shoot competitively."

"Sure." I sighed, forcing myself to smile since he was making such an effort to cheer me up.

"Great, I'll send you the camp schedule this week and you let me know which ones you can help with."

I thanked him as best I could and then walked with dragging footsteps back to the car.

"Back so soon? How did it go, honey?" Marion said, glancing up from her tablet.

"Um, okay, I guess. I can't start training right away, though."

"Oh dear, still not healed?"

"No," I said, flopping back against the seat. "I guess I knew my shoulder wasn't quite right. I can't believe I'm saying this, but Dad was right when he said I should have gone to another physiotherapist last year."

"Well, I suppose we don't have to mention *that* part to him," Marion said, the corner of her mouth curving into the slightest of smiles. "The most important thing is that you're on the right track now."

"Earl told me I need an easier bow," I said, choking on the bitterness of the words.

"That's fine." Marion navigated her mom-mobile out of the parking lot. "We can go shopping this week if you know what you need."

I shifted so I could rest my head on the window beside me and stared at the scenery whizzing by. The truth was I didn't know what I needed. What I wanted was to be completely healed and able to shoot exactly how I had before. If only I hadn't had that stupid accident, no, make that *two* stupid accidents.

But then you wouldn't have found Claudia, I reminded myself. *You wouldn't have gone up north to the ranch and you wouldn't have Red.*

I sighed. It was probably worth all the pain and effort then. Red was one of the most amazing things in my life. I wouldn't give him up for anything.

"I'll have to do some more research first," I said slowly. "I might get one of those horse bows instead. Earl thought it would be okay to practice with that…just to gain my strength."

"Sure, sweetheart, whatever you like." Marion said, navigating expertly around a car crawling along in front of us.

"Can we afford it, though?" I asked tentatively. "I know we don't have a lot for extras right now. Dad had to sell his car and everything."

Marion coughed and glanced over at me. "Astrid, we're fine. You don't need to worry about that. Your dad just wanted a change; he's in line to get one of the new Teslas when they come out, that's all."

"Oh," I said, frowning. They'd been so worried about losing *everything* last year. I'd stayed up nights worrying about all of us and now I come home to find out that they're perfectly fine;

better than fine, actually. I wished they could tell me what was going on, even just once. It was insulting to be treated like I was a two-year-old child that needed to be protected all the time.

Her phone beeped from the depth of her purse, the especially annoying tone that meant it was my dad texting her, but she was too conscientious a driver to pull it out and check it.

"Do you want me to get it?"

"No," she said quickly. "Just leave it. I'll check it at the barn."

But after that she seemed extra tense and nervous, gripping the steering wheel tighter and tighter until her knuckles turned white.

As soon as we pulled into Hilary's driveway and parked in front of the barn, Marion grabbed her phone and scrolled through the messages anxiously.

Her face fell as she read and, to my astonishment, her lower lip began to tremble.

"Marion, are you okay?"

"Yes, of course," she said, in that same over-bright voice she'd used earlier. "Just a change of plans, that's all. It appears that Nancy can pick your father up and take him to the club so there's no need for me to hurry back."

"Oh," I said, watching her face anxiously, not knowing what to say.

She sat there without moving, staring blankly out the window, fingers clutching her phone tightly to her chest. I couldn't just walk away and leave her like this.

"Marion, um, do you want to come in with me and see the horses?"

"Pardon?" She turned to look at me vacantly, eyes wide.

"Horses," I repeated, "do you want to come see them?"

"Yes, dear," she said in a distant voice. "Whatever you like." She nodded like something had been settled and got out of the car without saying another word.

I guess I might as well leave this here, I thought glumly, taking my battered practice bow from the back seat. There was no point of me having it at home if I couldn't even practice at the range. At least I could start getting Red used to it.

The horses were already eating breakfast and their waters were full, so I grabbed my brushes and went into Red's stall to make sure he'd had a good night and that he wasn't too traumatized after Maverick and Possum had left abruptly that morning.

"Hey, buddy," I said, slipping in beside him and running a hand over his neck. "How are you feeling?"

He looked fine, even more relaxed than he had the day before and he rumbled low under his breath when he saw me, searching my pockets gently for treats.

"Do, you want to help brush him?" I asked when Marion paused in the stall doorway.

"No, not today, Astrid," she said vaguely. "I didn't bring any gloves. Perhaps next time. I'll just look around."

"Okay," I said, sending her a worried glance. I brushed Red in silence for a few minutes, working my curry comb in tight circles over his shoulders and back to loosen his muscles and free up the dirt buried deep in his coat. He bobbed his head in appreciation, tossing half his hay into the center of his stall with a flick of his nose.

"Don't waste it," I told him, smoothing his fur back down with a light-bristled body brush and then using a fine goat hair finishing brush so that his copper coat gleamed.

"Come on," I said, when he looked perfect, "if you're not hungry anymore then let's go for a walk."

His hooves clopped up the aisle in a satisfying way, which was the signal for all the other horses to abandon breakfast and come rushing to the front of their stalls to watch us go. Ellie nickered anxiously, and Rabbit leaned over his stall door, banging his big front foot against the wood.

"Rabbit, you have to settle down," I told him firmly, "you can't act like this when Pender comes back from vacation. You'll terrify her."

He shook his head violently from side to side, ears flopping against his head like a dog. Then he spun around and barged back out into his paddock, kicking out abruptly so that one hind foot cracked loudly against a fence post.

"Honestly," I said under my breath, "do you have to be that dramatic?"

Red ignored all the chaos and strode calmly out into the sunshine, looking around at his new home with interest.

The first thing I noticed was that Marion had gone back to her car and was sitting with the engine off and all the windows down. She sat in the driver's seat staring straight ahead, her gaze fixed unseeingly on the far distance. She looked like she was a million miles away.

I shivered despite the warm air and led Red tentatively toward the car.

"Marion? Are you sure you're okay?" I asked in a small voice, coming up level with her window.

She jolted and looked up with wide eyes as if surprised to find herself in her car with a horse staring in her window.

"Oh yes, of course," she said. She lifted her tablet off her lap and set it in the passenger seat. "Of course, Astrid, everything's just fine. I'm just catching up on some work."

"Um, okay," I said doubtfully, "Red and I were going to go for a quick walk. Did you want to come with us?"

"Oh," she looked at her watch, "yes, no. No, I'm just going to finish up here and head out to do some errands. I'll pick you up after lunch, okay?"

"Okay," I said, uneasily, wondering if I should even be leaving her by herself. But she shooed me away with one hand, studiously picked up her tablet and started poking at the screen.

"Come on, buddy." I tightened Red's lead rope just as he was about to stick his head in the car window to investigate. Marion didn't look up and I hurried him away before he could snort horse-slime into her car or eat the seats or something equally bad.

My first goal was to check out the half-built indoor arena; I wanted to see it up close. I tugged gently on Red's rope until he stopped eating grass and moved slowly around the far end of the paddocks until we reached the edge of the wooden framework.

It looked very far from being done. The outer skeleton was up but the roof wasn't on and there weren't any walls or anything. Red and I picked our way around the perimeter. I wanted him to see everything so he wouldn't be scared when they started construction again, since the action would be happening right outside his paddock.

I probably needn't have worried. He just pulled me toward the young, spring grass growing right up against a discarded pile of lumber and began eating as if there was nothing in the world more important.

"Okay, okay," I said, pulling his head up and backing him gently up a few steps. "Let's not get pushy now."

We skirted a set of deep, rutted tire tracks down at the far end where some machinery had torn up the softer footing and headed down toward the far side of the barn where Ellie's paddock was.

Ellie nickered in surprise when we appeared unexpectedly and trotted over eagerly to see us. Red nickered back, and I let him walk up to her so they could sniff noses and he could reassure her that he hadn't abandoned her with all these strange horses.

Her blonde forelock covered one eye and she looked like a wild, gypsy pony.

"Hey, pretty Ellie. Are you settling in okay?" I scratched her behind her ear and, once she'd reassured herself that Red was still her friend, she turned and sauntered back into her stall to finish breakfast.

We carried on our way, following the gravel driveway up toward what I assumed must be the house. I let Red graze from time to time while I looked around with interest. Even though most of the fences were in need of repairs, there were actually pastures everywhere, enough for all our horses and more. To my right was a pretty meadow dotted with low-hanging trees.

"Oh, look, Red, it's another little barn; oh, and there's another."

We crossed into the meadow through a big gap where the fence had fallen and walked up to where two little barns stood about twenty feet apart. They were both similar; a big open stall area with enough room for two horses and attached to each was a small area that could maybe be used to store feed or tack. In fact, one of them had a saddle rack and a broken bridle hook above it. It even had a small plastic sign that had the name *Duke* engraved on it.

I wonder who he was, I imagined some girl from long ago carefully sticking his name on the wall, proud to be taking care of her first horse.

I leaned against Red's shoulder and scratched under his mane while he grazed; the tension of the morning draining out of my body limb by limb. It was amazing how one single half-day with my family, even if it had been a decent, interesting day, could sap my energy more than a week of doing heavy chores back on the ranch.

Finally, Red came up for air and we went back through the fallen gap in the fence and followed the road upward, past more overgrown pastures. I stopped when we came to a small, grassy paddock where the low, wooden fencing looked brand new, painted white and shining against the knee-high grass.

What lives here, I thought, leaning over the top rail of the little pasture. But the next second I had my answer. The tall grass parted in a wave of rustling and a series of dark, round shapes headed toward us.

Red pricked his ears and held his breath, eyes wide, his head and neck shot up until he seemed about ten inches taller than normal. And suddenly they were there in front of us. A group of Labrador-sized black and white animals making small bleating sounds and popping up one by one with their little cloven feet on the bottom rail of the fence, looking at me expectantly.

"It's okay, silly," I told Red, stroking his neck when he leaned back in alarm, "they're not cows, you don't have to worry.

They're goats, I think, or sheep…maybe. Anyway, they're definitely not cows."

They stared at us curiously with large, intelligent eyes. They were the size of goats, and had short, pointy ears that flopped partly to the side. They were all black and white, but some had patches, and some had the colours swirled together like someone had trailed a paint brush over their sides, mixing the pattern in swirls and blotches. They reached their noses out to me, begging for treats.

"Oh, you're adorable," I said, stretching my fingers out tentatively to scratch the nearest one on the neck. Its coat was sleek and soft, and it leaned into my touch, not afraid of me at all.

"Are you admiring my flock of sheep, Astrid?"

"Oh, hey, Mr. Ahlberg," I said, surprised to see Hilary's dad home in the middle of the day, dressed in jeans, a plaid jacket and muddy rubber boots. At least he seemed happier than he ever had before. "I thought they were goats."

"Don't worry, it's a common mistake. They're hair sheep so they do look a bit goaty."

"Well, I think they're great," I said. "What do you have them for?"

"It's all part of the long-term plan. The Harvest Bistro is going to be a farm to table experience where as much of the ingredients as possible are grown here in an ethical way."

"Oh," I said, drawing back, "but they're not…these guys aren't *ingredients,* are they?"

"No, no." He reached out to stroke the nearest sheep fondly under its chin, "We won't eat these ladies, just their offspring;

they're my foundation breeding stock. And it will be nice for the customers to come out and meet them, learn more about where food comes from."

"Hmm," I said, not wanting to hurt his feelings. I seriously doubted that people would want to meet the real animals whose children they were about to eat. I'd never eat meat again if I had to look all the animals in the eye. But I couldn't say that to him.

"Well, come up the hill and see what we've done with the house and the restaurant. I know Linea would love to see you."

"Sure, I'm just giving Red a tour of the property."

"He's a fine-looking animal, he seems much calmer than some of the other horses Hilary has staying here. That Rabbit is a little high strung."

"Yeah, well, he was a racehorse before, so I think he picked up some bad habits at the track."

We walked up the hill, Mr. Ahlberg striding along so fast I could hardly keep up, while he kept a running commentary about all his plans for the farm and restaurant.

"This fall we'll be more like a pop-up restaurant just for events and special occasions. Further down the road we'll be open for supper and lunch and, of course, we'll serve breakfast to our guests at the Inn, too."

"You're building an Inn, too?"

"That's Linea's department. She's renovating part of the house to be a bed and breakfast. We're not just starting a new business, Astrid. We're creating a community here; a whole new lifestyle change."

"Oh." I had no idea what he was talking about.

"Of course, it won't happen overnight. We need to take baby

steps, plan our work and work our plan, so to speak. Here's the house and here's Linea."

"Wow." I stopped as the gigantic white manor house came into view. Even completely surrounded by metal scaffolding it was clearly an impressive house and could have probably fit four or five normal-sized houses inside of it.

I imagined it was someone's version of a country mansion, part farmhouse and part millionaire's estate. It wasn't exactly the downsizing Hilary had talked about.

"Astrid!" Hilary's mom ran lightly down the front steps, her arms flung wide, ready to wrap me in a tight hug. "I am so, so happy you're here. You look fantastic. Poor Hilary's been a bit overwhelmed with her project, I'm afraid, she's so been looking forward to you coming home. We're not horse people, so we can only have so much input. And who is this big fellow here?"

"This is Red," I said proudly, as soon as she paused for breath, "he's my aunt's horse but I get to ride him."

"Well, he's lovely, look at that adorable chin hair he's growing. He's like a little goat."

I stifled a laugh and vowed that my very next chore would be clipping his excess fur, especially his beard, so he didn't look so scruffy.

"Well, Hilary's helping out with the church youth group, so we'll have to be your tour directors today. How about we show you the outside of the house for now, since this big guy can't come inside, and tell you all about our plans."

We skirted the outside of the massive house, keeping Red clear of the scaffolding and the equipment that lay scattered around everywhere.

Both the Ahlbergs were full of excitement; their words tumbled over one another as they told me about the renovations, both inside and out, and the gardens they were planting and the grape vines and the chicken house and the quail aviary and the bee hives and the rabbit hutches. It all sounded amazing but also like a lot of work; I wasn't sure how three people who'd never farmed before or owned a restaurant were going to manage everything by themselves. If I'd learned one thing staying at my aunt's ranch it was that taking care of many animals was hard work.

At the back of the house, I stopped dead in my tracks, my mouth hanging open. "Oh, wow."

"Fantastic, isn't it? It's the main reason why we had to buy the place."

I nodded, unable to find the words to describe how beautiful the view was. The house sat on top of a grassy hillside that rolled right down to the ocean. Down below was a sandy beach and a boathouse and a dock with a large boat tied to wooden pilings.

From our place on top of the hill, we could see far out to sea. Past the boats were a series of green and blue islands, and beyond that you could just see the mountains of the mainland, standing purple and white against the sky.

"This view is better than the one from our condo," I said, "it's amazing."

"I can't tell you how wonderful it is to wake up and drink our morning coffee out here just staring at that view." Hilary's mom laughed. "I have to pinch myself to make sure I'm not dreaming. Ronald has been out fishing nearly every day. Come on, take a look inside here, Astrid, this part's the restaurant."

"Oh, it's nice," I said, turning from the ocean and peering in a set of open glass doors. The part that was meant for the restaurant was a wide-open room lit by windows on all sides with a wood floors and a huge chandelier made of interlocked deer antlers hanging the middle. Even though the tables and chairs were draped with protective cloths, it still looked warm and inviting. I could imagine how amazing it would look when all the furniture was in place and it was full of happy customers.

"This whole wing here will be for the restaurant, the kitchen and the guest suites for the bed and breakfast and we'll use the west wing for us to live in."

"Wow, this place is so huge." I whispered, following them across the lawn to the other side of the house.

"It's certainly perfect for our needs," Hilary's mom said, smiling dreamily. "We should have done this a long time ago. This is much more in alignment with our values than the life we left behind. That's the house, and now we'll show you the chickens and the quails."

I looked at my watch and frowned. I hadn't realized how long I'd been away from the barn. It was already almost lunch time and Marion would be expecting me to be on time. I still had to clean Red's stall and give everyone lunch.

Still, I didn't want to be rude. I followed Hilary's parents to the chicken coop and admired the multi-coloured birds marching around inside, and then we went to the quail pen and did the same.

"Sorry, I have to go," I told them before they could drag me to see the bee hives. "I promise I'll come back for the full tour. I have to run and feed lunch now."

"Oh, absolutely, Astrid, I know how you girls are about your horse chores. We'll show you the gardens and the rest of the farm next time. Come for dinner and a sleepover and we'll give you a real tour."

"Thanks, I will," I said, leading Red back down the driveway toward the barn. I looked at my watch again and, when we reached the sheep paddock, I led Red over to the low fence. Feeling slightly guilty about not wearing my helmet, I hung the lead rope over his neck and attached it to the other side of his halter like a clumsy pair of reins, climbed on the rail and slipped onto his bare back.

He waited until I was settled and then picked up a brisk walk, or brisk for Red anyway, toward the barn.

Despite being late, it was impossible to stay worried when the day was so beautiful, and I was riding bareback past miles of rolling pastures on the best horse in the world. My thoughts drifted back to my meeting with Earl at the range. Surely, he couldn't be right about me not being able to practice. Everyone talked about pushing through the hard times and making their dreams happen; nobody talked about resting and lowering your expectations.

"Hang on, buddy," I said, just as we came in sight of the barn. Marion's car was already parked in the driveway, and I slipped off his back and landed lightly on the ground, hoping she hadn't seen me riding without a helmet. I didn't need her worrying about me when I was out here alone.

Luckily, she was at the far end of the barn when I got there and hadn't even noticed me at all. She was down in front of Ellie's stall, standing about a foot away from the little horse, her head tilted to one side as if she were studying her. She looked up as Red's hooves came clopping back down the aisle.

"Oh, Astrid, there you are. Good."

"Sorry, Marion, I still have to clean Red's stall and give everyone lunch. Are you okay waiting just a few more minutes?"

"Certainly," she said, turning back to stare at Ellie.

I put Red away and gave him his lunch and then quickly threw hay to the rest of the horses and checked their water.

"Um, Marion?" I said, skirting around her to put lunch in Ellie's stall. "Are you sure you're okay?"

"I brought gloves," she said unexpectedly, holding up her hands that were covered in a pair of half-worn leather gloves I'd never seen before. They weren't gardening gloves, either; they'd most definitely been purchased at a tack store; I recognized the brand. She caught my eye and sent me a shy smile.

I studied her more closely and realized she was wearing jeans and a cotton shirt; not at all the type of clothes she'd normally choose. She must have gone home and changed while I was out touring the property.

"Did you want to brush Red?" I asked her in surprise. "I still have to clean his stall so we have time."

"Actually," Marion paused and took a deep breath, "do you think I could brush this one here?"

"Ellie?" I paused. I didn't think Hilary would mind if Marion brushed her. Even though the mare was young she was very steady and had never put a foot wrong in all the months I'd handled her back at the ranch.

"Okay," I said finally. "I'll get her brushes."

I pulled Ellie's grooming kit from the tack room and grabbed her blue nylon halter and a lead rope. She probably didn't even need to be tied since she was about to be face-deep in hay, but I didn't want to risk her knocking over Marion by accident.

"Come on, Marion. I'll show you how to put her halter on."

I gently stroked the mare's shoulder until she came up for air and then slipped the halter over her head and tied her rope in a safety knot to the ring in the wall just beside her manger.

"Okay, so the first brush you need…"

I stopped when I saw Marion standing quietly beside me with the round rubber curry comb in her hand.

"Yeah, that's the one…now you move it in circular…." I stopped again as Marion leaned in and began currying Ellie's withers like she'd done it a million times before.

I edged backward out of her way and moved to the stall door, watching as she moved her brush in slow, rhythmic circles, dislodging a faint but steady stream of dirt and hair onto the shavings below.

Ellie snorted in satisfaction into her hay pile and leaned into Marion's brush strokes.

Thoughtfully, I left them alone and grabbed the wheelbarrow and a manure fork so I could clean Red's paddock and then tidy his stall. He was always a clean horse and preferred not to mess his stall up unless the weather was very bad. It was an easy job, but I took my time, giving Marion the space she needed.

She looks like she's done this before, I thought, glancing across the aisle at her. *Was she around horses when she was a kid? She never talks about her childhood much.*

When I came out of Red's stall, she was carefully combing out Ellie's long mane, isolating each golden strand and laying it on the mare's neck in perfect order. The mare's coat was already polished to a high shine.

"Wow, Marion, she looks great," I said, putting the wheelbarrow away and coming back to stand in front of where Ellie was tied.

She looked up and smiled, her eyes looking more tranquil than I'd ever seen them in all the years we'd lived together.

"Oh, hello, sweetheart. Thank you for letting me spend some time with her. She's such a kind soul; she reminds me of your Quarry. I do miss my visits to Claudia's farm."

"Claudia's? You went to see her after I left?" I asked, surprised.

"Oh, often. Whenever she was home from the hospital, I brought Caprice to see her nearly every day. It didn't take long before she convinced me to brush Quarry from time to time. Sometimes I'd just park my car there by the barn in the fresh air and work on my tablet. It was so peaceful out at the farm. I miss it and I miss Claudia."

I frowned at the heavy note of sadness in her voice. It had never occurred to me that Marion might miss Claudia as much as I did, that they'd become friends, and that she might be grieving the loss of Quarry and the farm, too.

"You can visit Ellie any time," I said on impulse, crossing my fingers that Hilary wouldn't mind. "And you can ride Red, too, if you want; he's very kind."

"Oh no, dear. Thank you, but I couldn't think of riding. I wouldn't know where to begin. I will take you up on your offer of brushing Ellie from time to time, when I have a spare afternoon. It's very soothing to spend time with her. Now, if you're all ready to go I just have to change and then we can head home and get ready to meet your father. His game isn't until later this afternoon, so he won't expect us until then."

Marion disappeared into the small change room and came out with all her barn clothes, including gloves and shoes tied into an air-tight plastic bag.

"Um, you can keep your boots and stuff here if you like," I told her, brushing some horse hair self-consciously off my dusty jeans.

"We'll see. I'll take these home to sanitize first and then perhaps we could find a place for them here. We'd better get going."

"Hang on one sec," I said, darting into the tack room and grabbing an apple off the counter. Red and I had a routine to uphold.

He took the apple gently off my palm, crunching it happily while I kissed his forehead and straightened his forelock.

"Goodbye, good boy," I whispered. "I'll see you tomorrow."

I felt a strange pang of longing as I left. I'd only been home a day but already this barn and rolling acres of property felt like home in a way that our condo probably never could.

We drove back into town where we showered and changed, and Marion dumped our laundry into the sanitize cycle on the washer.

I yawned, still tired from all the travel the day before and pretended to be enthusiastic when Marion handed me a kale salad with a pile of dried fruit and nuts sprinkled over it.

"There's Caesar dressing on it, too," she said, smiling. "Two tablespoons full; I thought we could use a treat."

"Great," I said weakly, reminding myself to be polite. "Looks delicious."

Actually, even with hardly any dressing, the salad wasn't bad at all. In fact, I kind of liked it; not as good as lunches back at the ranch, but still decent.

***

The entrance outside the racquet club was already packed with sporty, well-dressed people all shining with health and good looks, just like yesterday. It was lunch time and there was a food truck selling sprouted wraps and smoothies laced with algae and wheatgrass parked on the curb. It was doing a brisk business; the squash people had it surrounded like a pack of wolves on a wounded caribou. We threaded our way through the chaos, me keeping my head down and avoiding eye contact while Marion greeted people all the way to the door. She seemed to know everyone.

Inside was just as busy. It was hard to tell who was a fan and who was a player because half the people not playing had shown up in tech gear as well. Who would have guessed that smashing a little ball around a glass cage would have such a following?

"Marion, Astrid, good to see you." It was the Greek god from yesterday, Darius, looking impeccably perfect with not a hair out of place. He stared just as intensely as he had the day before, taking first Marion's hand in greeting and then mine. He seemed to have forgotten that I'd insulted him somehow the other night at the reception.

"Come, ladies, I will direct you to the best seats in the house. Marion, your husband will be playing his first match in about a half-hour. Shall I bring you some drinks?"

"Oh, no," Marion said, blushing faintly, "thank you but we can get them ourselves. I should go find Bruce."

"I insist. Bruce is still warming up with Nancy, but he said I must look after both of you today as his special guests. Shall we go find our seats?"

For a second, uncertainty flashed across Marion's face, but then she forced a smile and allowed him to lead us to the same spot we had yesterday. She'd brought cushions for us to line the hard bench with and we sat down while he disappeared to find us drinks.

"Well, this is a good turn-out," she said brightly, "you father will be pleased."

There were already matches going on in two of the glass playing courts, and the crowd had gathered around the one closest to us where two women were battling it out, moving at speeds so fast they didn't even look human.

"Wow," I said, leaning forward in spite of myself, "how do they keep going like that? It looks exhausting."

"Those two are world class players," Marion said quietly, "we were lucky to have the prize money to draw in talent like that. As soon as squash makes its successful Olympic bid, those two will be on the team for sure."

"Is that what Dad wants to do? Be on some international team."

Marion coughed and then laughed. "I'm sure he'd love it, Astrid, but right now he's just setting his sights on North America. We've developed an invitational exhibition circuit to introduce people to the game and develop new talent. Our goal is to petition to have squash included as an Olympic sport. It will be fully sponsored. Anyone who qualifies will get to spend all summer travelling across Canada and the States."

"Oh, I hope he gets to go," I said, probably too enthusiastically. The idea of my dad being gone all summer leaving just me and Marion alone sounded too good to be true.

"Well, he'll most likely qualify if he wins the rest of his games this tournament. But, of course, we wouldn't want to uproot you from your life at the barn and have you spend your whole summer on tour."

"No, thank you," I said quickly, glad for the millionth time that Aunt Lillian had allowed me to bring Red home. Without anything tying me here, I might have had to spend the entire summer in endless squash tournaments. This was definitely not my world.

A bell rang and the match between the two women was over. The one in the black skirt and tank top raised her hands up over her head, victorious while the one in yellow gave her a sweaty congratulatory hug and then stalked off to the shower area.

"Your drinks, ladies." Darius was back, handing us green smoothies and pre-made veggie-wraps covered in plastic.

"Thank you," Marion said graciously, slipping her wrap into her purse as soon as he'd turned away.

I set mine beside me on the bench, feeling hungry but cautious. Marion was always kind to me, but she noticed *everything,* and she had a phobia about eating too much. I'd have to wait until she was distracted to eat it; we may have just eaten lunch but that kale salad was long gone.

"Oh, there's your father," Marion said, and I turned to see

my dad striding toward the nearest glass court, dressed in another form-fitting outfit, swinging his racket aggressively from side to side. To anyone else he might look relaxed and unbeatable but, from long practice, I could see the tension in his jaw and the fevered expression in his eyes that he got when he was working on a deadline or was stressed out.

He's not sure he'll win, I thought in surprise, *he's actually nervous.*

He turned casually to the audience, scanning the faces closest to him. I was just about to raise my arm to let him know where we were when his coach, Nancy bounced up beside him, her ponytail swinging madly from side to side.

She laughed her high, glittering laugh and caught his upper arm, wrapping her fingers around his bicep and stretching up on tip-toe to say something quietly in his ear.

Are you kidding me?

Marion tensed beside me, drawing her shoulders up until they were near her ears, but she didn't say a word. And I didn't know what to say to make her feel better. Not looking at her, I reached for my wrap instead, unwinding the plastic and nibbling nervously at the edges.

I risked a quick glance at Marion, but her face was completely blank, totally devoid of any emotion. Only her hands, balled into tight fists in her lap gave her away. I shifted closer so our shoulders bumped lightly. After a rigid second, she leaned into me just the tiniest bit and let out an unhappy sigh.

Despite my dad's nerves, the match had a predictable outcome; he crushed his opponent and spent way too long striding around his cube, arms raised victoriously in the air while his exhausted rival crouched in a corner with his hands on his knees, wheezing and struggling open-mouthed to catch his breath.

Cheers and applause met my dad on all sides when he stepped out of the cube, and he beamed, glowing with satisfaction and the thrill of winning. Nancy met him, looking up into his face adoringly while she draped a towel reverently over his shoulders.

Anger blazed in my chest, and before I could stop myself, I'd climbed to my feet.

"Come on, Marion," I said abruptly, "let's go down there."

"Oh, Astrid," she said, looking alarmed, "we don't want to disturb him now."

"Yes, we do. We're his family and *you* belong down there. Now, come on."

She sent me a tentative half-smile and followed me down the steps to the spot where my dad was now being interviewed by a short, bald newspaper reporter in a tweed jacket. Who'd guessed that Squash would attract this much attention?

"Brilliant match," the reporter said, beaming at my dad. "To what would you say contributed to your sudden rise to being one of the top players in your division?"

"Oh," my dad said, trying unsuccessfully to look modest. "Squash is a game of strategy. Anyone who has an analytical mind like mine, the ability to make rapid-fire decisions, and the drive to win at all costs will be able to excel at this sport. I have all those qualities."

"Of course." The reporter coughed and straightened his tie. "Any final words of thanks?"

"Thanks?" My dad looked blank. "Oh, yes. Thank you to my

sponsors at WorldCor, and to my coach, Nancy, who drives me to succeed."

"Anyone else?"

"No…I can't think of…." He stopped, his gaze fixed on Marion and, to his credit, a faint blush stained his cheeks. "Oh, of course, much of the credit goes to my lovely wife, Marion, and my daughter, Astrid, for supporting me all the way. Come on over here, ladies."

We both stood rooted to the ground, and then the crowd parted until we stood beside him for a quick photo shoot. He draped an arm around both of us and Marion just looked dazed, and I managed to smile while leaning as far away from his sweat-soaked shirt as possible. The whole experience was incredibly uncomfortable.

Finally, we were released back to our seats while my dad went off to shower and change.

"Well, that was different," Marion said, but she looked pleased. She seemed to have overlooked the fact that he'd barely remembered to acknowledge her at all. I could see him forgetting about *me*, but Marion practically devoted her whole life to the man. He wouldn't be able to function without her quietly running his life behind the scenes.

The afternoon wore on and I found myself actually beginning to enjoy watching the matches and to understand how the game was played. My dad checked in with us, looking fresh and completely un-winded by his match, wearing an identical outfit plastered with sponsor names as he'd had on before.

He was only there for a few minutes before Nancy, smiling at me and Marion with her teeth bared and her blue eyes glittering under the lights, hustled him off to debrief and plan the strategy for tomorrow's game.

I liked her less and less every time I saw her.

Darius came and checked in on us at least once an hour, bringing snacks (which put him in my good books) and asking about a hundred times if we had everything we needed.

"What is *with* him?" I whispered to Marion when he was gone. "I thought he was like some star player. Why is he sucking up to us?"

"He's not sucking up, Astrid. He's just very grateful that the club facilitated his move to Canada and for the full sponsorship that your father organized with WorldCor. Socializing and being polite to sponsors is part of the package of being an athlete, I'm afraid. You'll have to remember that if you pursue your archery further."

If? I thought in alarm, *doesn't she mean* when *I become a professional archer? Why is she doubting me now?*

"He's just trying to thank us however he can," she went on, still talking about Darius. "You should be nice to him, Astrid; he's a war refugee, you know, and he lost most of his family. He's been through a good deal of hardship. I would have thought you'd get along with him because of the horses."

"I *did* ask him about them," I said, "but I think I offended him somehow. He just walked away without answering."

"Oh," Marion said thoughtfully. "Well, he's been through a lot, I suppose. He's only a few years older than you, Astrid, so he might be shy."

"He *can't* be my age," I said skeptically, "he practically has a beard."

"Well, I suppose a person grows up little faster when half their family is killed and they're left an orphan in a strange country."

Marion frowned in irritation and I looked away quickly, feeling small and guilty. It wasn't Darius's fault that he was that ultra-intimidating combination of beautiful and intense. It wasn't easy to be myself around someone like that. I vowed to be nicer to him the next time we met.

We managed to escape around dinnertime and thankfully, we didn't have to go out to any events that night. There would be one final dinner on Monday evening and then the whole thing would be finally over. I wanted things to quiet down and to see Caprice again. She must be miserable in the kennel all by herself.

"Well, that was a satisfying day," my dad said, jumping into the driver's seat of Marion's car and revving the engine enthusiastically. "What did you think of your old man, Astrid? Were you impressed?"

"It was a very good game, Dad," I said honestly.

"My opponent tomorrow is weak. I should be sure to take him and then, if I win on Monday, I'll qualify for the exhibition circuit. That would give you something to brag about."

"Um, yeah, that would be great."

"What would you think about touring all over with your dad? We could buy an RV and see the sights, be travelers for the summer?"

"Oh, um, that sounds like fun, Dad, but I have Red and am helping Hilary out at her new farm. And, uh, I'll be starting archery again soon."

Like a bucket of icy water had been thrown over us, an ominous silence fell over the car, wrapping me so tight I could hardly breathe. The hairs on the back of my arms stood up and I froze, one hand automatically closing on the door handle as if I were ready to leap out into traffic, to do whatever I needed to do to get out of the path of danger.

My dad didn't explode, though. After a long, tense moment, he breathed out through his nostrils in one hiss like an angry bull.

"Well, that's a shame," he said between clenched teeth. "I thought it would be a good bonding experience for us all as a family, but never mind, if you don't have time for us then I guess that's that."

I stared at the back of his head in astonishment, my mouth hanging open. This was the man who, *maybe*, voluntarily spent time with me twice a year, usually because Marion forced him into it. And now he was making me feel guilty for not wanting to spend the entire summer following him on tour where he most likely would completely ignore me the whole time?

"It's okay, Astrid," Marion said smoothly, turning around to send a tight smile in an effort to diffuse the mounting tension. "Your father just forgot that you'd already made commitments. We understand."

My father muttered something under his breath and I fixed my gaze outside the window, watching the trees roll by, waiting for the thud of my heart to go back to normal.

"Fine, I guess I'll go *alone*," he said louder this time, so we could both hear him. "Since this family is so unsupportive."

Marion inhaled sharply, and I just sat there, my stomach in knots and my whole body ridged with fear and shame.

I want to go back to the ranch, I thought desperately thinking

69

of Aunt Lillian's gentle, smiling face, *I should have never come back here.*

My dad looked around at us as if surprised to find himself in the middle of the roiling, dark cloud of tension that filled the car to capacity.

"Well, we won't worry about that until I've won my division," he said smiling, his mood changing abruptly from frigid to sunny. "I'm sure we'll figure out a plan that works for everyone. What do you say we order pasta tonight so nobody has to cook?"

"That sounds lovely, darling," Marion said, coming back to life as if nothing had happened.

"Astrid?"

"Okay, thanks," I said weakly, clearing my throat a few times to get the words out.

Marion had already pulled out her tablet and brought up the menu for a new restaurant they'd both started going to and put in our order.

"The usual for you, dear?" she asked my father and punched a few buttons when he nodded. "Astrid, how about a half-order of spaghetti with parmesan and I'll sub out the garlic bread for a salad?"

"Oh, I like garlic bread," I said automatically, without thinking, and then abruptly shut my mouth, closing my eyes and holding my breath.

Stupid, I told myself angrily, *how can you mess up so many times in such a short car ride?*

There was another long, weighty silence and then my dad said, "Well, it *is* a celebration, so I suppose a small indulgence wouldn't hurt. We have to keep our strength up, after all."

He laughed, and I opened my eyes to see Marion smiling up at him adoringly, looking like he'd said the smartest, funniest thing in the world.

I exhaled slowly, cursing myself for the garlic bread comment. I'd grown out of the practice of censoring my words and my eating habits. I couldn't let down my guard here like I could at Aunt Lillian's. It would pay to keep that in mind from now on.

Dinner was waiting for us at the front desk when we got home, and I managed to pick away at my smaller portion slowly so that I finished at the same time as everyone else. My dad magnanimously split the garlic bread into three pieces, handing the smallest piece to me as if it were a gift. I smiled back automatically like I was supposed to and nibbled on it as unobtrusively as possible.

Finally, my dad shuffled off to the den to work on his Sudoku puzzles and, after I'd helped Marion clear the table and load the dishwasher, I retreated to the safety of my room for the rest of the night.

But, even all alone with the door shut, I couldn't stop my hands from shaking. I didn't even know what was bothering me so much; it wasn't like anything had *happened*. Nobody had beaten me or even threatened me. But there was something about that constant terrible tension in our house that made me so anxious that I felt physically ill.

And my dad was acting more unpredictably than before. Back in the old days, he was just cranky and nasty pretty much all the time. I'd known exactly where I stood with him; he'd consistently despised me.

But this new dad who was nice sometimes and then became nasty at the flick of a switch is what made my hands shake with fear. Because the nice part of him was easy to like, you could see that the people at his club loved him. And that made the bad side of him seem so much worse.

I picked up my phone uncertainly and stared at the blank screen, not sure what to do. I just wanted to feel better.

Hey, are you still up? I typed tentatively and hit send before I could change my mind.

The response from Rob came back almost instantly and the flood of relief that flowed through me was so strong I nearly cried.

Just finishing homework, I have a paper due.

Um, it's summer. How do you have homework?

I take some college courses for fun. It will give me an edge when I apply for university.

Of course you do, I typed, laughing, *geek*. And then I instantly felt horrible because what if he thought I was seriously insulting him?

Guilty as charged. How is everything at home?

I hesitated, fingers poised over my phone, debating what to say. I couldn't tell him the truth. That I was scared and lonely and full of regret; it would be too embarrassing. Nobody wanted to hang out with *that* girl.

It's okay, I said finally, *the usual.* I hesitated again. *I miss the ranch.*

Tears sprang to my eyes and I pushed them away roughly with the back of my hand. This had been my decision to come home, nobody had forced me into it, and it was too late to turn back, so there was no point in crying about it.

There was no answer, so I got changed and pulled my laptop onto my bed, sitting cross-legged as I pulled up some of the horse archery videos I'd saved. I'd subscribed to this great channel that was run by this hilarious group of about ten brothers who lived somewhere overseas where it was all desert. The videos were in English, but they had accents and wore those robes that desert people wore, so I knew it had to be somewhere far away.

They were completely amazing, fearless riders who did all sorts of stunts and who rarely ever missed their targets. But their bravery wasn't the main thing that stood out; it was the obvious love that they had for their horses. I'd seen other videos where the archers were good, but they'd be kicking their horses with big spurs or yanking on their mouths or their horses looked thin or lame or just plain scared.

These riders weren't like that at all. They moved seamlessly with their horses, and could drop their reins completely and just use seat aids while their arms were free for shooting. And the horses were brave and beautiful and seemed to be having just as good a time as their riders. If Red and I were going to attempt horse archery, then it would have to be like that; I wasn't going to risk thumping around on his back or ruining his mouth or scaring him. I wanted it to be beautiful.

My phone pinged, and I glanced away from the video.

Just say the word, Astrid. I'll come and rescue you.

I drew in a sharp breath and then carefully studied the message a few times to make sure I'd read it right. Of course, he was just kidding. It wasn't like he could actually steal me away.

But still, I hugged my phone gratefully to my chest, feeling not quite so alone in the world.

Chapter Three

The next morning, I woke to the sound of Marion talking quietly on the phone right outside my bedroom door.

"Oh dear, well, I suppose we'll have to come and get her then. I'm not sure what we'll do with her, but I guess we'll make due. Is there any way you could just…. No, no, I understand."

I heard her sigh and move down the hall toward the kitchen to wake up the Keurig machine.

Worried, I slipped out of bed and padded down the hall in my bare feet.

"Everything okay, Marion?"

"It will be in a second," she said, taking a huge swig of coffee, closing her eyes gratefully as the liquid hit her throat. "That's better. Now I can face the day."

I laughed, feeling more like my old self, and poured myself a cup, ignoring her surprised look. "Me, too. You know this would taste better with real cream and sugar, right? Soy milk just isn't the same. Who was on the phone?"

"Oh, the kennel. They want me to pick up Caprice a day early. She's not happy there; she's barking non-stop and she won't eat. She's supposed to be on pain medication, but they can't get it into her. I'm not sure how we'll fit her in around your father's schedule, though. Today is a big day."

"Poor thing, she must be lonely. Can we go get her right now? I can look after her."

"I guess we'll have to. She hasn't had any breakfast yet, so she's probably starving. How fast can you be dressed and ready?"

"Two minutes," I said, dumping my cup of foul soy-milk-tainted coffee into the sink and heading for my room. I threw on the jeans and a t-shirt that had been designated for the barn and pulled my hair back into some semblance of order. There, I was ready.

Marion met me at the front door, looking like she'd spent an hour on herself rather than the two allotted minutes. She'd cultivated speed-perfection into an art form. Unfortunately, none of her skills had rubbed off on me at all.

It was just a short drive to the kennel, and the second we stepped out of the van, we could both hear Caprice's high-pitched barking coming from somewhere inside.

"That's her stress bark," Marion said, biting her lip. "I should have never left her here."

The front door was locked but when we rang the buzzer a few times, a harried looking young woman came to the door.

"Thank goodness you're here," she said, wincing as Caprice's barks ratcheted up another few decibels. "You've got to get her out of here. She's upsetting all the other dogs."

"She doesn't like to be left alone," Marion said, as we followed the woman past the outer play area to the kennels in the back, "she won't bark like this if someone stays with her."

"Well, we can't be expected to stay with her every second of the day," the girl said, rolling her eyes, "there are other dogs here and we have chores to do. We can't devote every waking moment to her. That's your job; you're her owner."

Caprice threw herself against the chain link door of her kennel as soon as she caught sight of us, forcing her little nose through the grate in a desperate effort to get to Marion.

"Oh, Caprice," Marion said, crouching down, "be calm, you'll hurt yourself."

She flipped the latch on the door and the little dog raced out into the hallway still barking and spinning in hysterical circles.

"Astrid, can you bring her stuff, please? I'm going to take her outside to the car so she calms down."

"Wow, that dog could use some training," the girl said to me, stuffing Caprice's dog bed, bowls, and accessories into a large print bag I recognized as the one Marion used to use for her yoga stuff. "You know, we do offer remedial classes. I could give you a brochure if you're interested."

"Um, no thanks. She's fine," I said, taking the bag awkwardly from her.

"She's not fine." The girl followed me to the door. "Dogs need to know their place in the world, their order in the pack. Your dog is anxious because—"

Anger rose up in me, quick and hot, and I spun around to fix her with a baleful stare, pinning her in place. "She's *anxious* because her owner died this winter, then she hurt her leg, and then my parents stuck her in an awful place like this for the weekend with someone who doesn't even like her. I'd hate it here, too."

I clapped a hand over my mouth, ashamed at how angry and awful I sounded. For a moment there, I'd almost sounded like my *dad*.

The woman's eyes widened, and she blinked at me in astonishment.

"Sorry," I said quickly, ducking my head. What on earth had come over me?

My face burned as I pushed through the door and hurried toward the car. I had a sudden horrifying image of the lady yelling at me or calling the police and lodging a complaint. But when I reached the safety of the car and turned to look over my shoulder the doorway was empty.

As soon as I slid into the passenger seat, Marion handed Caprice's trembling body to me. "It's my fault for leaving her there. I hope she didn't hurt her leg again when she was panicking."

We drove to the barn in silence, Marion gripping the steering wheel so hard her knuckles turned white. At every stoplight, she reached over to stroke the poodle's head, but Caprice didn't even notice, she'd fallen fast asleep the minute the car started, and she didn't wake up once until we'd reached the barn.

"I'm not sure what to do with her today." Marion frowned and slowly opened her door. "I did promise your father that I'd be there at the club to support him. I'd hate to leave her at home alone when she's in this state."

"I can watch her," I said quickly. "I don't have to go to the tournament. Hilary won't mind if I hang out here today, she's at rehearsals anyway, and I don't think Dad would care if I don't come."

"Oh, Astrid, of course he'd care. But, you're right, he will be very busy today; he's under a lot of pressure."

"I thought his therapist said he was supposed to be doing this to learn teamwork. When did it turn into a competition?"

"Well, yes," she hesitated, "that *was* how it started. But, I don't know, it seems to make him so happy and it does keep him occupied."

"Good enough," I said quickly, sending her a teasing smile, thinking at the very least that it kept him out of the house.

She coughed under her breath, not disloyal enough to make fun of him with me but her lips twitched the tiniest bit.

Caprice held her hind leg high off the ground when I set her down, but she wagged her tail and sniffed the air eagerly, taking in the familiar smell of horses, hay, and countryside; the smells she'd grown up with.

We walked slowly beside her, letting her pick her own pace into the barn and, once she'd sniffed up and down the whole aisle, she settled into her dog bed with a grateful sigh.

"Are you sure you're okay with this, Astrid? She'll need her medication after her breakfast. I hate to leave you all day with her."

"Marion, she's fine. Just go. Tell Dad good luck from me and I'll see you tonight."

"Right, here's some money for lunch then, order whatever you like, and have fun with the horses, dear. Say hello to Ellie."

Finally, she was gone, and I was miraculously alone for the entire day.

The horses were already eating breakfast so the first thing I decided to do was clean Red's stall. I slipped on his halter and led him carefully past the sleeping Caprice to one of the unoccupied stalls, the one across from Rabbit, and turned him loose. I'd noticed earlier that the unused paddock still had a good amount of grass growing, even after Rob's horses had spent the night there. I knew Red would appreciate the change of scenery. He didn't disagree; after checking the empty stall out briefly he headed outside and began to nibble at what was left of the spring grass.

I took my time cleaning his stall and paddock, savoring the fact that I didn't have to rush around or *be* anywhere. I raked his paddock until it was spotless and piled more shavings in his stall so he had an extra thick bed to sleep on.

When everything was in order, I looked at my watch and frowned. Hilary still wasn't back from her rehearsal and all the other horses still needed their stalls cleaned. She hadn't asked me to do it and I didn't want to step on her toes and start taking over. Still…I looked at my watch again.

Oh, what harm can it do? I thought, *I'm sure Hilary will be glad for the help.*

I slipped on Ellie's halter and led her to the grassy paddock next to Red. Then I cleaned her stall and paddock, remembering belatedly that she was the type to scatter manure into every last inch of her stall and then walk in circles, grinding everything up like a blender.

"Great, thanks, Ellie," I said, glancing over to make sure she and Red were still behaving themselves. Once her stall and paddock were finally clean, I did the same thing with Riverdance, who followed me obediently to the last free stall with a pleased look on his face. He was neat and tidy, of course, and left all his manure in a single pile in his paddock and, like Red, his stall was spotless.

"Okay, you two," I said, turning to Jerry and Rabbit, who were the only ones left, "are you going to behave while I clean your stalls?"

I left them both where they were and cleaned around them while they ate. I wasn't confident that they wouldn't run around like maniacs if I changed their routine too much, and I didn't want to risk anyone getting hurt.

Once everyone was clean and returned to their proper stalls, I swept the aisle until it was free of every last speck of hay and dust.

"Will you eat your breakfast now, Caprice?" I said, kneeling and petting her head. She'd slept like a log the whole time, only glancing up briefly whenever the horses clopped past her dog bed.

She opened her eyes sleepily and then stretched out her front paws and yawned, her little pink tongue curling up between her sharp teeth like a question mark.

I rummaged through her bag of supplies and pulled out a can of food that luckily had a pull tab on it; I would have been completely out of luck if it had needed a can opener. I dumped the gloppy mess of chunks and gravy into her bowl and then found her medication and stuffed the tablet deep inside the food with my finger, avoiding any contact with the smelly stew.

Caprice whined happily, stood on three legs and began to devour the food as soon as I set it down in front of her.

"There's a good girl," I said, going into the tack room to wash every last trace of dogfood meat off my fingers.

When I came out, Hilary's mom's car whooshed up to the front door with a spray of gravel and then shot off as soon as Hilary jumped out.

"Astrid!" she called in excitement, doing some twirly ballerina dance leap into the barn. She was still wearing tights, leg warmers and some gauzy blue mini-dress so I assumed she'd just come from dance class. She spun in a circle and flung herself across the aisle in a series of leaps and then floated gracefully down to a sitting position on the floor next to Caprice.

"You brought my favorite dog," she said, leaning down to kiss Caprice on top of her head.

"I cleaned the barn," I said, "I hope you don't mind. I have the whole day to just hang out."

"Wow," Hilary said, getting up and going from stall to stall, "of course I don't mind. Thank you so much. Sorry, I'm late, though, I have extra rehearsals going on right now since our show's coming up fast. You guys are coming to watch it, right?"

"We'll definitely come," I said, "I think Marion already bought tickets. Hey, since I've got everything done, do you want to go for a ride?"

"Ugh, yes, I guess I should," Hilary said, surprising me with a frown.

"You don't want to?"

"No, I do, but Jerry's been such a handful since we moved here, ever since we stopped being able to use the ring. I never liked riding on trails very much and it's hard to keep him exercised by just riding up and down the driveway."

"Well, let's use the ring then, he'll get used to the construction if we take the time to expose him to it."

"No, it's not that. The builders said that we shouldn't use it just in case they dropped nails or other sharp things into the sand. They said they'll drag it with magnets after they're done but to stay out before then. Hopefully, they'll actually start work again someday…I paid them enough."

"Oh," I said, glad I hadn't taken Red in there the other day. "We could just ride around the property then. I still haven't seen everything and Red needs to stretch his legs; he's used to being worked every day."

"Sure." She sighed and looked over at Jerry skeptically. "Maybe he'll behave better if Red's around. We've just been riding by ourselves since we moved here, and he doesn't like it."

"Rob hasn't trailered over to ride with you?"

I glanced up to see her standing there with a funny look on her face.

"Nope," she said abruptly and then disappeared into the washroom to change her clothes before I could ask anything else.

I carefully moved Caprice's bed into the tack room, wondering if she'd start barking like back at the kennel if I went for a ride, but she just curled up and went to sleep, probably happy to be back in a barn, in *any* barn, again.

I brushed Red's already gleaming coat, sighing at the little goat-hair beard I'd forgotten to trim and picked out his feet and slipped on his bridle, leaving him free of his saddle again. Liza had told me I would have to start using my saddle if I wanted Red to get used to it, but I was feeling too lazy to start now.

Hilary was still brushing Jerry, her forehead knit in a series of worried lines as she ran the brush with excruciating slowness down his side. Jerry tossed his head up and down a few times, his eyes wide with excitement. He was obviously dying to get out of his paddock.

"Oh, sorry we're taking so long," she said when she heard Red's hooves clopping down the aisle. "You can go on ahead if you like; or maybe we could just skip it and ride another day when Jerry's calmer. We can go bake cookies or something instead."

I stared at her, wondering who this girl was and what she'd done with my friend. One thing was sure, there was no way I was going to be stuck inside *baking* on such a nice day when all I wanted to do was play outside.

"Don't worry, Hilary, I'm not in a rush. I have the whole day. I'll take Red outside and let him graze while you get tacked up."

She sighed loudly and slid open Jerry's stall door to go and get his stuff from the tack room, grimacing at me weakly as she passed. She was clearly anxious about Jerry being in high spirits, but I was sure that once we hit the trails she'd see how wonderful it was.

Finally, Jerry was tacked up and Hilary reluctantly led him over to the mounting block.

"Okay, Jerry, *stand*," she said to him, her voice wavering, as his head shot up and his eyes bugged out at something invisible off in the distance. He ignored her, snorting loudly through both nostrils and turning so his shoulder bumped into her, sending her staggering backward a few feet.

"Ouch, Jerry, quit it," she commanded, backing him up sharply a couple of steps. He obeyed, looking astonished to find she was somehow still attached to him by his dangling reins, and then he reached over and nudged her hard with his nose. "Come on, stop being such a jerk," she said, her voice trembling as she finally got him lined up beside the mounting block.

Privately, I thought he was being pretty typical; it was she who was acting out of character. Hilary was normally a beautiful, confident rider, but she looked terrified of him today. What was going on?

She gathered her reins and scrambled onto his back in one swift move, jamming her feet in the stirrups and bridging her reins across his neck as if waiting for him to explode. He did look a bit intimidating with his head in the air and his back hollowed and his pink-tinged nostrils fluttering excitedly in the air.

"Okay, crazy-pants," Hilary said, taking a deep breath and reaching one hand carefully forward to scratch his neck with the tips of her fingers, "we're just going to walk okay, just *walk*."

Jerry jigged forward a few steps then stopped dead, jamming his front feet into the ground and spraying gravel in all directions. He stood rooted, eyes widening as he caught sight of the rising edifice of the indoor arena towering over the far side of the barn. He snorted loudly, that sharp cracking sound that signals danger, and the muscles on his neck bulged.

Hilary's face went white with fear, but she didn't panic, she kept petting his neck and talking to him softly, and I could see her struggling to regulate her breathing.

"Come on, Red," I murmured, leading my half-sleeping horse to the mounting block and slipping up onto his sunshine-warmed back, "let's show him there's nothing to be afraid of."

Once I was on, Red looked over at Jerry with mild interest and then turned and ambled up the driveway past him in the direction we'd taken yesterday, his head bobbing and his ears at half-mast.

Behind me there was the sound of scrabbling feet and then Jerry's nose appeared right next to my thigh, so close I could feel his hot breath through my jeans. His long legs hit the ground like they were made of springs as he bounced along in our wake, his short grey mane bobbing up and down on his neck with every electrified step.

"Are you okay, Hilary?" I asked, looking uneasily at her grim expression.

She nodded to me briskly and took a deep breath. "I hate trail rides," she said, her voice still tight with fear. "I've never liked them. And I hate that I'm afraid of my own horse out here. I'm supposed to be a good rider and I feel like I don't even *know* Jerry when he's like this; he feels dangerous."

"He's definitely excited," I said thoughtfully, "but don't you think that will go away with more practice? Wasn't he like this the first few times you showed him off the property?"

"Well, yes, I guess so." She bit her lip and grabbed the reins as he danced sideways, craning his neck at something invisible in the grass. "Actually, he was awful at his first show. He dumped me in the warm-up ring and then stepped through his reins and broke them. It was mortifying."

"But you survived, right? And that was in front of an audience, too. This isn't nearly as bad as that must have been. And think of what a much better horse he'll be once he's confident out here."

She glanced over, looking at me strangely. "That's good advice, actually. When did you get so smart about horses?"

I shrugged. "I don't know. Justin knew just about everything there is to know about horses; maybe I picked up some stuff.

And just think, Hilary, we'll have so much fun this summer exploring your property and all the trails."

"I guess so." She laughed and loosened Jerry's reins a millimeter. "If you say so. I haven't explored much since we got here. I've been too busy to do much of anything."

Jerry's steps slowed, and he let out a big sigh, reaching over to gently nip Red on his neck.

"Hey," I scolded, "you stop that. Red didn't do anything to you."

"Oh, he's not being mean. That's what he does to the other horses when he wants to run. I think he's asking him to play."

I looked down at Red's pricked ears and then over at Hilary. "It's up to you. Do you want to trot?"

"No," she said firmly. "I do *not*. I'm barely surviving the walk."

Luckily, Jerry was much too interested in looking at the world around him to argue with her beyond a few irritated head tosses. He passed us, striding along ahead of me and Red with his long legs, his eyes bright as if this was the best day of his life. He craned his head at everything but thankfully kept his feet on the driveway. Red finally picked up on Jerry's energy and got a spring in his own step, arching his neck and breaking into a slow trot now and then to keep up. He was comfortable, like riding a big pillow, and I sat on him easily, enjoying myself completely.

We travelled much faster today than Red and I had on our own. We came to the break in the pasture fence and Red turned automatically toward it, probably remembering the good grass he'd had there the day before.

"Do you want to go in and explore?" I asked Hilary, easing Red to a stop.

"Oh, I suppose it couldn't hurt, I guess. I haven't looked in here yet."

As soon as Jerry had passed through the gap in the fence, we turned right and followed the fence-line around the massive pasture, the horses wading up to their knees through the thick grass. I let Red take a bite now and then, but Hilary was still too nervous to let Jerry stretch out his neck, even though he looked much more relaxed already.

"Hey, this fence actually looks pretty decent in most places," Hilary said, studying the boards with a critical eye.

"The shelters are in good shape, too," I said. "I checked them out yesterday."

"This field is huge," she added as we continued to follow the fence-line downward into a small wooded area with a small stream running through it. "We could even divide it in two."

We stopped to let the horses drink, but Jerry had other ideas. He took a quick sip and then lifted his big front foot and brought it down hard onto the surface of the stream, sending water spraying in all directions.

"Jerry," Hilary cried, kicking him firmly in the sides to get him to move forward. She tugged at his reins, but he completely ignored her, much too happy with his new game to listen to her until we were all completely drenched. I was doubled over with laughter, my face buried in Red's mane to protect myself against the spray of muddy water.

Red didn't even move out of the way, even though his head and neck were drenched. He pretended nothing was happening and kept on drinking until he was finished, only lifting his head to stare at his weird friend in bemusement.

Finally, Jerry had had enough, and he stepped daintily out of the water and shook himself from head to tail like a dog, nearly unseating Hilary and sending her flying, before dropping his nose to crop at the grass growing nearby.

Hilary, soaked from head to toe, sent me a glare. "And *this* is why I hate trail riding," she said, wiping muddy water off her face.

"Oh, come on," I said, struggling to hold in my laughter. "That was hilarious. You can't get an experience like that riding around in the ring."

"Exactly," Hilary said primly, but the corner of her mouth curved up into a reluctant smile.

Jerry was much more content now and Hilary let him stride along with his neck stretched out, his movement elastic and relaxed.

The fence down at this end was in good shape, too, and Hilary brightened up when she saw how little work there was going to be in to get this pasture in working order again.

"I think Jerry will settle down a lot more if he can have real turnout," she said. "He's the type of guy who needs to stretch his legs. He was always a bit high-strung at Claudia's when the weather was too bad for him to go outside."

"Maybe it will help Rabbit, too," I added, "he looks…upset right now."

"Yeah." Hilary frowned. "He doesn't seem very happy, does he? I'll have to do something before Pender gets back. She'll never be able to ride him like he is."

We came out of the wooded area and back into the lush, rolling pasture. The horses picked up the pace. Red's ears were pricked, and his steps high and light.

"Do you want to trot now?" I asked Hilary. "Red would love it."

"Okay, fine," she said, "but if this jerk dumps me on the ground, you're picking me up and carrying me home."

"You're a brilliant rider, Hil," I said. "You're not going to fall."

And she didn't, Jerry picked up the trot easily and didn't ask for more, his eyes were bright and his ears pricked, but he looked relaxed, too. Red trundled along in his wake and finally broke into a gentle canter in order to keep up with his big friend. Jerry flicked an ear back at us but didn't bother to pick up his own pace.

I left Red's reins loose on his neck, only holding on to the end of the buckle so I didn't drop them completely while he churned along rhythmically beneath me. I was so used to riding him bareback by now that speed didn't faze me at all.

Hilary slowed Jerry to a walk when we came to the end of the pasture and turned to me with a wide smile on her face.

"Wow, that was actually fun," she said. "Jerry was great."

"See, I told you so," I said breathlessly, bringing Red up beside her.

"You were right. Now, let's see what else we can find."

We went back out through the gap in the fence and continued up the driveway toward her house. When we passed the sheep paddock, Jerry snorted at the waving grass suspiciously, but the sheep were at the far end and too busy grazing to give him much of a reason to spook.

"Let's turn here," Hilary said as the house came in sight, she pointed to a narrow trail that led off to the right into a stand of young, pine trees. "I've seen this path before and it was on my list of things to explore. I'm so glad you're here, Astrid. I haven't had any time to do any fun stuff since we bought the place. Everything has been so crazy and stressful lately; we had to move and build the barn, and then there was that whole thing with the indoor. And I've had to be at rehearsals almost every day."

"Wait, what happened with the indoor?"

"Oh"—Hilary waved her hand breezily in the air—"it just turned out to be more expensive than I'd budgeted and I ran out of money. No big deal. I paid them and everything, but they said they had some other job to do first and I'd have to wait. The contractor is a little cranky."

"Did you tell your dad?"

"Um, sort of; he's busy right now with the renovations and the restaurant. I told him I was handling it."

"Well, you are good at pretty much everything, Hilary. I'm sure it will be fine. It will be ready in no time."

The young forest gave way to larger and darker trees, big spruce and cedars that towered above us. The land dropped away abruptly, leading us steeply downward into a valley where moss grew on all the tree trunks and giant ferns grew up around us on all sides. It was a few degrees cooler than it had been up above, and damp, and a strange silence enveloped us. Even the horses seemed to take softer steps, as if reluctant to disturb the forest floor.

"Wow," Hilary said in a hushed voice, leaning backward in the saddle to stare upward at the massive trunks, "these trees must be ancient. They're definitely old growth. I wonder why it didn't get logged."

"Some of it was," I said, pointing to a gigantic stump that was bigger than Red and Jerry combined. It had deep grooves carved like a ladder on two sides and I remembered from history class that long ago, before chain-saws existed, the loggers would have to climb up these huge trees and cut them down with axes and hand saws. Sometimes it would take days or weeks to cut down a single tree.

We came to another little creek with ferns and a few pale flowers growing along the bank. This time Hilary urged Jerry through it without letting him stop. Red dropped his nose to sniff the water, flicking his head a few times to find a clean spot to drink and then he slurped delicately like a deer, and then ruined the image by lifting his head and sticking his tongue out, letting the water dribble out of his mouth and down his chin, dripping off his goat-like beard. I made another mental note to cut that thing off as soon as we got back.

We headed upward on a winding track and soon, we were out of the old growth and back into smaller pines and cedars. The ground under the horses' feet went from dark earth to sand, and then the path widened and the trees fell away completely, leaving us in a wide open meadow.

"Where are we?" I called up to Hilary, but she just shook her head.

"I don't know, but it smells salty. I think we're down by the ocean."

She was right. The land rose steadily up a low hill and when we reached the top, we could see the jewel-toned blue of the ocean stretching out in front of us in an endless expanse.

"Oh, wow," I said, and then pointed up the hill far to our left where the massive house was only a small square on the horizon, "look, there's the house and the restaurant."

"Okay, that makes sense, I know where we are now. Should we keep going?"

"Definitely." I nodded firmly. "Let's follow the trail wherever it takes us."

The horses pricked their ears excitedly when they saw all that water stretching out in front of them. I was certain Red had never seen the ocean before in his life and I wondered how he'd handle it.

"Are you okay if we trot?" Hilary asked over her shoulder. "Jerry wants to go."

"Sure," I said, happy that she was comfortable enough to suggest it.

Jerry broke into a trundling, forward trot, legs flashing and mane bobbing in excitement, and Red broke into a nice canter, snorting happily under his breath. I went with him easily, but I could feel a slight ache in my seat bones this time. My muscles were definitely going to be sore tomorrow.

The footing changed to deeper sand that bogged the horses down as they plowed through it and finally, they dropped to a walk of their own accord, blowing from the unaccustomed effort. We were right next to the ocean now, hooves sinking into the damp sandy beach that ran alongside the shore. They stopped and stared out at the wide expanse of ocean with fixed expressions, and I could only imagine what they were thinking.

The sea was calm; only a few gentle waves lapped at the shore, but it was still magnificent.

"I can't believe I didn't even know this was here," Hilary said. "This place is like paradise. I've never ridden a horse on the beach before."

"Me, neither," I said breathlessly, relishing at the soft breeze tugging at my hair, and running up and down my arms. The horses didn't want to get too close to the water, so we rode halfway up the beach until it turned too rocky and then picked our way back up onto the grassy lawn.

We passed the dock where the boat lived, too big to fit in its boathouse as Hilary's dad had confessed to me during our tour. He planned to build another one as soon as everything else was finished. And then we followed the trail back into the woods on the other side, heading upward through a poplar grove that opened up into yet another meadow.

"Hey, Hilary? What's that thing up ahead?"

Hilary looked over to the right to where a huge grassy mound of dirt stood tucked in the woods, almost as high as our heads.

"Oh, I think the old owners were going to build something here years ago. They brought in a lot of fill and dumped it but then never finished whatever the project was."

"It would be a perfect backdrop for archery," I said enviously.

"Oh, go ahead," Hilary said, shrugging. "I doubt we'll develop this area any time soon. We can ask my parents, but I'm sure that as long as there aren't any horses or humans around who could get shot here, it would be fine."

Looking at the grassy berm, I shivered with the possibilities. Earl had said I shouldn't practice too much until I had the lighter bow, but there was nothing stopping me from practicing quietly on my own. It would be a good place to teach Red, too.

The trail led onward until we came alongside more broken-down fence posts, these ones in much worse shape with whole sections of fence lying on the ground.

"We're at the lower fields now," Hilary said, "we're circling back toward the barn."

She was right; soon, we came to the driveway again and we followed it downward until we reached the barn. I was glad to see it. As much as I'd loved our ride, I was sore and my jeans were chafing in places I didn't want to think about. I looked down at my watch and wasn't surprised to see that we'd been gone for nearly two hours.

I slid down off Red and groaned when my feet hit the ground, feeling the ache all the way up into my knees, hips, and back. Red looked tired, too. He was used to trail rides, of course, but we'd been stuck in the ring nearly all winter and hadn't had time to get back in shape before our move to the island. Riding through that deep sand and trotting up and down hills was not the easiest thing for him.

I hobbled to Red's stall and led him inside before removing his bridle and giving him a scratch on the neck. I was surprised to see that there were a few spots of sweat on his chest and lower neck and more on the insides of his hind legs.

"Do you need a bath, Red?" I asked him, but the spring air was still a bit chilly and he dove back into his hay pile with such happiness that I satisfied myself with just giving him a good curry and picking out his feet.

Hilary had taken Jerry back outside after pulling off his tack and was hosing him down, carefully washing every last bit of dirt and sweat from his grey coat. He didn't seem to mind. His eyes were half-closed, and his ears flopped to the side as he enjoyed being fussed over.

I cracked open the tack room door to check on Caprice, but I needn't have worried; she was still curled up in her bed. She looked up when she saw me and wagged her tail a few times before snuggling back into her cushion.

"Good girl," I whispered, and then tip-toed past to hang up my bridle, and put my brushes and helmet away.

"Hey, do you want to sleep over tonight?" Hilary said, poking her head inside the tack room. "We can order pizza and watch horse movies that make us cry."

I laughed. "I'd love to, but I have to go this squash party that my dad's club is hosting. I promised I'd go, especially after I bailed out of watching him play in the finals today."

"Sorry, what sort of party?"

"Squash," I laughed again. "Hey, you should go with me. It will be completely boring, but I guarantee the food will be good and you can keep me company."

"I don't know, would your parents mind?"

"No. Well, I'll ask Marion just in case, but I'm sure they would think it's okay. Come on, it will be fun. You can hang out by the cheese table with me and keep me from eating everything."

"Don't start with that." She sent me a meaningful glare and disappeared only to reappear a second later carrying all her tack. "Okay, if Marion says it's fine then I'll go. Did you invite Rob?"

Her back was to me as she hung up her saddle, but something in her voice made me look up from where I was kneeling next to Caprice and pay attention.

"No," I said slowly. "I didn't even think about bringing anyone until just now. I also don't think I want to subject him to my dad yet."

"Okay," she said quickly. Without looking at me she grabbed a few carrots from the bag off the counter and ducked out into the aisle.

That was strange, I thought. But I didn't have much more time to think about it because there was the sound of car tires crunching on gravel and Hilary's excited voice calling out that Marion was here.

Marion agreed right away that Hilary should come to the party. "That's a perfect idea," she said. "Should we pick you up at seven o'clock?"

But my step-mom's smile dropped away completely when she saw the state of my jeans.

"What?" I said, glancing down and then bursting into laughter. The whole inseam from my thighs to my knees was caked with a combination of dirt, horse sweat, and bits of hair, and I guessed that the back of me wasn't much better.

"Oh no," Marion said, putting a hand up to her mouth as if she was going to be physically sick. "You definitely *cannot* get into my vehicle like that. No. Change first and put those in a garbage bag. How on earth could you have possibly gotten so dirty?"

"We went for a trail ride and I forgot to bring extra jeans," I confessed. "We left home so fast this morning that I didn't bring something to change into. Sorry, it's all I have."

"Luckily, I have emergency towels in the car," she said crisply, wrinkling her nose like she was trying not to gag. "You'll have to sit on those. Can you *please* use your saddle when you ride, Astrid? Honestly, I just want to throw those jeans out."

She turned toward the car and as soon as she was rummaging

in the trunk Hilary wheezed with the laughter she'd been holding in. "Same old Marion," she whispered, keeping a hand over her mouth. "I swear I don't know how you turned out so normal living with those two."

She helped me gather up Caprice's stuff while I took the little dog outside for a quick walk on the lawn next to the barn.

Marion covered the passenger seat with about five layers of towels and ordered me not to touch anything when I got in the car. She even laid another towel over my lap so she wouldn't have to look at all that dirt sitting in such close proximity to her. And she rolled all the windows a quarter of the way down to let out the barn smells.

"Honestly, Astrid," she said, "I don't know why you had to pick a sport that involved so much…debris."

"I thought you liked horses," I said, waving goodbye to Hilary through the open window.

"I do, but they'd be so much nicer without all the hair and dirt."

I like their hair and dirt and the way they smell, I almost said out loud, but I stopped myself just in time. Marion was on my side after all so there was no point in arguing with her. She couldn't help being so weird.

"How did Dad do in his match?" I remembered to ask.

"Fabulous. He won his division and he's very pleased. That means he qualified for the tour this summer."

"Wow, that's great. When does he leave?"

"Nothing's been finalized yet. Do you know what you're planning to wear tonight?" she asked, abruptly changing the subject.

"Um, no." I looked at her blankly. Planning my wardrobe was usually the very last thing on my mind.

"Well, I laid some things out on your bed for you to try. After you've showered and we've…disposed…of those jeans, I'd like you pick something nice."

"Sure," I said, resigning myself to an evening of dressing in things that didn't fit right and eating things I'd be lectured over later. At least this time Hilary would be there.

Marion hurried me up the elevator from the carport.

"Stay there," she ordered and left me standing in the front foyer in my dirty clothes holding the stack of towels I'd sat on while she ran inside and grabbed my fluffy bathrobe from my room.

"Here," she said, handing me the robe and a plastic bag. "Put your jeans in here once you've changed…and the towel you were sitting directly on. The rest you can just leave out here. I'll take care of it."

She disappeared inside with Caprice and I reluctantly changed, glad that nobody was around to witness this. Good thing we lived on the top floor and didn't have any neighbours.

I folded myself in the bathrobe and said goodbye to my comfortable jeans. I had the feeling I was never going to see them again.

I guess I'll have to ride in a saddle from now on, I thought wistfully, *I don't have that many extra pants to spare.*

I padded inside and went directly down the hall to the big bathroom and scrubbed every last trace of barn from my hair and skin, borrowing heavily from the arsenal of smelly soaps and body washes that Marion kept on hand for emergencies. When

I finally emerged, smelling like roses, I wrapped my hair in a towel and went to my room to see what awful things Marion had left out for me to wear.

To my surprise, there were three spring dresses on the bed, all of them in pretty colours, although the odds that any of them would actually fit me were slim.

Sighing, I tentatively pulled on a floral print one first, surprised at how easy it was to get on. I walked barefoot to the mirror and stared at my reflection looking at myself critically from side to side.

Well, besides the flowers, that's actually not too bad, I thought, liking the way it draped down my body without hugging too tight. The flowers were a bit much though; not my style at all. I slipped it back over my head and tossed it onto the bed.

The blue one was so dark it was almost black, in a silky soft, stretchy material that hung just right when I put it on.

Wow, I thought, turning side to side to get a good look, *this colour is beautiful. It makes my eyes look darker, too.*

I picked up my phone and took a quick picture of my reflection in the mirror, sending it to Hilary. One of the few times I'd risk sending a photo of myself out into the world.

What do you think of this one?

Fantastic, she wrote back right away. *You're beautiful.*

Well, I wouldn't have gone that far, Hilary was always way too kind to me, but still, it looked pretty nice.

I slipped it off and hung it carefully over the back of my chair before reaching for the third dress, this one in a pale green, but I knew as soon as I slid it on over my head that it was all wrong. The fabric wedged tightly around my shoulders and it was only by a mixture of wriggling and squirming that I managed to inch it down over my body at all.

I looked at myself in the mirror, feeling sick. This was the real me, awkward and bulgy. The colour made my skin fade to a jaundiced yellow hue and the tight fabric made all my extra curves stand out in sharp relief. Disgusting. I was a complete mess; I didn't know why I even bothered.

"Astrid?" Marion called from outside the door, "did you get a chance to try on the dresses?"

"Just a minute," I called, struggling to pry the awful dress over my head. I twisted and turned, scraping the fabric painfully across my hips and then again when it got hung up on my shoulders. Finally, it came loose, along with the sound of multiple threads breaking. I yanked it off and flung it to the bed in a heap, grabbing my robe again just as Marion walked in the door.

"Did you find one you liked?" Marion asked, taking in my disheveled hair and red face. She dropped her gaze to the dress that lay twisted in a knot on the bed. "I'm sorry, I didn't know your size anymore. You've changed so much while you were away."

"The blue one," I interrupted, looking away. I refused to cry in front of her over a stupid dress.

"That was my favourite, too," Marion said quietly, "should I...should I take this one away then? It didn't fit?"

"It's too small," I said, still not looking at her. "I'm sorry."

She picked up the green dress slowly and then hesitated in the doorway, twisting the material in both hands nervously, looking like she wanted to say something important but didn't know how.

"Okay, I'll leave you alone then. I'll make us a snack to tide us over until dinner," she said finally, shutting the door softly behind her.

Come on, pull yourself together, I told myself. *Sometimes clothes fit and sometimes they don't. There's no reason to be a baby about it. It's not the end of the world.*

But it took a long time before I could look at myself in the mirror again.

Chapter Four

I felt better by the time we had to leave to pick up Hilary. My dad had come home long enough just to get showered and changed and escort us down to the car.

He hadn't minded at all that Hilary was coming, and he'd complimented me on my outfit; both rare events that left me feeling more positive about the night to come.

Hilary wore a simple dress, had her hair up in a messy bun and barely any make-up at all, but she somehow managed to look completely stunning and about five years older. If she hadn't been such an amazing friend I might have been jealous. But it wasn't her fault she was always flawlessly perfect; inside, she was still the same goofy Hilary that I loved.

"Thank you for inviting me," she said politely to my parents, "and congratulations on winning your division, Mr. Kendrick."

"Well, thank you," my dad said, beaming at her in the rearview mirror. "I had some tough competition tonight. We're always happy to have you along, Hilary. You're a good influence on Astrid, you can keep her on the straight and narrow path."

Hilary kept her smile fixed in place, but she nudged me subtly in the ribs to let me know she thought he was ridiculous and that she was on my side.

The drive to the log-style restaurant where the banquet was held wasn't long and soon we were climbing out, my dad greeting bunches of strangers with hearty slaps on the back and Marion doing the same with air-kisses. Hilary and I hung back, nodding politely and avoiding any small talk as we made our way slowly inside.

"Do you know anyone here?" she whispered.

"Not a single person," I said softly. "Oh, I've met that guy there; that's Darius, who is some sort of squash star."

"Who? You mean the Greek god there?" She gripped my arm tightly, pulling me to a stop. "That's not something you forget to mention to your best friend, Astrid."

"Huh?" I looked over at Hilary, but her eyes were glued to Darius and, annoyingly enough, I saw that he'd spotted us and was headed our way.

"Introduce us," Hilary hissed at me. Her cheeks flushed and her eyes had a glazed, fevered expression in them that was entirely unlike her.

"Um, okay," I said lamely as he approached. He went to greet my parents first, but his eyes kept flicking back to Hilary and when he had the chance he shifted over to us.

"Hey, Darius," I said, "this is my friend Hilary. Hilary, this is Darius."

But instead of greeting each other like normal human beings, they just stood there, staring at one another as if they were playing that game of frozen-tag where you had to stay motionless as long as possible. All the swagger and charm drained out of

Darius's face and he looked impossibly young and vulnerable.

"Um, Hilary?" I said, right at the point where it couldn't possibly get more awkward than it already was.

"It's nice to meet you," Hilary said in a voice that sounded like all the air had left her body.

Darius shook himself like he was coming out of a deep sleep. He went to reach for her hand and then stopped himself just short of touching her, his fingers hovering mid-air between them.

It was my dad, completely oblivious to whatever was taking place, who saved the situation.

"Let's go inside and find our tables," he said, coming up and punching Darius good-naturedly on the shoulder. "We don't want to miss the speeches."

We followed them inside, Hilary walking woodenly beside me with a far-off look on her face, a small smile playing over her lips.

"Oh, there's Susan," I said in surprise. I should have guessed that the Ling's might be there, since WorldCor was a pretty big sponsor of the club.

She looked up and caught my eye, smiling and waving us over.

"Astrid," she said, giving me a genuine hug. "You look super. I missed you at school last year."

Even though we'd never been exactly friends, I'd always liked Susan. We moved in completely different circles at school so had never spent much time together outside of WorldCor parties. She was smart and had a wickedly sarcastic streak, so I'd always been grateful that she'd never turned her sharp tongue on me, even when it became obvious that I had that ridiculously painful crush on her out-of-my-league older brother.

"Come sit down," she said, pulling out a chair. "Tell me about what you've been up to."

It turned out that we were sharing a large, round table with Darius, the handsy coach Nancy, the Lings, and a few other people I half-recognized from my dad's work. There was a brief flurry of activity around the table as everyone found their seats.

Susan pulled me down beside her and Hilary sank to her seat on my other side without saying a word. The second my dad reached the table, Nancy appeared out of thin air and planted herself beside him. Marion raised an eyebrow but sat down quietly on his other side silently, a smile fixed on her face.

I wasn't sure how it happened, but Darius somehow managed to slide himself next to Hilary, even though I was positive someone else had been sitting there a moment before.

I filled Susan in about my time at the ranch, and Hilary sat beside me pretending to listen and smiling automatically whenever I turned to include her in the conversation.

Our dinner arrived, and I mostly concentrated on my delicious plate of ravioli while the general conversation turned to squash. My dad held court at the far end of the table, telling stories and cracking old-person jokes while both Marion and Nancy looked up at him like every word coming out of his mouth was the most brilliant thing ever.

I didn't mind, though; everyone looked like they were having a good time and it *was* nice to see my family actually happy for once.

Hilary was more like her old self by the time we were halfway through dinner, although she hardly ate anything. Even though

Darius was beside her, he spent most of his time talking to a guy on his right; as far as I could tell he and Hilary didn't so much as glance at one another.

Finally, dessert came, a silky hazelnut *crème brûlée* topped with deliciously burnt sugar, and then the lights dimmed, and someone tapped on a wine glass to start the speeches.

Various people took turns getting up on stage to thank sponsors and hand out awards and things. It wasn't as boring as I'd expected; many of the speakers had had quite a bit to drink by then so they were pretty funny. There were slideshows of things that had happened over the year, and I actually found myself laughing at all the silly jokes with everyone else.

When I glanced over at Hilary at a particularly funny part she was watching the stage, but her face was pale and immobile in the dim light, and she'd placed both her hands on the table as if she were ready to push herself upright and bolt at any moment.

I was about to ask her if she was all right when I noticed that Darius's hands were on the table, too, and that his left one had slid over to lay next to hers, and their pinkie fingers were touching slightly in a way that could have been an accident but probably wasn't, and for some reason that small thing made me flush and look away as if I were seeing something I shouldn't be.

When I glanced back again they weren't touching at all and maybe I'd just imagined it.

There was an announcement, and when I turned back to the stage, it was my dad climbing the stairs, and Marion and Nancy were both applauding madly; Nancy added in a few of those high-pitched obnoxious wolf whistles that made Marion shy away like a startled horse.

"Thank you, everyone," my dad said, "for making our club's inaugural year such a successful one. Every single one of you should be proud. Because of your hard work, we have one of the finest facilities in North America, a credit to our city. Because of *you,* we are poised to host world-class international competitions, creating an economic benefit to the Island we love and putting our city on the global map."

"I'm pretty sure we were already on the map," Susan whispered under her breath and winked at me, grinning.

I laughed and poked her lightly in the ribs. My dad's speech wasn't *that* bad, and it was nice to see him excited about something rather than being just manic and angry all the time. It made him seem much more human, and I felt a rush of something like affection for him. But then, of course, he had to ruin it.

"On a personal note, I'd like to thank our coach, Nancy, who is passionate about our great sport and works tirelessly to both make us better players and to promote squash to the world. And, of course, I'd like to thank my family, my wife Marion, and my daughter, Astrid, for putting up with me. Ladies, I have a surprise for you."

At that, I sat up straight and went very still, like a rabbit sitting frozen in the middle of a road with an oncoming car barreling toward it.

The lights dimmed, and an image popped up on the screen behind him; a huge grey motor home splashed with sponsor logos across the side.

"Welcome to our new home for the summer."

It can't mean what I think it means. I thought numbly, *he can't be serious.*

Hilary came alive beside me, putting a hand on my shoulder. "Astrid, what is he talking about?"

"I don't know," I said miserably, "he didn't say anything about this before."

My hands shook under the table and I had the sudden feeling I was about to be sick.

I looked up to see Marion watching me, her face pale and tense. She made eye contact with me and then shook her head slowly back and forth. I could only hope that it meant that there'd been some mistake. Marion would take care of it; she always did.

"Wow, Astrid, that sounds like a good time," Susan said dryly, "good luck with that."

"Yeah, thanks," I said flatly, remembering what I liked least about Susan. She was fun but not exactly supportive.

I glanced over at Marion again, but she now looked so calm that I almost managed to convince myself everything would turn out okay.

My panic had mostly evaporated by the time the event ended and I was able to say goodnight politely to everyone at my table without dropping to the floor in hysterics.

I just have to hold it all in until I get to Hilary's, I thought, *just a little bit longer.*

Chapter Five

"Could you drop us off at the barn, please?" Hilary asked when we turned into her driveway. "I have to do night-feed before we go to bed."

"Oh, but you'll get your nice dresses dirty," Marion said, "and your shoes."

"We'll be careful, I promise," Hilary said. "I swear I won't let Astrid get so much as a smudge on her."

"Let the girls have their fun, Marion," my dad said jovially. He was still glowing from his win earlier and from the party.

Marion laughed and shook her head. "All right, then. I'll pick you up tomorrow afternoon, Astrid. You can call when you're ready."

Hilary thanked them again for the invite and then we hurried out of the car, Hilary tugging on my arm so I just had time to grab the backpack I had stashed in the back seat.

We waited in the dark entryway of the barn, holding our breath until the car turned around and crunched back down the driveway. The horses nickered quietly in their stalls, feet shuffling through the shavings, all of them probably wondering why we were being so slow to bring their dinner.

"Oh, Astrid," Hilary whispered, "this is awful. What are we going to do?"

"I'm not sure," I said, my hands shaking.

"Can you refuse to go? You can just stay here with us for the summer."

I paused, hope blooming in my chest. But I couldn't just ask Hilary's parents to take me in for an entire summer when they were clearly up to their ears in renovations. They'd always been so good to me and I didn't want to be a burden…again.

"I don't know," I said, too tired to even think about it anymore. "Maybe Marion can talk him out of it. We should give these guys their night feed."

I flicked on the aisle light and padded in my flats to the hay room.

I held the hay out carefully in front of me, not wanting to get any on my dress and tip-toed to Red's stall where he waited patiently in front of his manger.

Hilary followed me slowly and when I turned around to go back for more she was standing right behind me, looking completely miserable.

"Hilary?" I said, stopping in confusion. "Are you okay?"

"N…no," she said, tears pooling in her eyes. "No, I'm not. Astrid, you *can't* go. You have no idea how far in over my head I am on this project. I told my parents I could handle it but…but I honestly have no idea what I'm doing."

"What? Hilary, you're doing a great job."

"No, I'm not. I love horses so much, but this is not how I thought it would be. I hardly have to time to do any of the other things I like. I'm good at a lot of things, Astrid, but figuring out when grain and hay and bedding needs to be ordered before it actually runs out and coordinating the vet and the stupid farrier who you have to book months in advance, that stuff I'm terrible at. And that mess with the indoor; I don't even know if they'll come back at all."

"Hilary, you'll figure it out. You're good at *everything*."

"That's so not true," she said miserably. "I make mistakes all the time and sometimes I think I must be crazy. Like what happened tonight…."

"What?" I asked in confusion.

But instead of answering, her lower lip trembled and then she began to cry, tears rolling silently down her cheeks.

I stared at her in horror, not having a clue what was the matter, but finally, I remembered that friends were supposed to comfort one another when they were upset, and I went and wrapped her in a hug. She turned and pressed her face into my shoulder, sobbing and sniffling until finally she took a deep breath and pulled herself upright.

"Sorry," she said, wiping her eyes with the back of her hand and smiling at me through her tears. "I don't know what's wrong with me."

"Tell me what's going on?" I said. "Was it Darius? Did he say something to you?"

"No, well, sort of. Astrid, do you believe in fate?"

"Um, I don't know," I said lamely, wondering if maybe she'd gotten into the wine at dinner while I wasn't watching. Hilary had a tendency to be dramatic, but she'd completely lost me this time.

"Astrid," she said, clasping her hands together, "the second I saw Darius it was like a lock clicked open inside my chest, as if he was the only person in the whole wide world who carried the key. And the crazy thing is I think he felt it, too. Does that make sense?"

"Do you mean that you *like* Darius?" I said in astonishment. "I know he's beautiful and everything, but you don't even know him. Plus, he's *old*...well, older than us anyway. He hangs out with my dad so he's probably a jerk, Hilary."

"He's nineteen," she said dreamily, turning to stare out at the darkness, "and I turn seventeen in a few months, two years isn't much. And besides, it has nothing to do with *liking* him. This is something bigger than us, I told you, it's fate. God must be directing us together."

Jerry nickered sleepily in his stall and I turned slowly back toward the hay room.

"Hilary." I sighed, wondering how to say this gently. "I'm no expert on boys, but back at the ranch I watched nice, normal girls fall in love with Kade on a daily basis. He was beautiful and charming, but that didn't mean he'd make a good boyfriend at all. He made them crazy and he left a path of broken hearts in his wake wherever he went."

"Do you think Darius is like that?" She frowned at me, looking more like her old self and less like a lovesick puppy.

"I honestly don't know him; I just want you to be careful, is all. Take your time and actually find out what kind of person he is."

I wasn't sure exactly where all this good advice of mine was coming from. It wasn't like I had any real experience to back it up.

"I guess you're right," Hilary said reluctantly. "It's not like this is the first time it's happened to me, either. I thought the last one was fate, too. And that didn't work out at all." Her head shot up and she clapped a hand over her mouth, staring at me wide-eyed.

"It did? You never told me that."

"Oh, it was a long time ago," she said quickly. "I was young and stupid, and I'd just prefer to forget it."

"Okay," I said slowly, wondering at her sudden mood shifts.

"You give great advice, Astrid. That all makes perfect sense and I feel much better now. Come on, let's go make popcorn and stay up late watching movies. Everything is going to be just fine."

I wasn't sure if she was exactly *fine,* but I was glad she wasn't crying anymore. Before we left, I snuck into Red's stall and kissed his forehead carefully and wished him goodnight.

To save our shoes we walked barefoot up the driveway, walking on the edge of the gravel on the soft grass and laughing and stumbling the whole way.

We changed into pajamas and made popcorn with extra butter and stayed up watching horse movies that made us cry, and Hilary didn't say one more word about Darius or fate. Not even once. And that should have worried me more than anything.

Chapter Six

The next day, when my alarm went off at six like usual, Hilary groaned and burrowed back under her covers grumbling until she fell back asleep.

Well, I guess that leaves me to feed the horses, I thought, crawling out of the guest bed and rummaging in my backpack until I found the clothes I'd packed the night before. I dressed quickly in the chilly morning air, pulled my hair back into a messy pony-tail, and padded downstairs.

My paddock boots were still in the barn, but I wasn't about to walk barefoot all that way this morning. I slipped on a pair of rubber boots that were by the front door and crossed my fingers that nobody would mind that I'd borrowed them.

I slipped outside and inhaled deeply in the chilly, morning air, and lifted my arms in a big stretch, luxuriating that I got to spend another entire day in the country.

I took my time walking down to the barn, wishing I had my aunt's dog Jake loping alongside me or even Caprice. Sometimes it was just nice to have a dog around keeping you company.

The horses were dozing outside in their paddocks when I

arrived; Rabbit was closest, and he raised his head and nickered sleepily when he saw me.

"Hey, everyone," I whispered, rolling open the big front doors and letting the early morning sunlight filter into the barn.

Huh, huh, huh, the horses said in a chorus, shuffling through their thick bedding to stand at the front of their stalls, heads hanging into the aisles.

I fed them hay first, dropping flakes into each stall and making sure that everyone was eating before I went to mix grain. Hilary had soaked beet pulp the day before and the feed chart was neatly written on a white board in the tack room so it was easy to mix their supplements together.

I dumped everyone's feed into their buckets, and then stood back and closed my eyes just listening to them eat; there was something incredibly soothing about the sound of horses crunching their breakfast.

I grabbed the wheelbarrow and pitchfork, but before I started cleaning, I texted Rob.

Hey, are you up yet? I sent. *Still want to go for a ride?*

Of course I'm up, he sent back, *just finishing chores now. How many free spaces do you have left in the barn?*

Um, three, why?

Okay, I'll bring them all then, as long as you don't mind helping me exercise. See you in a half hour.

Great, I wrote.

Help him exercise? I thought, slipping my phone back into my pocket and lifting the wheelbarrow. *What does that mean?*

I picked around the horses without moving them out of their stalls, and had everything cleaned and swept and the feed room prepped for evening grain by the time Rob's trailer rumbled up the driveway.

A bubble of nervousness rose up inside me; I hadn't seen Rob since Christmas and I didn't know what to expect. But it dissolved the second I saw him and his dad again in person.

"Astrid," Rob said, coming over to give me a tight hug as if it hadn't been months since we'd seen each other last. "I'm glad you're home. Help me unload these beasts?"

"Sure." I laughed and inhaled quickly before he pulled away, savouring the warm, earthy scent of him. He was dressed in breeches, half-chaps and a blue polo shirt, and I felt underdressed in my oldest pair of half-worn breeches and a scruffy t-shirt with a hole in the armpit.

"Good to see you, kiddo," his dad said, wrapping me in a warm hug, too. "Glad you're home to keep this boy in line."

"Oh, I doubt he needs that," I said, laughing, and we went around to the back of the trailer to where Rob was already dropping the ramp.

"I'll hand you Artimax," he said, opening the back door, "and I'll bring Ferdi, and then we'll come back for the other two, okay?"

"Sure," I said, "I'm not sure where we'll put everyone, though."

Artimax sauntered out of the trailer like he'd done it a million times before, completely ignoring the hysterical tantrum Rabbit was having.

"Wow," Rob said, frowning over his shoulder at the big thoroughbred. "That horse needs some exercise. He looks miserable."

Artimax followed me easily to the barn and into the stall beside Red. I slipped off his halter and he sauntered around, sniffing every inch of the stall like he owned the place, and then strode outside to get what was left of the grass in the paddock.

Ferdi danced at the end of his lead rope, swiveling his head around to look at the other horses pressing against the front of their stalls, bobbing their heads excitedly.

"Come on, kid," Rob said to the horse encouragingly, leading him into the next empty stall. As soon as he was free, Ferdi bolted outside to stand next to Artimax, pressing near the fence to be as close to his friend as possible.

"He's a bit of a sensitive soul," Rob said, laughing. "Come on, you can take Possum inside, she's gentle, and I'll tie Maverick to the trailer and tack him up there."

Possum was beautiful. She was the daughter of Aunt Lillian's stallion Fox, and her mom was a mare out of Doc, so Possum had the best of both worlds. She had a coat like buttermilk and black tipped ears just like her mom. She was wearing a cotton sheet to keep her clean, and her long black mane and tail looked fluffy and well-brushed. She followed me obediently to her stall, and waited until I removed her halter before she daintily turned and went outside to search for grass.

Maverick was a whole different story. He followed Rob obediently enough, but his ears stayed back the whole time and he stomped along as if he was resentful being asked to do anything at all. His nostrils and lips were pinched together, and it almost sounded like he was grinding his teeth. His ears flicked forward briefly when Rob unbuckled his halter, but then he wheeled around and marched outside, shaking his nose up and down at the other horses.

"He's like a cranky old man, isn't he?" Rob's dad said,

shaking his head. "I'm not sure how far you'll get with that one, son."

"Oh, he'll be fine," Rob said mildly. "We just have to find a job for him to do that makes him happy."

"Well, I'll head out then. I'll leave the trailer here. Text me when you're ready to go."

"Thanks, Dad," Rob called and then turned to me with a grin. "Okay, cowgirl, who are we going to ride first?"

"What's with this *we* business?" I said, laughing up at him. *Had he grown taller this year?* "I'm just riding Red. The rest of these are up to you."

"Ha, we'll see about that. Okay, if you want to ride Red first then I'll take Maverick. They probably move at about the same speed. You using the saddle today?"

"Yeah, I guess I'll have to," I said ruefully. "I'm so sore from yesterday, and Marion is going to throw out every pair of jeans I own if I come back with them all horsey. Plus, Liza said I'm supposed to be practicing with it."

I went to find my boots and brushes while Rob grabbed the horses hay nets from the trailer and pulled off Maverick's cotton sheet to get him cleaned up. When I came back out, Maverick was already tacked up and I had to hustle to get Red ready.

It actually took me a few minutes to remember how to adjust the saddle properly on Red's back and settle the girth into just the right place so it didn't pinch and gave his elbows plenty of room.

I led Red to the mounting block and stared at the stirrup for a second before stepping into it and swinging on his back. I rotated my legs and ankles back and forth, adjusting to the strange feeling of all that leather between me and his back. The stirrups felt weird, like they were too short, and I dropped them down another hole until it was almost like not having them at all.

"This isn't so bad, is it?" I asked Red, letting the reins out to the buckle so he could wander over to investigate a patch of grass that had caught his eye. I turned in the saddle to watch as Rob led Maverick to the mounting block. Maverick stood like a rock, but he had a hard, resentful look in his eye as Rob swung up, as if he were only there because he was forced to be. He submitted to his rider with a flared nostril and an irritated shake of his head.

I frowned, wondering if somehow the young horse was in pain or if he had just been born with an awful personality. I didn't know very much about him. Aunt Lillian had thought he'd be a good candidate to send down here for some reason. Surely, she would have told Rob if Maverick had a past injury, though.

"So, your plan with this guy is still kind of the same as mine with Red?" I asked tentatively.

"Yep, just get him happy moving forward. That's pretty much my plan for all the horses, actually. A bit of ring work and a lot of conditioning work. That's the way most horses should be brought into condition anyway. Plus, they love it."

"Liza said something about that, too. She called it a weird name, though. The camping school or something like that."

"I think you mean campaign school." Rob laughed. "That's the old name for it, but it just means training out in the countryside to get them happy moving forward. That way they build muscle and stamina naturally and they don't get ring sour."

Maverick did look a tiny bit happier as he headed up the driveway; his ears unfolded slightly from where they'd been pinned against his head, but he still didn't look bright and interested in the world like Red did.

We let them walk at their own pace up the driveway which, compared to my ride with Hilary yesterday, was snail-slow. I didn't mind, though. There were still a million sore places on my body, and even though Claudia's expensive saddle was as comfortable as possible, it still took a bit of getting used to. Even with the longer stirrups, my legs couldn't hang quite so freely as they did bareback, and it was harder to feel the subtle changes in Red's back as he moved. Still, I was happy just being out here in the sunshine spending time with my favourite horse and one of my favourite humans.

"Let's go this way first," I said, leading him through the break in the pasture fence. "This field's actually in decent shape; the posts are good and there's not that many spots where the boards are down, so it shouldn't be too hard to get it in working order again. Poor Rabbit is going nuts without turnout, though."

"Yeah, I'll bet," Rob said. "I'm not sure why Hilary doesn't have pasture here yet. She's been here for months. It wouldn't take much to fix it up."

I shrugged. The last few days had been so chaotic that I hadn't asked Hilary about the details of her project yet, but she did seem to be having some issues.

When we came to the little stream, Red dipped his head down to drink at the edge, but Maverick tromped through as though it wasn't there, not interested in drinking, playing, or exploring.

"Well, at least we know he's not afraid of water," Rob said, letting Maverick lead the way.

"This is a good place to trot or canter," I told him, "if you want to. We just follow the fence back up to the top."

"Yeah, let's do it then." Rob urged Maverick into a trot and then up into a rolling canter that Red had no trouble keeping up with. In fact, he picked up the pace on his own and pulled up beside Maverick before moving to pass him.

"Good boy, Red," I said, giving him the reins fully and allowing him to move forward in a thundering gallop. Both stirrups came loose and slipped off my toes at the same time, but it didn't matter; I was better off without them.

Rob looked over and grinned at me. "Come on, Maverick," he called, "don't let them beat us." Maverick flattened his ears, tossing his head at Red as if to tell him how disgusted he was with this whole outing.

When we came to the end of the fence, Red reluctantly slowed, then came back to a trot, and then a prancing walk, arching his neck proudly and snorting.

"You're such a good boy," I said, petting his neck enthusiastically. I was glowing with happiness; so far, the saddle hadn't slowed him down there at all. He felt pretty much the same as he had when I rode him bareback.

We let them walk on a loose rein up the driveway and then turned into the forested trail the led us lower and lower into the rainforest section of the property.

"Wow," Rob said, "this is great. This is just like the trail at Claudia's."

"That's what I thought, too," I said. "I love how it feels so ancient in here, like we've stepped into a time portal back to prehistoric times and a dinosaur could walk out any minute."

Rob nodded, craning his head backward to look up at the giant, mossy trunks towering overhead.

The horses' footsteps were completely muffled, and the chattering bird calls faded away behind us. We walked along not saying a word, just breathing softly with the rhythm of the woods around us. The space felt sacred somehow, as if the ancient trees were alive and watching us, protecting us.

When the trail rose upward again, taking us into the younger forest we both sighed as if we'd woken up out of a deep sleep. The path widened for a few steps and Rob moved up beside me, reaching over to run his hand down my bare arm just for a second before easing Maverick on past me.

I looked after him, surprised, my arm tingling from the unexpected contact, my skin already missing that brief moment of warmth. I sighed and shook my head; it wouldn't be good for me to get too attached to him. Things changed so quickly in this world and I didn't want to risk getting hurt. Look what had happened with Susan's brother Thomas; I'd made a fool of myself.

But Rob's not Thomas, said a voice inside, *you can trust him.*

We followed the trail out of the woods and up onto the grassy hillside that overlooked the ocean.

"Wow." Rob brought Maverick to a halt so he could marvel at the view. "Hilary's family sure lucked out on this place. It's got a bit of everything."

"I know. And she's been too busy to explore it so far. She's been stressed out by this play she's in."

"What night are you going to watch it?" Rob asked, still staring at the ocean, "We should go together."

"Yeah, I'd love that," I said, my voice sounding a hair too eager. I blushed and reached down to wind a lock of Red's mane around my finger as a distraction, my heart speeding up. "Um, maybe let me make sure my dad's not going, too. I'm not sure if Marion bought tickets already."

"Oh." Rob looked over at me, surprised. "Does it matter if he's going?"

"Well," I hesitated. "I'm not sure if…well, I don't think you want to be there if he's going."

"Huh," Rob said, shrugging. "Well, let me know, I guess. Should we do some trot work here?"

I nodded, willing to do just about anything that would distract me from this moment of exquisite awkwardness. Had I sounded like I was backing out of wanting to go with Rob? Did he think I meant I'd be embarrassed of *him* and not my dad?

Both horses picked up the trot at the same time and I had to focus to stay balanced. Red was electric underneath me, his neck arched and his ears pricked in fascination the closer we went toward the water. I realized too late that I should have shortened my stirrups, there was no way I would reach them like this and I didn't want them banging Red in the sides.

Maverick moved forward obediently enough but he still looked cranky, wrinkling his nostrils and shaking his head sideways at Red when we came too close.

Their hooves sank into the sandy soil, leaving a trail of prints that curved toward the ocean. This time Red didn't hesitate, he strode boldly down the beach right up to the water lapping at the shore.

The ocean wasn't as calm as it had been yesterday, the tide was in so we had less beach to play on and the water was darker and more turbulent, little whitecaps poking up and down across the surface. Still, the waves were tiny by anyone's standards, and Red marched right down until he stood ankle deep in the ripples, reaching his nose down to splash lightly in the salty water.

Maverick trudged up beside him and stood there with his ears at half-mast, a bored expression on his face as if to say he'd seen oceans a million times before and they didn't impress him a single bit.

"What is *wrong* with that horse?" I said, laughing. "He acts like he's a hundred years old rather than a baby."

"I think it's just his personality," Rob said, and I was glad to see that the awkward moment had passed and he was back to his old, smiling self. "Give him time, he'll come around."

I stopped and put my stirrups up two holes, frowning at the way it already made me feel constricted; still, I didn't want to keep losing them. I'd either have to adapt or take them off the saddle completely when I got back.

We trotted down the beach and then walked the horses carefully when the trail turned rocky and headed up toward the woods again.

"This is the place I wanted to show you," I said as soon as we'd reached the spot where the grassy berm stuck up out of the ground. "Hilary said she thought it would be fine if I shot my bow here some time. I had this crazy idea that maybe this year I could do some mounted archery on Red."

"Oh," Rob said, his eyes widening with interest. "That sounds like fun. That would be a great way to bomb-proof the young horses, too. We'd have to make sure we don't accidentally shoot them, though."

"Yeah, first priority." I laughed. "Casey and I did a whole bunch of research one night when were on foal-watch at the ranch; you can get these foam-tipped arrows to start with that are safe to use around horses. I was actually thinking about ordering some online."

"How many bows do you have?"

"Just one practice bow but it's not the right type to use on horseback anyway; it's too long. We'd need shorter bows, and with a lighter pull weight to start with, like the ones kids use."

Halfway across the meadow we picked up a trot again and kept going until we reached the driveway. We let the horses walk on a loose rein all the way back to the barn.

"You did so good with your saddle, Red," I said, reaching down to scratch under his mane with my fingernails. "Hang on, I'm going to take a picture for Liza just to prove I'm actually using it."

I pulled out my phone and leaned way back so I could get about forty photos of Red's neck and ears from different angles, just managing to capture the pommel of his saddle in the frame so she could see that I was actually riding with a saddle as promised.

"Isn't that a good one?" I asked, showing the photo to Rob but he just shook his head, raising his eyebrows and sending me a mocking smile.

"What? You've sent me plenty of pictures of your horses so

don't act all superior," I said, reaching out and punching him gently on the shoulder.

He ducked away laughing, that smug smile still on his face.

I looked up to see Hilary waiting for us in front of the barn, standing there with her arms crossed tightly over her chest and a frown on her face.

"You should have woken me up," she said sharply. She glanced between me and Rob quickly and then looked away, a blush staining her cheeks.

"Oh, sorry," I said, surprised at her tone. Hilary almost never got upset over small things. "I wanted to let you sleep in. I did all the chores, too."

She dropped her gaze to the ground at her feet and bit her lower lip. "You didn't have to do that, Astrid. I'm perfectly capable."

"Hilary," I said, jumping down off Red's back. "What's wrong with you?"

She took in a deep breath and held it in, puffing out her cheeks as she continued to stare at the ground. Finally, she shrugged and let the air out with a whoosh, shaking her head. "I don't know. I'm sorry, you're right. Thanks for doing chores."

She shot another quick glance at Rob and then looked away.

"Isn't it okay that we're riding on the trails?" I asked her, frowning. She was acting like she didn't *want* Rob there with his horses, but that was impossible; they were friends, weren't they? Or was she just mad that we'd made plans without her?

"Yes," she said, her face softening, "yes, of course it is. I must still be tired; just ignore me."

She turned to Rob like she was steeling herself for a fight but when she spoke her voice was soft. "You brought the whole gang, hey? Is everyone ridden already?"

"Nope, just the first round," Rob said, swinging lightly to the ground and smiling at her gently. "You want to come on the next one?"

She hesitated and bit her lip. "Sure," she said finally. "Yeah, that would be great. Who's next?"

"You take Jerry, I'll take Ferdi, and Astrid takes Artimax?"

"Oh, no," I said, shaking my head. "I don't need to go with you guys. I'll just put Red away and then hang out here."

"Come on"—Hilary grabbed my hand and pulled me inside, seeming more like her old self—"you're not bailing on me. And it was *you* who insisted that trail riding was good for the horses' souls."

"Uh huh, but I already rode *my* horse. Now I want a shower and breakfast and to go back to bed," I said, only half-joking. My stomach had started to rumble about a half hour ago.

"What kind of horse person are you?" Rob asked me, not for the first, or probably last, time.

"A sore one," I said, "but I guess that as long as you're absolutely sure Artimax won't toss me off in a ditch somewhere then I could give it a try."

"No, he's rock solid. And I'll be right there; I'll walk you through it. You'll love him."

I reached down and put a hand on Red's chest. He was mostly cooled out, but his fur was still sticky with half-dried sweat. I didn't want to leave him like this two days in a row.

"Just a quick shower for this guy," I said, "and then I'll tack up."

"Okay, and I may have left some pastries for you guys in the tack room," Hilary said over her shoulder.

I showered Red outside the front door, spraying him down carefully with lukewarm water and using the rubber horse-squeegee to strip all the excess water off his coat. He shook like a dog as soon as I was done and followed me back to his stall with a contented snort, his tail switching back and forth rapidly the way horses do when they're ready to roll.

"Not in here," I told him, leading him right through his stall and out to the paddock beyond, "you'll get stuck against the wall if you roll inside."

He whipped around as soon as I slipped the halter off his head, pawed at the earth a couple times and then dropped to the ground with a deep groan, rolling on his side and then kicking all four feet in the air while he itched his back in the sand.

Beside him, the rest of Rob's horses had come outside and, like rolling was contagious, they all dropped to the ground one by one and rolled, too.

Red lurched to his feet, circled a few times, and then dropped down again on his other side, the clean side, to repeat the process, rising up with a huge shake that sent dirt flying up around him in a halo. He snorted, gave one final shake and then marched back into his stall, ready to work on his hay pile again.

"Sorry it's not pasture, buddy," I told him, "we're working on it."

"Coffee?" Rob appeared in the aisle outside Red's door.

"Yeah, thanks," I gratefully took the paper cup he handed me, inhaling deeply before taking my first sip. "Did Hilary say something about pastries?"

I followed Rob into the tack room where Hilary was sorting her tack with one hand while balancing a cheese croissant in the other. I helped myself to something oozing with raspberry filling and closed my eyes as the sweetness hit my tongue.

Artimax didn't mind me brushing him and tacking him up. I hadn't spent much time with him last year when Rob had first bought him, and he'd always intimidated me slightly with his overwhelming personality, but it turned out that he was completely sweet.

He stood solidly while I worked over his speckled coat, but every time I picked up a new brush he had to turn around and sniff it all over before I could keep brushing him. He also had a weird habit of licking me whenever I got close to his head. He'd turn and look like he was going to nip my arm and then he'd just lick it instead. It was bizarre, but he didn't seem to mean any harm and it made me laugh, so I just ignored him and kept on getting him ready.

I looked at the horse boots Rob handed me skeptically and held them up to Artimax's legs to figure out which way was up. They were battered leather that looked like they'd been through the wash a few times. There was soft fleece on the inside and they had buckles instead of the Velcro I was used to. Finally, I strapped them on as best I could and hoped I'd done it right.

The soreness that I'd felt right after my earlier ride on Red had faded to a dull ache so I was able to climb into my saddle with reasonable finesse. Artimax was a bigger horse than Red and his stride was longer, but it didn't take long before I felt fairly confident that he wasn't going to toss me off his back.

Hilary looked way more relaxed on Jerry than she had the day before and he, too, was less prancy, even with all the new horses in the barn.

We started out in the same way as before, letting them walk on loose reins and stretch out and take in the new scenery. We turned into the little pasture and followed it downward to the stream. But these horses knew all about water and they didn't even hesitate; even Jerry didn't fool around splashing like he had before.

When it came time for the uphill trot section, Artimax strode out powerfully, throwing me backward behind his motion so that I accidentally popped him in the mouth.

"Sorry, boy," I whispered, quickly getting myself organized and moving with him rather than against him. As soon as I found his rhythm he was steady and easy to follow.

"He'll duck his head at first when you canter," Rob called back. "Don't fight him, just give him his head for a second and he'll settle in. He's honest and you could canter him on a loose rein forever without him taking advantage of you. Liza thinks it's more of a strength and balance issue than a vice; we're working through it."

I gulped nervously and involuntarily leaned forward when Artimax sprang into a canter, but I did as Rob said, letting the reins slide lightly through my fingers a good six inches while Arti shot his nose forward and down. Then I gradually took up the reins until I could feel a light contact with his mouth and was relieved to find that he was ready to listen to me.

Wow, I thought, carefully adjusting his stride to something less enthusiastic. *He's fantastic.* After that, I wasn't afraid at all.

By the end of our ride, Hilary seemed completely back to her old self, laughing and joking with us and looking as confident as she ever had on Jerry. The nervous girl from yesterday and the snappish girl from this morning had disappeared.

I came back to the barn, completely tired and happy, but when Rob suggested that we ride yet another round of horses I had to suppress a groan. I'd been a hard worker at Aunt Lillian's place, but I usually just rode once a day, and I had to admit that I didn't work Red very hard when I did ride him. Now I realized just how out of shape I was; I was sore in places I didn't even want to think about.

"Do you do this every day?" I asked Rob, dropping to the ground and wincing as pain shot up through my ankles and knees.

"Yeah, when I'm lucky. When school and other stuff doesn't get in the way. I would ride twenty a day if I had my choice."

"Okay, well, you are completely crazy then," I said, laughing.

"Maybe a little," he said, not looking sorry at all. "Come on, just one more round and then we can hang out for a while before my dad comes to pick me up."

"But who am I going to ride? You have Possum and Hilary has Ellie, but I don't want to pull Red out again. He's not even fully dry yet."

"You can ride Riverdance," Hilary said from her spot on the lawn where an already freshly bathed Jerry was cropping mouthfuls of grass as fast as he could, droplets of water dripping off his grey sides.

"Sadie's horse? I can't ride him while she's not here; and he's too good for me anyway. I don't want to wreck him."

"You won't wreck him." Hilary laughed. "He's super well-trained, but he's easy going, too. Sadie said I should take him out a couple times a week just to stretch his legs and I've just been too busy to do it, she won't mind."

"I don't know," I said doubtfully, thinking of how stern Sadie was when something displeased her.

"Hang on, I'll text her and make sure it's okay then."

I slid my saddle off Artimax and hung it up on one of the folding racks in the barn aisle, and then pulled his boots off before carefully hosing him down, all the while worrying about what Sadie would say. On one hand, I wanted her to say no; Riverdance was an ex-bullfighting horse, elegant and well-trained with big soft, intelligent eyes and a knowing expression. He reminded me of a younger version of Claudia's horse Quarry, who I'd learned to ride on. Bottom line; he was too good for me and I didn't want to ruin him.

On the other hand, it was one thing knowing that about myself and another thing completely for Sadie to say it in a horrified text. Sadie was kind but she was strict, too, and Riverdance was her prized possession. I couldn't imagine her—

"Yep, she says its fine," Hilary said. "Just use his own tack and give him lots of carrots."

"That's all she said?" I asked skeptically. No dire warnings about being careful with his mouth or bouncing around on his sensitive back?

"Nope, that's it. She watched you ride Quarry all summer, Astrid. She trusts you to take care of her horse and not do anything stupid. And it's my first ride on Ellie since she arrived here. I'm probably not breaking out of a walk."

"I'm good with an easy ride, too," Rob said. "Apparently,

we've got to build you guys up slowly. I want you nice and fit this summer to help condition these horses."

"Oh great," I said, groaning out loud. "I'm going to need more pastries then."

We took a short break to fuel up on snacks and glug down the bottles of water Hilary had stocked the fridge with.

Then I took a deep breath and grabbed Riverdance's custom-made wooden grooming box, the one with his name engraved on the side in gold letters, his supple leather halter and a carrot, and slipped into his stall.

"Hey, buddy," I said almost reverently, holding out my hand so he could sniff it. I'd handled Riverdance a ton back at Claudia's, turning him in and out and cleaning his stall, but this felt different, as if I were meeting him for the first time.

Huh, huh, huh, he said under his breath and then caught sight of the carrot and pricked his ears, standing to attention with his front feet close together. He arched his neck and bobbed his nose politely, encouraging me to hand it over.

"You're so pretty," I said, breaking off a piece of carrot and holding it outstretched on my palm.

He took it gently, his whiskers barely brushing my skin, and crunched it slowly, half-closing his eyes, savouring each bite.

When he was done, I slipped the halter over his head and tied him lightly to the ring in the wall. I ran my hand down his golden neck, marveling at how silky smooth he was; he didn't have any remains of a winter coat like Red did. It didn't take me long to brush the non-existent dust off him, pick his feet, and carefully buckle his expensive-looking leather exercise boots onto his legs.

"Do you think Sadie would mind if I used my own saddle?"

I asked doubtfully, looking at the buttery soft leather of Riverdance's saddle. Quarry's old tack was nice, but this looked almost brand new. "I don't want to scratch this one."

"Oh, Astrid, stop worrying about every little thing," Hilary said in exasperation. "You're not going to wreck anything. You are perfectly capable of not ruining an eight-thousand-dollar custom-made saddle." I could hear laughter in her voice.

"Great, thanks a lot," I muttered, setting the saddle carefully on Riverdance's back, "that's very reassuring."

I did the girth up loosely and carefully slipped the plain snaffle between his teeth. He accepted it politely, opening his mouth obediently and let me adjust all the fittings until everything lay flat and perfect. I arranged his long forelock between his eyes and then laughed when he turned to me, expecting a treat.

"Is this the point where Sadie gives you more carrots?" I asked, tightening his girth one more hole and leading him to the mounting block. I'd put some chewy molasses horse cookies in my pocket and I broke a piece off and fed it to him, laughing when his eyes widened in surprise and he bobbed his nose up and down excitedly.

I led him tentatively to the mounting block and waited for the others.

"I've always liked him," Rob said, eyeing Riverdance appreciatively. He ran a hand over the horse's shoulder. "Sadie brought him from South America, right?"

"Yeah, Brazil. Sadie's brilliant on him."

"Well, she's a great rider; he's probably a lot of fun, too. Don't worry, you'll do great."

I smiled and nodded, not feeling quite as nervous as I had before. Grooming Riverdance had settled me down and I felt like we'd made friends. I'd never seen him put a foot wrong with Sadie and he was always an easy-going type of guy so most likely I would survive this ride.

Possum had been eyeing him up and now she arched her neck and squealed, striking out a front foot and batting her eyelashes at him.

"Uh-uh," Rob told her, "now is time for working, not flirting. You can do that on your own time."

Possum made a chortling noise under her breath, but she stood obediently while Rob swung up on her and let her walk in big circles on the driveway.

"Okay, buddy, here goes nothing," I said, climbing the block and getting gingerly onto his back. It wasn't elegant, but I made sure not to thump down on the overly expensive saddle, and Riverdance stood rock-still and at attention until I'd picked up my stirrups and adjusted my reins.

I'd barely brushed my calves against his side and he was off, arching his neck and mouthing the bit, his stride powerful and electric underneath me. It was like driving a sports car rather than a pick-up truck, and it was exhilarating and scary at the same time. He felt full of compressed power just waiting for an outlet.

"Breathe," Rob reminded me, "and he might do better on a looser rein, he's expecting to work right now and you want him to get into relaxation mode instead."

"Right," I said, inhaling and exhaling deeply, and consciously asking my muscles to relax. Riverdance responded right away, swivelling an ear back, and then dropping his neck down and blowing his own breath out loudly through both nostrils. The energy leaked out of him until, finally, it was like sitting on Red when he was at his most relaxed.

"Ooh, thanks for the tip," I said, "that's much better."

Hilary came out, looking nervous and gingerly tightened Ellie's girth before stepping onto the mounting block. She paused, stroking Ellie's neck a few times before taking a deep breath and climbing carefully into the saddle.

Ellie didn't flinch; she was a green horse comparatively speaking, but she *had* had a few months of training under her belt back at the ranch and she was sensible. She just turned around and sniffed half-heartedly at Hilary's boot before moving off in a slow walk.

And that's how our ambling ride went. Both baby horses followed Riverdance resolutely up the trail, looking around at the new West Coast terrain with mild interest. They didn't mind crossing the streams or heading up and down hills, and they barely looked at the sheep when we passed, which made sense since they were used to cattle and donkeys back home. When we arrived at the ocean they pricked their ears and snorted in excitement, but they didn't threaten to bolt or act silly at all.

Rob was grinning from ear to ear. "Your aunt breeds awesome horses, Astrid. These guys are so smart and so solid; this is the type of horse every kid should grow up with."

Even Hilary was smiling and lavishing praise on Ellie, her own nervousness evaporating with every step. We kept the horses at a walk, although they probably could have easily handled faster gaits, and arrived back at the barn in excellent spirits.

We'd taken longer than we'd planned, and Rob's dad was

already there when we got back so there was no time for hanging out and eating more pastries. We untacked quickly and got busy helping him get his horses loaded in the trailer.

"Same time tomorrow?" Rob said to both of us, but his gaze settled on me.

"I have rehearsals tomorrow," Hilary said quickly, "but you guys go ahead."

"Okay," I said, ignoring my protesting muscles, "that would be great. I'll text you tonight."

We waved as the truck bumped down the driveway and then both collapsed cross-legged on the cool cement in the open doorway.

"That was fun but exhausting," Hilary said, leaning her head back against the barn wall. "I don't know how he does that every day. I'm plenty fine riding one horse a day let alone four or five. He used to ride extra horses for Liza, too, and I've never heard him complain or say that he was tired. Not once."

"Yeah, he's pretty great," I said, pressing my damp hands against the smooth, cold floor of the alleyway.

Hilary made a small noise in her throat and then pushed herself upright. "I should feed lunch," she said and turned away abruptly, her boots loud on the concrete floor.

I pulled myself slowly to my feet and stretched my aching muscles, frowning at Hilary's retreating back. Something was definitely up with her.

"Hey, Hilary?" I said tentatively, following her to the hay room and standing in the open doorway. "Are you okay? You know you can tell me anything, right?"

She broke open a bale of hay and turned, giving me a funny look. "Thanks, Astrid," she said, grabbing an armful of flakes. "I mean it. You're a good friend; the best. I'm fine, though, nothing to worry about."

"Okay," I said slowly, "and you're all right after that thing with Darius last night? You were acting strange."

"Was I?" she asked, opening her eyes wide to look innocent. "I guess I was a bit distracted; it's all the stress from the play and the indoor and everything. And plus, he's the best looking human being I've ever seen in my entire life and I think we were meant to be together on a cosmic level."

"What?" I groaned internally. "Hilary, we've been over this; he's old!"

"Astrid, he's practically the same age as us," she said, sounding irritated. "Anyway, it has nothing to do with it. When I looked at him it was like a bolt of lightning hit me. Like I was drowning but being rescued at the same time; it was awful but wonderful, too. You know what it's like, right?"

"No…" I said slowly, not having a clue what she was talking about, but then I thought of that time, back at Susan Ling's lake house before the accident and my summer with Quarry, when I'd first noticed Rob. He was balanced on a rope swing curving far out over the dark water. There had been something about the way his body arced through the sky and the way the setting sun touched his skin; I'd never seen anyone look as beautiful or as free. But it had been a tranquil moment, an inspiration, nothing like the fire and fury Hilary said she'd felt last night.

"Well, maybe," I conceded. "So, what happens now? Are you actually going to see him again? Your mom is going to freak out."

"Oh, I'm not going to worry about the details," she said airily, "it will all work out just like I want it to."

She smiled, her eyes glittering, and I had the sinking feeling that when Hilary set her mind to something she wouldn't rest until it happened. I only hoped she would take some time to think about it logically before things got too serious.

"Okay, I'm ready for a shower and a real lunch," Hilary said abruptly, "I'm starving. And, I forgot to tell you that Marion called this morning after you'd left. She asked if you wanted to stay the night with us again. She said she'll drop off some extra clothes for you after dinner."

"She did? I guess, if it's okay with you and your parents. That would be great."

"Of course it's okay, it's better than okay. If I had my way you'd live with us full time."

"Yeah, I could probably go for that."

We fed the rest of the horses their lunch and walked side by side up to the house in a tired silence.

I was *almost* too exhausted to worry about Hilary but not quite. And I couldn't help wonder why Marion had wanted me to stay here tonight. I was always glad to hang out with the Ahlbergs, of course, but I didn't like the last-minute decision; something didn't feel quite right. Were she and my dad arguing about the road trip? Had he actually expected that we'd pick up everything and go with him? Knowing my dad, the answer was probably yes.

"Don't worry about it," Hilary said, guessing my thoughts, "maybe they just wanted a quiet dinner alone, like a date night."

"Ew, maybe, I guess so."

"Come on, my dad's been testing out all sorts of recipes that he wants to use at the restaurant. We can be his guinea pigs."

That didn't sound too bad at all.

Chapter Seven

Dinner was as fantastic as we'd hoped, even though none of the food matched each other in a traditional way. Hilary's dad had made like ten different dishes for us to sample; everything from lasagna and sweet potatoes to roasted quail and an Asian fusion noodle dish that had what looked suspiciously like octopus pieces in it. He had even made two different soups. But most of it was delicious and we just tasted a bit of everything and went back for seconds of the things we liked. He'd even had us fill out little cards to say which flavours we liked best and what we didn't like and why.

We ate in the half-renovated restaurant section of the house, sitting around the one table that had been set up, overlooking a view of the ocean. It was one of the most interesting dinners I'd ever had, and I ended up discovering some new foods I liked, though octopus was not on that list.

Marion arrived just as we were starting dessert.

"Come in, come in, sit down," Mr. Ahlberg said happily as Marion stood poised in the doorway, looking equally horrified of the half-finished room as she did of the table laden with five different desserts. "I have a raspberry gelato that will blow your socks off."

"Er, no," Marion said stiffly, averting her eyes from the table, "we have reservations at a restaurant."

"Come on, Marion," Hilary said in her most wheedling tone, "it is probably the best thing you will ever taste in your whole entire life."

Marion wavered for just a second and then stiffened her spine and shook her head. "I couldn't but thank you, it looks delicious. Astrid, may I speak to you outside?"

"Um okay," I said, pushing back my chair slowly.

I followed her out to the porch, my stomach twisting anxiously.

"Astrid, the Ahlbergs have said that you can stay here for a couple of days. Would you be okay with that?"

"Yes, of course. But why?"

"I want to talk with your father about our plans for this summer. I thought it would be best if we worked it out ahead of you coming home."

"Like, you mean so he could yell at you without me around?" The words came out of my mouth before I could stop them, but I wasn't taking them back. I cared for Marion more than any other person on earth and I was sick of seeing her pushed around. I gulped and took a deep breath. "I'm not leaving you there to deal with that alone, Marion."

She stared at me, astonished, and then looked away, her expression unreadable. "Astrid," she said carefully, "I just want to have a grown-up conversation with your father; is that too much to ask?"

"No," I said, drawing back from her in surprise, feeling stung.

Marion stared down the driveway, lost in her own thoughts.

"He's somehow gotten himself set on the idea that we're both going with him this summer and he's not thinking clearly about your responsibilities here at the farm. He'll be disappointed when I tell him we can't go."

"But, maybe I could help you," I said, "we could think up a plan together, as a family. Maybe we could meet him on the road somewhere this summer and plan some short vacations together that don't last the whole summer."

"Yes, I suppose," she said.

Another piece of the puzzle fell into place. "Marion," I said in astonishment, "do you *want* to go?"

"Oh, well"—she frowned and looked out across the lawn—"it would be nice to spend some extra time with your father, dear, but it wouldn't work out logistically. I wouldn't feel right leaving you on your own, even though I'm sure you would be very responsible."

My mind whirred over the possibilities; it didn't make any sense to me that Marion would actually *want* to spend extra time with my dad, but apparently she did. I didn't want to be the one standing in her way, but I also couldn't sacrifice my entire summer. I needed to think more.

"Two days," I said, "and then you come pick me up no matter what, even if he's angry. I'm part of this family, too, and I don't want you to have to deal with him on your own."

Again, there was that brief flash of emotion in Marion's eyes, but she just nodded and turned away, her head down as she navigated the porch steps.

I watched her get into her car and drive slowly away, waiting until her car had disappeared completely before I headed back inside.

"Everything okay, Astrid?" Hilary's mom said as I came in.

I opened my mouth to tell her everything was fine, just like I did every other time she asked. It had always been an unspoken rule between Marion and I that we never talked about my dad's anger or irrational mood swings. And now I wasn't so sure whether that was to protect *him* or to protect us.

Hilary's family had taken me in many times over the years and, though they must have guessed that my home-life wasn't great, I'd always been too embarrassed to share any details, even with Hilary.

But now all three of the Ahlbergs were staring at me with a potent mixture of worry, love, and compassion, and I realized that these people had often been more of a family to me than my own parents had been. I could trust them to be on my side no matter what.

"No, everything's not fine," I said, taking a deep breath. "I need your help."

"Oh, honey," Hilary's mom said, coming over and wrapping me an extra tight hug, "we thought you'd never ask."

We stayed up late into the night, eating popcorn and playing Monopoly in front of the TV, discussing our plans for the summer and how to best convince my dad that this was the best idea for everyone. And I felt lighter and more alive than I had in years.

And late that night I got another surprise, my first email from Liza complete with lots of photos of Folly, baby Figaro, and Quarry doing all sorts of cute things.

"I promise I'll come down and visit in a few weeks," she wrote, "things are so busy here right now that I can't leave. But I'm thinking of you guys all the time and I'm working on a plan so you can get your dressage fix. Justin sends his love, too. Liza."

I poured over the photos, studying not just the horses but the familiar barns and landscape behind them, feeling a pang of homesickness so bad that I had to bite my pillow to keep from crying.

For the millionth time, I wondered if I'd made the right decision to come home.

Chapter Eight

The next morning, after we'd fed the horses, I had a quick breakfast with Hilary and her family, and then waved them goodbye as they went off to take Hilary to her rehearsals and do some errands for themselves in town. I could have gone, of course, but I'd jumped at the chance to be able to spend the day with the horses instead.

Once the car was out of sight I flopped down on the sitting room couch, excited to be alone in such a fantastic place. This room had become my favourite. It didn't have a view of the ocean, but there was a window seat that looked out into a small, sculpted garden, and the inside walls were lined with hundreds of books. It had a quiet, safe, homey feel that made me want to spend all day in there curled up reading.

It was still early enough that the builders hadn't started their daily round of hammering and shouting yet. It was perfectly quiet, like the inside of an art gallery.

I pulled out a book at random and sat down with a satisfied sigh to read, but it wasn't long before I sat up again, too restless to sit around; I wanted to explore.

The Ahlbergs had told me I was free to poke wherever I wanted, and so I walked quietly through the guest wing of the house, opening doors and peeking in at the rooms that had already been renovated. There were ten bedrooms in all in this wing plus the four on the other side of the house. Plus, there was the nice sitting room that was for guests and the big living room that was just for Hilary's family. The big restaurant kitchen I knew very well since we ate there every day, but there was another, smaller kitchen on the Ahlberg's side of the house, and a solarium with stone benches and an empty pond that was still waiting to be filled with plants and fish.

I grabbed myself a snack of leftover pie and looked at the clock on the kitchen wall. I still had time before I had to do paddocks and meet Rob for a ride. I had just enough time to go and explore the beach. We'd passed by it on our rides, of course, but I hadn't gotten to explore the rocky area near the dock yet. It looked like it would be a perfect place to find some tide pools.

Slipping on my boots, I hiked down the hill to the ocean, inhaling deeply as the salty breeze whipped around my face, buffeting my clothes and pulling my hair in all directions. Today, the ever-changing ocean was dark and knee-high waves crashed against the shore. Gulls cried overhead, turning in large circles, their eyes trained downward to the sea.

I climbed carefully up onto a pile of rocks that had been carved into latticed geometric designs by a hundred years of salty water running across it. As I suspected, a trough of water had collected into a shallow trench on the top and I crouched down eagerly beside it to peer into the pool.

The cool thing about tide pools was that they might look

empty at first, but gradually you saw they were teeming with tiny, living creatures. I didn't get to spend nearly enough time at the beach growing up, but I'd been on enough class trips to the ocean to know what to look for.

My shadow, and probably the vibration of my footfalls, had alarmed the family of anemones gathered on one side. But, as I sat quietly, they gradually began to stretch their arms out again, looking like pale upside-down jelly fish with their long tentacles undulating just under the surface.

"Are you hungry?" I asked them, looking around until I found a tiny discarded crab shell at the side of the pool. I picked it up by one claw and dipped it into the pool just by the anemones waving tentacles. It paused and then reached out and snatched the crab from my fingers, drawing it deep into its core and disappearing completely. The other anemones, sensing somehow that there was dinner on the menu, stretched out their arms toward their friend, hoping to get some food, too.

"Hang on, hang on," I said, searching the rocks until I'd found more of the little discarded crab shells. I fed the creatures one by one until they'd all disappeared, and then smiled in satisfaction.

An especially large wave smacked against the rock I was perched on, spraying me with a fine mist of sea water. I wiped my face and leaned cautiously toward the ocean side of the rock, staring down into the sharp crevices that lined it. The ocean made a sucking, gurgling sound against the stone as if it were a living thing speaking a different language, something dark and guttural.

Starfish, I thought, spotting four or five dark, purple stars suctioned tightly to the sides of the rock. I leaned over carefully until I was flat against the boulder, the spray from the waves speckling my face and arms as I reached way down until I could just touch one purple creature gently with the tip of my finger, marvelling at the smooth surface.

Out in the ocean, there was a loud splash and I pushed myself back up, watching a few sea lions playing no more than twenty feet away.

I live in the very best place in the world, I thought, sighing with happiness. *The ranch was wonderful, but this is worth coming home to, no matter how awful the other stuff gets.*

I got to my feet and brushed my hands together, and headed back up the hill. It was another beautiful morning and my walk down the driveway to the barn had a magical feel to it. I stopped to visit the sheep, scratching their chins and the spaces behind their ears, promising next time that I would bring treats.

The horses barely looked up from their breakfasts when I came in so, even though it took longer, I just cleaned around them, not wanting to disturb their morning routine.

I cleaned the paddocks that Rob's horses had used the day before and wished again for us to have a working pasture.

Soon, I told myself, *Hilary said it's next on the list.*

I swept the aisle until there wasn't a speck of hay on it and went into the tack room to make sure the evening beet pulp was soaked and that my tack was clean and organized.

On inspiration, I grabbed my unstrung practice bow from where it had stayed propped up in the corner by my locker for the last few days and took it over to Red's stall.

"Hey, buddy," I said, sliding open the stall door and slipping inside. "Do you remember this?"

Red lifted his head briefly from his hay, sniffed the wooden limbs of the bow, half-interested to see if they were edible, and then went back to his food.

"You're not too worried about it, huh? Well, maybe we'll try it out this afternoon."

The rumble of a heavy vehicle approaching made butterflies dance in my stomach. I slipped out of Red's stall and went outside to meet them.

"Morning, Astrid," Rob's dad said, jumping out of the truck and handing me my coffee and a paper bag that smelled like freshly baked pastries. "I've got to be somewhere pretty quick this morning, so come help us unload."

"Sure," I said, setting my snacks aside reluctantly to take Artimax's lead rope. Rob had only brought three horses today, and the plan was to ride Red and Maverick first, and then Artimax and Possum; Ferdi had been left behind at home since he was scheduled for a lesson in their own ring later that afternoon. Rob ran his crew on a tight schedule, carefully balancing ring work, conditioning work, and rest days to keep the horses from getting burnt out.

Balancing a pasty in one hand and a curry comb in the other, I worked over Red's coat in tight circles, bringing up the dirt and hair in tufts. He was in a good mood that morning, as always, and leaned into my curry comb when it hit the places that needed extra scratching, especially the spot right next to his withers, and the one behind his ears, and the one just to left of the base of his tail. So, basically, everywhere.

"Weirdo," I told him affectionately. "Maybe if you'd shed out as nicely as Riverdance and Jerry you wouldn't be so itchy."

"He will next year," Rob said from the stall beside me. "The babies are like that, too; Maverick, especially. Once they adapt to the warmer climate down here, they'll shed earlier in the season every year."

I whisked all the debris off and then smoothed his russet fur down with the body-brush until it practically glowed in the early morning light.

***

"Let's do our normal route and then take a closer look at the fencing in the pastures," I said. "Maybe it will speed up Hilary's fence-building project if we figure out what parts can be saved. I think Rabbit's going to go nuts if he doesn't get a break from his paddock soon. He's starting to chew at the boards in his paddock now. He's eaten almost all the way through one."

"That's not a good sign," Rob said, "he's a horse that needs to move almost all the time."

We ambled up the driveway and then turned right through the break in the fence.

"This is the most obvious choice for a pasture," I said, eyeing the fence for any breaks or rotten boards, "but if we fence it off then we lose a huge section of our trail ride. We almost need a track around the outside for trotting and cantering."

"Hmm, it would probably be too expensive to build a track. Maybe the best would be to just put gates at each end. That way we can at least use it for speed work when there aren't any horses in here."

"Yeah, maybe we could just turn some of them out at night

and use it to ride in during the day."

"That's a good idea. That's what I did at home last summer during the heat wave; the horses just hid in their stalls during the heat of the day and went out as soon as the sun went down."

We rode along in comfortable silence for a few minutes and then followed the trail steeply downward, crossing the little stream.

"You okay to trot and canter?" Rob asked as we came to the open, uphill part of the ride.

"Yes, definitely, let's go."

Before Rob could answer, I gave Red a light nudge and leaned low over his neck. He was already on his toes waiting for the cue, and he sprang forward into a sudden gallop with more speed than I'd expected, making me yelp with surprise and grab for his mane. But, this was trustworthy Red, not Folly, and I made myself give him the reins and let him choose his speed and his footing, losing myself in the thundering of his hooves and the powerful surge of his hindquarters rocketing us across the ground.

The fence-line came up faster than I'd expected and I sat up, playing with the reins and gently asking him to come back to a canter, and then down a trot, and then a walk.

"Wow, that guy has a real motor when he wants to use it," Rob said, trotting up behind us on a scowling, panting Maverick who sent a scathing glare in Red's direction. "We couldn't keep up."

"I've never gone that fast," I admitted, still glowing with euphoria. "He felt totally fine, though; he was listening to me the whole time."

Red blew through his nose contentedly and dropped his head to grab a mouthful of grass—a self-reward for all his hard work.

We headed up the driveway, stopping to say hello to the sheep who crowded the fence-line making the deep *baaing* noises that was their way of begging for treats.

Red went right up to the fence to greet them, softly touching noses to a big black and white one that put her front hooves up on the boards and stood on her hind legs to get closer to him. Maverick snorted at them and wrinkled his nose in disgust, flattening his ears as he marched past without giving them a second glance.

"That's quite the horse you have there," I teased, moving Red up beside them again. "He's like a cranky old man, waving his cane, and yelling at kids to get off his lawn."

Rob burst out laughing and reached down to scratch Maverick's neck. "Oh, he's coming around. Just yesterday he took a carrot from me without spitting it out. He did glare at me the whole time he ate it but still, it's progress. I'm hoping that he perks up when we start jumping, maybe that's what he'll like."

"*Maybe*," I said doubtfully, privately thinking he would be lucky to find a single thing in the *world* that cranky Maverick would enjoy.

We kept at a peaceful walk until we'd come out of the rainforest section and were on the path that led to the ocean.

"More canter?" Rob asked, glancing over his shoulder with one eyebrow arched in a challenge.

"Absolutely," I said, touching Red lightly with my calves. This time we kept it slow and steady, the deepening sand dragging at the horses' hooves as they plowed toward the ocean.

We dropped down a gait when we reached the beach but kept a steady trot right to the edge of the waves, letting the horses splash playfully in the retreating surf. Or, at least Red splashed playfully; Maverick tromped through the waves like they didn't exist, his nose lifted to avoid any splashing water. He edged out of the ocean as soon as Rob let him and marched up the beach in the exact direction of the exit trail as if he was ready for this pointless trail ride to be over.

Hmm, that's pretty smart, I thought, *he knew exactly where to go and he's only been here once before.*

We sauntered back to the barn, and I put Red into his stall for a snack and a drink of water while he waited his turn for the shower.

While Rob was getting Maverick washed down, I went into the tack room for my own snack and was delighted to see that the bag was still half-full of my favourite raspberry danishes, the ones filled with a deliciously gooey, cream-cheese mixture.

"They're my favourite," I called out the door, "how did you know?"

"Something about the way your eyes light up whenever you eat one." Rob laughed. "And the fact that you've literally said, wow, these are my favourite pastries, like a thousand times."

"Did not," I protested, biting into one and closing my eyes in blissful pleasure. Was there anything better in the world?

"Ha, liar!" Rob laughed and pretended to spray me with the hose as I ambled over.

"Don't get the danish wet," I said, turning sideways to protect it from splashes. There was nothing more depressing than a water-logged pastry.

Maverick glared at both of us, not pleased about his bath, or laughter, but his nose twitched slightly when he caught sight of my danish and, like a miracle, his pinned ears unfolded, and he actually pricked his ears in my direction.

"Ooh, do you want this?" I asked in surprise, glancing at Rob. He turned the water off and stepped back, letting the lead rope go slack.

I broke off a tiny piece and stepped closer to Maverick, talking to him softly. "Here, boy, did you want to have a piece? I'm not sure if you'll like it but it might be better than the healthy carrots and apples that mean Rob keeps forcing on you."

Maverick made a *whuffling* sound under his breath and stepped forward. His nostrils flared as he reached out curiously to sniff the small piece of pastry in my hand. He wiggled his lips and was just about to take it off my palm when he caught sight of the rest of the uneaten danish in my other hand. He moved before I could react and snatched the entire thing, narrowly missing my fingers. He gulped it down in one bite, bobbing his nose up and down and swirling his ears around as if he was the cleverest horse on the planet.

"You little brat," I said to him in astonishment, "you ate that whole thing, you thief." And then both Rob and I burst into laughter that built and built until I couldn't stop and we were both doubled over with tears streaming from our eyes.

Maverick ignored our mocking completely, licking every last bit of sugar off his lips before reaching out to search my hands for more. Only when he was completely sure there was nothing left did his ears snap backward into their signature style and he lowered his head grumpily to finish his bath.

"We found out what he likes," I wheezed, wiping the tears from my eyes. "He can be a taste-tester in Hilary's dad's kitchen. He can specialize in desserts and pastries."

"He could go on T.V. as one of those animal chefs," Rob howled, "we could teach him how to use a mixer—"

"—and wear a chef's hat and an apron," I said, snorting with laughter, not caring how ridiculous we were being. I'd hardly ever laughed this hard in my life; my ribs hurt and I could barely breathe, and I was sure my face was blotchy and red. But it was also wonderful, and all the tension that I usually held in my body evaporated in that fit of hysterical laughter. I felt, well, I felt *good*.

"You're crazy," I said to Rob, and he stuck his tongue out at me.

"Right back at you," he said, stripping the water from Maverick's fur with the squeegee and leading him inside.

I gave Red a short bath, just enough to take the layer of sweat off and put him back away, apologizing for not spending more time on him. Then I tacked up Artimax while Rob got Possum, and off we went again.

"You know, I've been thinking," Rob said when we got to the first pasture again. "What if we used electric fence for this section here? Then we could just fence off a big chunk in the middle and still use the trail on the outside."

"Electric fence? What's that?"

"Plastic fence with bits of metal woven in it; it looks like big pieces of tape that you attach to posts and then you run an electric current through it. It probably would be too risky to use it for someone like Rabbit, or Ferdi, but the rest of them would be fine. Red and Ellie and Riverdance could stay out there, no problem. And, best of all, it's cheap. I think I even have an extra electrical box at home we could use, it's solar powered and everything."

"Really?" I said in delight. "Could you bring it tomorrow? I mean, if Hilary says it's okay. I'm not sure if she'll go for it, though; she wants the place to look exactly like Claudia's did."

"Oh, well, then she'd better get on it. The horses need pasture in the worst way. Rabbit is a couple days away from losing his mind."

He sounded frustrated and I turned to him in surprise. "She's doing her best," I said, feeling defensive. "She's never built a farm before, you know."

"I know. But, Astrid, if you moved Red to a new farm would you build him pasture first or a fancy indoor arena?"

"Pasture," I said without hesitation.

"Right, because the pasture is for him and the indoor arena would be something for *you*, right, not Red."

"Well, sure, I'd want to make sure he was happy first."

"Exactly, and that's why you're a better horse person than Hilary."

"Come on, that's not fair, and Hilary's a much better rider than I am."

"Maybe, but that has nothing to do with being a horse person. You care about what the horses think, Astrid, and you take time to figure out what makes them happy."

I didn't have an answer for this and it felt disloyal to Hilary to agree with him, so I took the easy way out. "Come on, let's trot," I said, letting Artimax stride out ahead of Possum. He was a larger horse than her, and fit, so I kept him at a nice, comfortable collected trot so she could keep up. He bobbed his nose a few times to ask if maybe I didn't want a bit more speed but was polite about it when I told him he'd have to wait.

We rode them right into the ocean up to their knees, laughing as they snorted and pranced and arched their necks at the *shhhhhh* sound of the waves sucking backward across the sand.

"When are you bringing your archery stuff out here?" Rob asked when we reached the grassy berm.

"My bow's in the barn, but I've been too busy to use it yet. I've been looking online for a cheap horse-bow, too."

"Well, let me know when you're ready; I'm dying to give it a try. Artimax would love it."

"Really? That would be great. I don't exactly know what I'm doing, though; I've been watching these videos online, so I think I know how to set everything up. I can show you when we get back if you like."

"Like how not to shoot your horse in the neck?" Rob asked, his voice filled with laughter.

"Definitely that. Plus, the horse archers use shorter bows than I do, and the technique is different from regular archery. I know you can get foam-tipped arrows to start out with, to prevent accidents. Did I already tell you about my meeting with Earl?"

"Your coach? No, what happened?"

"He basically told me I'm not ready to start practicing for real. I'm still supposed to take it easy."

"Oh. How long until you can start training again?"

I bit my lip, struggling not to show how much this bothered me. "No idea. He said to get stronger first and then we'd see. He wants me to help with summer camps, too."

"You know what would cheer you up?"

"What?" I asked suspiciously, not liking the glint in his eye.

"Canter-trot transitions. Lots of them."

"Sure." I laughed. "Why not."

Again, I had to remind myself not to fight against Artimax when he ducked his head in the upward transition and rooted at the reins. I let the reins slide lightly through my fingers, not giving him anything to pull against and, once he'd stretched out his neck and snorted, I inched them shorter so I had a light feel of his mouth again.

We brought them back down to an active trot for a few minutes, skirting the boggy area on the low side of the pasture, and then asked for more canter on the uphill. This time the transition was smoother, more relaxed, and I put the reins in one hand so I could reach down and pet his neck. We walked at the top of the hill, letting them stretch down, and then headed across the driveway to the next pasture. This one was flatter, and we did upward and downward transitions the whole way, something the horses seemed to love.

We rode back to the barn in companionable silence, and then stopped when we saw a large, black vehicle sitting in the driveway and the sound of high-pitched kid laughter coming from inside the barn.

"Callie, don't touch them. Remember, they're not our horses."

"I want to pet the Palaminoooo…" the child-sized voice rose up to a frantic pitch that made me wince. *Wow*, I was sure I'd never have been allowed to be that obnoxious. I had barely been allowed to have an *opinion* in my house let alone have a tantrum.

"Well, you can't," the mom-voice said firmly, "if you can't

behave then I'll have to drop you off at grandma's and visit the horses without you."

This was followed by a sullen silence and the sound of small boots clomping toward us.

A small girl stamped her way out of the barn and I couldn't help but laugh at her furious expression. Despite the scowl on her face, she was completely adorable; dressed like a miniature rider in tiny breeches and paddock boots. Her hair was braided into two pigtails with ribbons on the end. She even carried a pint-sized sparkly pink crop in one tiny fist, which was a bit terrifying given her murderous expression.

But all that changed as soon as she caught sight of us. Her face lit up and, with a shriek of delight, she launched herself toward the horses, waving her whip in the air as she ran. Before we could stop her, she'd wrapped herself around Possum's front leg while the little mare snorted and rocked backward in alarm.

"Easy," Rob said, laying a hand on Possum's neck and immediately the mare relaxed, stretching her nose down to ruffle the little girl's hair.

"Callie, no!" A woman, dressed in breeches, paddock boots, and a pink polo shirt hurried out of the barn, her face white with shock. She darted to her daughter's side and pried her free of Rob's horse, giving her an angry little shake.

"Oh, my gosh, I'm so sorry. She has no manners at all. Callie, you could have been killed."

Suddenly, I realized why they seemed familiar. It was the family I'd met on the ferry coming back to the Island. Callie was the little girl who'd almost thrown herself overboard to see the whales. Maybe the mom should use one of those harness things with a leash that some parents used on their kids. The child clearly had a death wish.

"I'm so sorry," the woman said again. "I'm Annie, and this is my daughter, Callie. We didn't mean to barge in, but rumour has it that you're going to have a boarding barn here and I was hoping we could talk and maybe get our horses on the wait list for when you're open for business."

"Oh, hi," I said, awkwardly shaking the outstretched hand she offered me. Her grip was like a vice, not painful but powerful, and I knew she must be strong even though she was rail-thin.

"Um, we're not the owners," I said, jumping down from Artimax, "but I can give you Hilary's number, if you like. There is some space left in the barn. The indoor isn't finished yet, and we still have to work on the pastures." I hoped I wasn't stepping on Hilary's toes by sharing all this information with a stranger.

"You're Nori Anderson's mom, aren't you?" Rob said quietly, and I turned to him in surprise. "I'm so sorry about what happened to Illumination."

The woman, Annie, went even paler and looked quickly down at her daughter. "Callie, go find your sister," she said firmly.

To my surprise, the little girl obeyed without arguing, trotting back toward the car.

"Sorry about that, we're all still so upset about losing Lumi. Nor-Nor...I mean, my daughter Nori, hasn't been the same since it happened. She's the reason we're considering switching barns. She can't even walk past his old stall, and she refuses to think about riding another horse. She's been awful, quite frankly, and I'm at my wit's end. I hoped a change of scenery might do us all good."

Finally, the little girl, Callie, came trooping back towing her sullen-looking older sister by the hand.

Nori stopped dead when she saw Rob, her jaw clenched spasmodically, and she turned her head sharply away as if she'd been slapped.

"I was busy, *mother*," she snapped, "what's so important that you had to drag me all the way out here?"

Annie raised her eyebrows at her daughter. You could tell she wanted to snap right back at her but was playing the part of this patient mom figure in front of strangers. "Honey," she said patiently, "these folks might have room to board the horses this summer. What would you think of maybe moving them here?"

"Why should I care?" Nori said peevishly. "Do whatever you like with your horses. Leave me out of it."

Annie flushed and bit her lip, clearly embarrassed.

"I have my own pony," Callie announced, breaking the awkward silence. "His name is Mister Sox."

"I know," Rob said, "I've seen you two at a couple of shows."

"Oh," she said, looking impressed. "He has stockings that go up past his knees." She turned to me knowingly as if this should mean something fantastic.

"Um, great," I said, edging past her toward the barn.

"That's Artimax, isn't it?" Nori said flatly, studying the horse with a practiced eye. "You won Training Level at Chilliwack last year."

"That's him," Rob said, looking over fondly at his horse.

"You moving him up to Prelim this summer?"

Rob shrugged. "Not this year. He needs to be fitter and that would be a big step for him. We're just going to hang out at Training Level for a while."

She frowned and shrugged impatiently. "You should move him up. Darla says horses go stale if they're showing below their potential. You'll waste him."

"That sounds like something Darla would say," Rob said easily, "but we're just going to take our time. There's no need to push him."

Nori huffed and rolled her eyes but didn't say anything more.

They followed us inside and I stamped down my irritation at this interruption to my day.

I took Artimax to his stall and shut the door tightly behind me to keep everyone out. Which meant that they all followed Rob and hovered outside of Possum's stall instead.

"This is an adorable horse," Annie said, "is she a warmblood of some sort?"

"Oh, *mother*," Nori said scathingly, "open your eyes; she looks nothing like a warmblood. How do you even survive being so stupid?"

There was a shocked silence and I guessed that even Nori knew that she'd gone too far because she muttered a quick, "sorry, Mom," under her breath and walked away to stare at the horses across the aisle, coolly assessing Jerry and his friends with a critical eye.

Rob was telling Annie and Callie all about Possum, but I kept a good eye on Nori to make sure she wasn't getting into any trouble.

She stood with her arms crossed over her chest, and then turned and sighed, and walked over to where Red was standing half-asleep with his head hanging out in the aisle.

"Hey, big guy," she whispered, not realizing I could hear her.

"You're a sweet one, aren't you? You have a very wise face."

I stopped brushing Artimax, surprised at how different she sounded when she wasn't being an arrogant little brat. She sounded almost human.

"Oh, Nor-Nor," her mother said, and I saw Nori cringe and grind her teeth. "You found a chestnut just like Lumi."

"That's it, I'm done here," Nori snapped, pushing away from Red sharply. "He is nothing like Lumi. Nobody is, and I'm sick to death of you."

And with that, she stomped out of the barn and a few seconds later the car door slammed. Twice.

"I am so, so sorry," Annie said, close to tears. "I know there's no excuse for her behavior, but honestly, she's not usually like this. I thought it would do her good to come out to a different barn, but it was obviously a mistake."

She looked over at Red and bit her lip. "He does look a little like Lumi," she said, "it's something in his eyes, so wise and kind. Nori blames herself for what happened, of course, but she won't talk to me about it. She won't talk to anyone."

"Nori's sad," Callie added solemnly, "she cries all the time now."

"Anyway," Annie said briskly, putting a hand on Callie's shoulder, "we've taken up too much of your time. I'll leave you my card just in case a space does open. It was nice to meet you both."

She led a subdued Callie out into the sunshine and a few minutes later they drove down the driveway.

"Wow. What was that?" I said as soon as I was sure they were gone. "That family is crazy."

"Annie's nice," Rob said, "and Nori used to be okay, intense and competitive, but not like she was today."

"What happened to her horse, though?"

"It was a pretty bad accident. He fell and broke his leg at an event. It was awful. They had to put him down right there and Nori pretty much went crazy; they had to get a doctor to sedate her to let the vet near him."

"That's horrible," I said, turning to look at Red who was still hanging his head over his stall door, lower lip drooping as he drifted into his afternoon nap. I couldn't imagine if something like that happened to him.

It almost happened to Folly, though, I thought, *it could have easily been her put down at that show.*

"*Was* it her fault?" I asked timidly, still thinking about my own accident.

"Who, Nori? No, it was just a fluke, I think. He slipped and fell and caught his front cannon bone with his hind hoof; it's something that could have happened to him galloping in the pasture. I mean, some people said they'd been pushing him too hard; he wasn't very old and they'd been moving him up pretty fast. But, it's easy to judge from the outside, right?"

He frowned and ran his hands down each of Possum's legs checking for heat, cuts, or any weird bumps. It was something he did to all his horses after every ride, even light trail rides, and it was pretty impressive. I made sure Red was brushed clean or bathed after every ride, but I would have no idea what to look for on his legs save for obvious gashes and lumps. Rob seemed to almost listen to his horses with his hands.

After the horses were put away, the barn tidied, and everyone was eating lunch, we sat down side by side on the cool concrete floor and leaned our backs against Red's stall. I pulled out my phone and opened the first video.

"These are my favourite ones," I said, finding the series I liked with the brothers in the desert. "I love that the horses are having a good time, too. And, see, some of them aren't even using saddles, either. That takes a whole different type of balance to shoot a bow off a galloping horse without having stirrups."

"Wow," Rob said, "these guys are pretty impressive. And you're right, those horses are having a great time."

"Yeah, I want Red to love it; I want to do it right."

"You will," Rob said, leaning his shoulder comfortably against mine as we pulled up more videos.

And we sat that way for the rest of the afternoon.

Chapter Nine

I spent that night with the Ahlbergs, and the next morning, Hilary and I wandered down to the barn to meet Rob after an excellent breakfast of crepes stuffed with glazed pears and covered in chocolate drizzle, courtesy of Mr. Ahlberg.

The sun was out, but the wind had picked up and we shivered in our t-shirts from the salty breeze rolling up from the ocean.

"I can't wait until I can afford a golf-cart so I don't have to do this walk twenty times a day," Hilary grumbled, rubbing her arms briskly to stay warm.

"Or what about an old truck like I had back at the ranch? I loved that truck."

"Yeah, I'm not sure if my parents would go for that," Hilary laughed. "But that reminds me; have you taken your learners test yet to get your driver's license? I'm thinking that I should get it as soon as I can. I'm kicking myself for putting it off so long. It's like a three-year process before I can actually even drive a horse trailer myself."

"No, not yet. It won't help me much when I'm not allowed to practice on anything here. I can't imagine driving anywhere with my dad or Marion; I would die from the stress."

"Ack, no, definitely not. But maybe my parents would help us. They want me to take one of those safety driving courses."

"We should take it together, then. That is, if I'm still around this summer."

"Don't say that, Astrid. It will work out."

Rob was already at the barn tacking up Ferdi when we arrived. He looked up and sent me that warm, heart-stopping smile that always made me feel like I'd won the lottery.

Hilary cleared her throat loudly beside me and disappeared into the tack room.

Red pricked his ears and nickered excitedly when he saw me headed his way, and my heart melted like it did every time he looked at me with those soulful eyes. Okay, it might have had something to do with the fact that he'd finished his breakfast hay and was ready for a snack but still, I was a hundred percent sure that he was glad I was his person.

We groomed and tacked up, and then took the horses out front to start our ride. But, as soon as I swung up into the saddle, Red swivelled around and pricked his ears at a vehicle racing up the driveway toward us way too fast, tires scattering gravel in all directions.

I squinted and then groaned under my breath.

"Hey, Astrid, isn't that Marion's car?" Hilary said.

"Yes," I said nervously, "I think so. I hope nothing's wrong."

But it wasn't Marion who got out of the car; it was my dad and he had company. Walking beside him was Darius.

"It worked," Hilary squeaked, turning bright red, and then pale and back again in quick succession. She clutched her saddle with both hands, looking dizzy. "He's here."

"What worked?" Rob asked, glancing at her in confusion. He

167

looked over at me when she didn't answer, but I just shrugged and shook my head. I wasn't about to tell him that Hilary had probably being praying non-stop to meet Darius again.

"Astrid," my dad called out, raising a hand in the air.

"Hey," I said weakly, wondering anxiously what this was all about. Had Marion managed to convince him that a family road trip was the worst idea in the world?

"Turns out Darius here is an old hand with horses," my dad said, clapping Darius on the back hard enough to make him wince. "I decided to drop in and see for myself what's keeping you so busy. Got to keep tabs on you sometimes, make sure you're not getting into trouble."

He squinted at us as he got closer, obviously trying to recognize who Rob and Hilary were in their helmets.

"Robert," he said formally, frowning and skirting around Ferdi's outstretched lips as they reached playfully for his jacket. Darius didn't hesitate, though; he stepped right up beside the big horse and laid a hand on Ferdi's neck, stroking it lovingly.

Beside me, Hilary made a squeaking sound. "Astrid, he likes *horses*," she hissed in a voice that hopefully only I could hear.

"Do you ride?" Rob asked politely, since Darius was practically whispering in Ferdi's ear and the big horse was lapping it up.

"I used to," Darius said, his expression darkening. "My uncle bred Arabian horses, back home. I spent every summer on their ranch with my cousins."

Arabians. I looked up with interest, and the thing that had been bothering me about him clicked into place. I knew now why he'd seemed familiar. He looked exactly like that family from my archery videos.

"Darius," I said in astonishment, "are your relatives into horse archery by any chance? Do they live in the desert somewhere?"

His face turned to stone, dark and foreboding and ready to fracture into pieces at any second. He looked much older than his nineteen years and something like rage glittered in his eyes. Ferdi snorted and nudged him with his nose, and just like, that the clouds passed. Darius took a few deep breaths before speaking.

"Yes," he said carefully, "my cousins could do anything with horses, but mounted combat and archery were something they loved especially."

"Oh," I said, full to the brim with so many questions but afraid to open my mouth again.

Way to go, Astrid, I told myself fiercely, *Marion told you that he'd lost most of his family. Maybe they're all in refugee camps now. Maybe they even had to sell all their horses. And you had to go and bring it up.*

"I watch their videos," I said finally to fill in the silence. "I'm trying to teach myself."

Darius looked up, his eyes bright with emotion. "It is a tradition that goes back *thousands* of years in my country. Our horses' pedigrees trace back to the time of pharaohs. It is hardly something that just anyone can learn on a whim by watching a…a video."

"I…I know," I stammered, blushing, "but I have to start somewhere. Don't I?"

"Do you?" he said quietly and then he rolled his shoulders as if shrugging off the weight of painful memories. He opened his mouth to say more, but my dad had already tired of the conversation and had moved on over to stand beside me.

"So, this is the new man you've been hanging out with," he said in that too-loud jovial voice and it took me a panicked second to realize that he meant Red and not Rob. He stepped up and gave Red a hearty pat right between his eyes that would have sent a more sensitive horse bolting for cover. But Red just snorted and popped his ears forward in surprise and then reached down to itch his forehead roughly on my dad's shoulder, nearly knocking him over.

I'd never seen Red be anything but gentle with both horses and people, and at first, I was too surprised to rein him in, and then I realized that my dad was actually smiling, and then he was *laughing* and using both hands to scratch Red on the forehead and behind his ears. I had not seen that coming.

"Well, Astrid, I can see you kids have work to do so we'll be running along now; we're just on our way to the club. Your stepmother has some crazy idea that you can't leave your responsibilities here to go on the road with me this summer, is that right?"

I gulped, my hands slick on the reins. Red shifted underneath me uneasily and I let out the breath I'd trapped in my lungs. "Yes, sir," I said quietly, "I need to take care of Red and I promised I'd help Hilary out here this summer."

"I couldn't do it without Astrid," Hilary said, finding her voice, "especially with the play coming up. She's so good with the horses, too."

"Well, if you and Marion don't want to come on a victory tour with your old man then I guess I'll have to go by myself; live the bachelor life for a while, hey Darius?"

Darius laughed obediently, but I didn't think he was even listening. He probably hadn't gotten over me reminding him about being a refugee. He'd somehow migrated over to Hilary and was petting Jerry softly on the neck without looking up. Hilary sat there silently, her face flushed beet red and her eyes fixed on Jerry's dark silver mane.

I cleared my throat and took another deep breath. "Dad, um, Hilary's family said I could stay here for the summer if I wanted to. So that, um, Marion could go with you. I'm sure she wants to—"

"Your *step*mother has made it quite clear that going on tour with her husband would be an inconvenience," he said, his smile dropping away.

Even though I knew he was wrong, I wisely said nothing. They must have been fighting over this—*over me*—but couldn't risk him changing his mind about letting me stay behind.

"All right, son, if you're done fooling around with the horses, we should head out to the club. *Time's* a wasting."

"Yes, I am ready," Darius said softly, but it looked like he could have stood there forever.

"Wait, Darius," I said quickly, still embarrassed but not wanting to let this opportunity escape. "I'm so sorry I brought up your family. But do you think you could give me some tips sometime on teaching Red to be a good archery horse? I want to do it properly."

Darius hesitated, his face clouding over again. Then he looked over at Ferdi and the longing in his face was obvious. He must miss horses very much.

"Oh, of course he'll help," my dad said impatiently, when the silence stretched out too long, "we have a few weeks before we hit the road anyway, don't we, son?"

Darius nodded, but he didn't look exactly thrilled about it.

We sat there silently until the car had made an abrupt U-turn and sped back down the driveway with a spray of gravel, and then Ferdi started to paw the ground impatiently.

"Come on, let's ride," Rob said, letting the big horse lead the way up toward the trails.

It was a very quiet ride; both Hilary and I stayed lost in our own thoughts while Rob helpfully pointed out to her all the repairs and modifications needed.

"See, if you ran the electric here then you could keep the track to ride on and the inside would be for grazing. You could have this ready in a few days."

Hilary nodded vaguely, but her thoughts were miles away; now and then her cheeks flushed, and secretive smile played across her lips in response to some inner thought…I was pretty sure she wasn't thinking about pasture.

I was depressed over my conversation with Darius, too. I should have handled it better, been more sensitive. I had no idea what awful things he'd been through during the war, but it hadn't been right for me to bring it up so casually. I hoped that his cousins and the fabulous horses they rode were okay.

As soon as we got back to the barn and I had Red untacked and put away, I sat down in the aisle and pulled those archery videos up on my phone and scrolled through the dates carefully.

The last one was five years ago, I thought anxiously, *why haven't they posted any new ones?*

I had a sinking feeling that I knew the reason why.

Chapter Ten

When Marion came to pick me up that night after dinner, I knew I'd been right about them fighting. Her face was pale but there were blotchy rings around her eyes like she'd recently been crying. Marion never cried.

I'm going to fix this if I can, I thought, feeling a surge of protectiveness.

Marion didn't say much on the way home and she disappeared into her office as soon as we got inside.

I went and showered quickly and changed into my new form-flattering yoga pants that also doubled as cycling gear since I wasn't about to strap myself into those spandex biking pants with the padded bum that Marion had first suggested.

I knew my dad was in the living room reading from a stack of sports magazines and I stood in the hall for a few minutes, gathering my courage. Finally, I took a deep breath and stepped into the living room.

"Dad," I said, twisting my hands nervously together. "Do you think we could go cycling?"

He looked at me incredulously and I thought he'd say no.

Then his face transformed into a smile and he jumped to his feet with frightening speed. I had to wonder what high-test fitness supplements he was on. It was like Folly when she was on her high-performance horse feed; so full of energy it was scary.

"Of course, Astrid, that would be great. Go find Marion and tell her we leave in ten minutes."

"Actually," I said nervously, "do you think we could go alone? I mean, just the two of us?"

"Oh," he said, looking nonplussed, as if the prospect of spending time alone with me was alarming. "Okay, sure. Let's do it."

We didn't say much on the ride down the elevator. We stood as far apart as possible, both fiddling with our bikes and adjusting our helmets until the doors opened and we wheeled right through the lobby.

"You switching that horse of yours for a bike, Astrid?" the doorman said, laughing, before he caught sight of my dad. He frowned and stood up straighter, adjusting his tie and looking like he'd rather be anywhere else but there.

"I'd never trade in Red," I laughed, hurrying past him so my dad wouldn't linger. "See you later."

"Do you know that man?" he said, frowning, when we made it outside into the cool evening. He made it sound like an accusation.

"Uh, yes, Dad, and so do you. That's Dom's son Carlo, he's been working here with his dad for years. His daughter takes riding lessons."

"Oh," he said, grudgingly, "I didn't know that."

We walked down the bike path that ran along the seawall and

then swung up and peddled easily. I'd been nervous about riding a bike again; it was my first time in years but, once I was on, it was surprisingly easy to find my balance. The path was flat so I didn't have to touch the confusing array of gears and the feeling of coasting along was exhilarating.

For once, my dad wasn't racing to get anywhere, he cruised along beside me, looking over at the glass-still water from time to time, lost in his own thoughts. It was peaceful and gradually the nervous energy running through my veins quieted and a strange sensation of peace enveloped me.

We rode for about an hour, hardly saying a word, and then turned around and retraced our steps, marveling at the purple-splashed sky reflected on the water.

We stopped at a picnic table on a rocky outcropping overlooking the ocean and I pulled out the snacks I'd brought for us; rice cakes and a bit of cheese and fruit.

"Thanks." My dad ate a few things and then reached into his pannier and pulled out some chocolate power bars and tossed them on the table. "Here, I brought dessert. Don't tell your stepmother."

He grinned down at me, and I couldn't help but smile back. *Now*, I thought, *now's the time.*

"Dad," I said, taking a deep breath, "I think you should take Marion on the road with you."

He stopped mid-chew and looked at me curiously; no trace of anger or irritation on his face–yet. "Well, I offered to take you both, Astrid. But you said you have the horses to take care of and couldn't go."

"I know, I'm sorry. But that doesn't mean Marion can't go.

Hilary's parents offered to let me stay there for the summer. They need a lot of help getting their new place ready, and it would mean free board for Red for the summer, too. I think Hilary's overwhelmed."

"So, you mean you'd be the hired help?"

He raised an eyebrow and I couldn't tell if he was serious or not.

"No, Dad, it's not like that. You know the Ahlbergs; they've always been like family to me."

I stopped, not wanting to remind him just then of the many times Hilary's family had taken me in for the weekends when he was home from business trips, to keep me safely out of the way.

Maybe he was thinking the same thing because he nodded thoughtfully and looked out over the ocean with a sigh. "They're good people," he said quietly. "And it's a good offer. But what makes you think Marion wants to come along? I don't want to uproot her for the summer, either."

"Oh, Dad," I said, wondering how he could be so clueless, "it's the thing she wants most. She seems sad right now and I think that maybe this trip would cheer her up."

He sat up and looked at me, a mixture of irritation and concern flickering across his face. "Marion, sad? That's not possible; she has everything she wants. Did she tell you that?"

"Of course not," I said quickly, hoping I wasn't getting Marion in trouble. "She didn't have to; I can see it in her face. And I know she was looking forward to going with you and being a part of things. She wants to help you."

"Oh, well, I'm not sure how much help she can be in this case. Nancy has all the logistics handled."

"Oh, I'm sure she does." I regretted the words as soon as I said them, knowing I'd crossed the line.

But surprisingly the outburst I'd expected didn't come. He just opened his eyes wide with surprise, confusion flickering across his face. "Nancy's just my coach, Astrid," he said quietly, "that's all; she's doing her job. And she happens to be very passionate about squash."

I coughed and cleared my throat nervously, knowing I had to tread carefully.

"I'm sure Nancy's a good coach," I said finally, "but Marion can help, too. I know she wants to be a part of everything. *She's your wife, not Nancy, and she wants to go on this trip.*"

He frowned, and I could see my window of opportunity closing. "That's about enough, Astrid. I assure you that your stepmother and I are capable of handling our own lives. We don't need your input."

I looked quickly down at the table and breathed slowly in and out. *Well, I gave it my best shot, anyway. I can't do much more than that.*

"Of course I'd prefer if she came," he said finally, breaking the silence. "I'd been looking forward to spending more time together this summer. Let me talk to her and think it over. You're sure the Ahlberg's offer to have you stay there is firm?"

"Definitely. Hilary practically begged me to stay and help her."

"All right, let's head back now before it gets dark."

Well, that wasn't as bad as it could have been, I thought, *there's a good chance he'll talk to Marion tonight. I hope she agrees to go. She needs this.*

Our ride back was silent, but my dad seemed more lost in thought than angry. He smiled briefly at the doorman when we went back inside and clapped me companionably on the shoulder when we put our bikes away in the foyer.

"Good ride, Astrid," he said, "we should do this more often."

And, actually, despite the few sketchy moments where his old anger had bubbled close to the surface, I agreed with him.

Chapter Eleven

The next morning, I woke up early and stumbled, half-awake, to the kitchen to see if I could find any hidden carbs. After last night's adventure, I knew my dad must have a secret supply of power bars stashed somewhere.

I stopped dead in the doorway and rubbed my eyes because there was my dad and Marion sitting at the breakfast table like a normal couple drinking their coffee, and there were actual eggs and ham and croissants on the plates around them. Nope, it wasn't an illusion; they were really there.

"We never had a real welcome-home breakfast for you, Astrid," Marion said, "we thought we'd sit down as a family and discuss our plans for this summer."

"Really?" I said, warm and fuzzy feelings starting in my heart. I pushed them down firmly, though, it wouldn't do to get too excited too early. Who knew how this was going to go?

I sat down and poured myself some coffee, and then looked at the food on the table and worked out the best plan of action. What I *wanted* to do was load up my plate, but instead I carefully took half a croissant, one small, fried egg, and a couple pieces of ham, looking up warily to find them both watching me. They looked away quickly, though, and then smiled at each other in a way that was almost cute.

I concentrated on eating my food in small, non-greedy-looking bites, and waiting for them to drop whatever announcement they'd planned on me. Would I get to stay with Hilary and her family for the summer, or would I be stuck in boring squash-world for an eternity?

"So, Astrid," Marion said finally, "how would you feel about me going on the road with your father this summer?"

I looked up at her smiling face and relief washed over me. I was so glad I hadn't ruined this summer for her.

"That…that sounds great, Marion," I said, waiting to make sure it meant I was truly off the hook before getting too excited.

"And you're sure you're comfortable staying at Hilary's place for the entire summer? You've been gone so long, and we've hardly seen you since you've been home."

And whose fault is that? I thought, and then pushed the uncharitable feelings away. We had different lifestyles, that was all. It was nobody's fault that I'd been born into the wrong family.

"Yes, I want to stay there," I said, hoping I didn't sound too eager.

"You'll keep up with your physio and you'll follow's Earl's instructions about how much you practice?"

"Yes, absolutely," I said. "I found a horse-bow online to order, too. I was hoping to try that this summer."

"Well, as long as Earl says it's okay, then you should go ahead and order it. We only have a few weeks to get everything organized before we leave."

And, just like that, it was done.

After that, things moved quickly. A permanent guest room was made up for me at the Ahlberg's, and my stuff was toted over in a series of trips and packed away.

The gigantic grey and black motorhome splashed with squash logos arrived and spent a week living out on the street in front of our condo since it was too big to fit into the underground parking.

It was pretty amazing that something so plain on the outside looked like a first-class hotel room on the inside. It had a full kitchen with granite countertops and a bedroom with a king-sized bed, and in the middle section, the walls slid out to reveal a full-sized living room with loveseats and a huge television that popped out from the wall. For a very brief moment, I was almost sad I wasn't going to get to ride across the country in it. Almost.

Chapter Twelve

With less than two weeks to go before their departure, Marion went into overdrive fitting in a million appointments for me; it was like she thought they were going away for a year and not just a few months.

I had the dentist and doctor for check-ups plus physio, chiro, and a sports therapist who told them exactly what Earl had said; that I had to build up my strength slowly. By the end of the first week, I was dying for them to leave so my life could get back to normal.

Since there wasn't any bus service from their farm, Hilary's parents had agreed to drive me to volunteer at one of the week-long camps at the range. I was a bit sad that I couldn't do more, but I knew it was a lot to ask them to shuttle me around when they were already so busy. Especially since I still needed to go to physio once a week. I was lucky they were driving me anywhere at all.

Hilary, too, was a whirlwind of activity; she had rehearsals for the play, but she also had the extra dance, singing, and acting lessons on top of that, plus her church group. Between being ferried around all over the city, riding, and taking care of the barn, she barely had a moment to slow down.

After another non-stop morning of errands, including an agonizing hour spent trapped in a salon getting my hair cut, it was a relief to walk into the quiet, cool barn and feel my tension drain away.

I slid open Red's stall door and moved up beside him, running my hand down his smooth coat. In the few weeks we'd been here the last of his winter fuzz had shed out and his muscles were starting to develop in a way that made him look extra handsome, if I did say so myself.

"You want to go for a ride, buddy?" I asked, leaning in to give him a kiss on the neck, inhaling his rich, horsey scent.

I brushed him slowly and took time to get his mane and tail lying perfectly flat and even, admiring the multi-coloured strands in his thick tail. From a distance, it just looked red, but up close there were mahogany, gold, and chestnut threads all mixed up in a shimmering cascade.

Like grains of sand on the beach, I thought, *each piece is different.*

I was just going to get his saddle when Hilary's mom's car pulled up fast, stopped abruptly, and sat idling in front of the barn. I stood there, waiting for Hilary to get out, but when the doors stayed firmly shut and nobody emerged I quickly went to the tack room. If they were having a private conversation I didn't want to be standing there staring. I ducked back into Red's stall without looking back.

Finally, I heard the car door open slowly. "Hilary," her mom said warningly, "the doctor told you that you needed to rest. You can come down to the barn later."

"It's okay, Mom," Hilary said, her voice thick with tears. "Can you come back and pick me up in a bit? I want to talk to Astrid."

I slowly slid the door to Red's stall open and peeked outside.

"Oh no, Hilary. What did you do?"

She limped unsteadily toward me on a pair of crutches, her eyes red and puffy, and the rest of her face pale with pain.

"Are you okay?" I said, moving toward her and wrapping her in a gentle hug.

She stood stiffly, her gaze trained on the ground, lower lip trembling.

"No," she said tearfully, "Astrid, I'm not okay. This is all my fault."

"What happened?" I asked, not liking how miserable she looked.

"Oh, I fell during practice. I landed wrong and twisted my ankle horribly. I'm out of the play and I've ruined everything."

"Oh my gosh, Hilary, I'm so, so sorry. This is awful."

"No, it's okay. I brought it on myself. This is what happens when you're a terrible person." Her voice broke and she wobbled on her crutches.

"Come on, what are you talking about? You're the best person I know. It was just an accident."

"Astrid," she said, drawing in a deep breath, "can we go outside and sit down? I need to tell you something."

"Um, okay," I said, my stomach churning with all the possible things she had to tell me. She didn't want me to move in. She was kicking Red out. What other awful thing could it be?

She wasn't very good on the crutches and it took us a while

184

to get outside to the picnic table. When she sat down she looked even paler and, to my horror, she began to cry; big silent tears ran unchecked down her face.

"Oh, Hilary. What on earth is wrong?" I said, sitting down close beside her. I wrapped an arm around her shoulder and gave her a tight hug. She leaned on me for a moment, letting herself cry and then pushed herself away from me abruptly.

"Don't hug me, Astrid, not until you hear what I have to say. I've been such an idiot."

"Don't say that. You're the most brilliant person I know, Hil. What happened?"

"Let me get this out now, Astrid, otherwise I never will. You deserve to know."

"Know what?"

She took a deep breath and then the words tumbled out in a rush. "After you left last winter, everything fell apart. I mean everything. Claudia died and that whole mess with Cole being a psycho and me having to move Jerry. And I wasn't thinking straight, everything was mixed up in my head, and I made some mistakes. At first, I...I thought it would just go away if I didn't say anything. It was just a stupid kiss and it didn't even mean anything...at least not to him. But it didn't go away, and I just feel so guilty all the time."

"Wait, what on earth are you talking about? Did something happen with Cole?"

"Ew, Astrid, no, not Cole, I'm not *that* crazy."

She looked down at the table and dug a fingernail into the wood, pulling up a thin sliver of paint. "It was last winter, before we came to visit you up at your aunt's place. I'd started keeping

Jerry at Rob's and we were spending all sorts of time together. I didn't mean for it to happen, but I just, well, I started to notice him; how nice he was, and how kind with the horses, and how good-looking he was. And it grew from there."

"What grew?" I said weakly. "You and Rob, were *together*?"

"No, no," she said quickly, "nothing like that. It was all me, Astrid. I fell for him *hard* and that feeling got worse and worse until I couldn't think of anything else. I thought for sure he felt the same way.

"I started spending all sorts of extra time over there. I was miserable after Claudia died, and Rob was so nice and comforting. He was like the only safe port in a terrible storm. I only felt normal when I was around him and I knew that we were meant to be together."

"Oh," I said, my face burning.

"But, Astrid, it was all me. Honestly, I don't even think he noticed that I liked him until I, well, I kissed him."

She stopped, her face flushing again and her eyes brimming with tears.

"You kissed him," I said dully, my heart thudding in my chest, an ache spreading out across my body until all I could feel was pain. Anger, betrayal, sadness. My dad had been right, there *had* been something going on between them this past winter when they'd come to visit. He'd sensed it somehow and tried to tell me. I'd been such a blind idiot to think that Rob would like me over Hilary.

"It was awful, Astrid. I practically pounced on him, and he was so surprised but polite about it, too, the way he is, and him being nice made it worse. He apologized and then I apologized, and I was so mortified that I didn't go see Jerry for a week. But Rob was so good about it and said we should just forget anything had happened. And then we came up to see you, and I wanted to tell you so badly, but I couldn't, and the worst part was that I still liked him, even though it was obvious he'd choose you over me in a heartbeat. And part of me was so jealous of you, Astrid. And I'm sorry for that, I couldn't help it."

"You were jealous of me?"

"Of course I was; I'm not perfect, Astrid. You always think I'm this nice, wonderful person, but lots of times I'm not. Sometimes, I'm not good at all inside."

"So, you kissed Rob and that was it?" I said, struggling to understand the whole story.

"I wish it was," she sighed. "After I got home from visiting you, the feelings just got worse and worse. I couldn't stand to be around him if he didn't like me, but when I wasn't near him I felt like I was going to die. I actually cornered him and told him how I felt, and I wanted to kill him when he told me again that he wasn't interested. After that, I begged my parents to let me move Jerry here even before the barn was ready. I thought that if I wasn't around him all the time that those feelings would go away."

"Did they?" I asked, already guessing the answer.

"No. Well, not right away. I was fighting them hard, though. I finally told my parents how awful I felt, and I told my pastor at church, and they helped quite a bit, but the feelings didn't go away completely until the other night when I met Darius. And now it's the exact same thing with Darius as it was with Rob. I just met the guy, but all I can do is think about him all the time.

There's something wrong with me, Astrid. I hate feeling like this.

"When I told my mom what was going on, she said I needed to tell you, but I put it off, knowing that you'd be so mad. I should have told you sooner, though. I'm so sorry."

"Okay," I said dully, not able to process anything she'd said past the hurt that was eating a hole away inside of me. Hilary was the person I trusted most in the whole world. What did it matter if she was *sorry* if she was able to hurt me in the first place? "I'm going to go ride now."

"Astrid, wait." Hilary looked panicked. "We need to talk about this more. I need to make it up to you somehow."

"I'm going to go ride Red," I repeated and turned my back and went into the barn. I didn't know exactly what I was supposed to feel, but I was just numb; my overwhelming urge was to get as far away from her as possible. I needed time to think on my own.

Red was exactly where I'd left him doing exactly what I expected him to be doing; eating. Because he was a solid, dependable friend who would never let me down when I least expected it. Not like some other people I could mention.

I finished tacking him up and, as an afterthought, I grabbed my bow from the tack room.

"Come on Red," I said, sticking a handful of arrows in my quiver and clipping it to the pocket of my breeches. I wasn't wearing a belt and my worn-out breeches weren't nearly as sturdy as jeans so the quiver sank nearly to my knees in an annoying way.

Clink-clink-clink rattled the arrows in their plastic sleeves, not used to being jostled around so rudely. Red snorted and tilted his head at the noise, one eye staring at the quiver in alarm.

"It's okay, buddy," I whispered, picking up my bow in the other hand. I climbed carefully on his back, trying not to hit him with my bow, sit on my quiver, or dump my arrows all the while aware that Hilary was still crying softly at the picnic table and watching me at my clumsiest.

My face burned and I looked anywhere but at her as we headed up the driveway.

"Astrid, wait," she said, snuffling tearfully, but I didn't look back.

Instead, I took a deep breath to block her out completely; this ride wasn't about *her*, it was about me and Red, the only friend who mattered to me now. I willed myself to relax, releasing the death grip my calves had on his sides and letting my legs hang long, the reins stretched to the buckle.

Red flicked an ear back as the tip of my bow accidentally banged against his hip but didn't pause his steady march up the driveway. All these rides with bigger, faster horses had woken him up and he was moving out with much more animation than he'd ever had before. I knew Liza would be happy with our progress. Suddenly, I wanted to see her more than anything; I needed someone to talk to.

"What do you think, buddy?" I asked, hitching the bow up again so it didn't hit him. I reached down to scratch his withers. "Do you like it here? Is it worth staying here, or should we find somewhere else to board you? Maybe we never should have left Aunt Lillian's at all."

Red didn't answer, but his head bobbed up and down as we headed downhill through the pasture, eager to reach the little stream so he could have his drink and then go for a canter; his favourite part of the ride.

As soon as he was through the stream, he broke into a trot and then a canter, but a few strides along he sprang to one side, snorting in astonishment and even giving a small sideways buck.

"Red," I said, in shock. I had never, ever seen him kick out like that. "What was that about?"

But as soon as I turned around, I realized what must have happened, the bow had twisted around and jammed him in the side as soon as he picked up speed. There was even a line on his side where it had roughed up his fur.

"Oh, I'm so sorry. That was my fault, wasn't it? Let's just walk."

I petted his neck soothingly and repositioned the bow carefully over my shoulder for the fifth time. I was clearly going to need some sort of bow sling before next time. It was much too awkward to keep it safely out of the way.

Anger at Hilary and guilt at myself for hurting Red, even slightly, swirled together inside me, but it wasn't until I reached the cool air of the rainforest that I began to cry. I stopped Red beside one of the ancient moss-covered stumps and slid off him. As soon as my boots hit the damp ground of that ancient forest the tears began to fall, and I sat down with my back up against the dead tree, keeping Red's reins clutched in one hand.

As a rule, I was not much of a crier; it had always been safer at my house to keep my emotions in check, and though I felt many things on the inside, I generally tried not to express them around witnesses. But Red was a different kind of witness.

"I know it's stupid, Red." I sniffled. "It was just a kiss. But, it just feels so awful. Hilary *knew* how much I liked Rob, and she went ahead and did it anyway; she didn't even care about me."

And what would have happened if Rob hadn't said no, I thought miserably, *she would have happily been with him right now without even giving me a second thought.* That's the part that hurt the worst.

I sat there feeling wretched and probably would have stayed curled up there all day if Red hadn't bumped the top of my head with his soft nose. He whuffled his lips through my hair and then touched my cheek gently. And then he dropped his head and nudged the pocket of my breeches, smelling for the apple snacks I usually kept there.

"No, Red, it's not time for snacks," I said tearfully, pushing his big head away. But he was back about three seconds later, his nose working as he scented out his cookies, trying to reach them through the fabric of my clothes.

"Oh, fine, you piglet." I laughed despite myself and stood up, brushing the black, loamy soil off my breeches and fishing in my pocket until I found a soggy treat.

"Red, why are my breeches covered in horse slobber?" I said, attempting to sound angry.

He looked at me innocently with wide eyes, crunching his treat and then bobbed his head, ready for more.

"No more until we get back. Come on over here. I have to figure out how to get back up on you."

Technically, I could get on from the ground, but Claudia had drilled into us that you always used a mounting block to get on a horse because it could hurt their backs if the saddle twisted on them.

I found a decaying stump that was roughly the right height and scrambled up onto him. Before I'd even settled properly in the saddle, Red turned around and bumped the toe of my boot with his nose before starting through the forest of his own accord. I wiped my eyes with the back of my hand and left the reins resting on his neck. I wasn't worried about *him* doing anything stupid.

We headed up the hill and, when we reached the sandy stretch, Red moved into a slow trot, snorting contentedly and stretching his neck down. This time I kept one hand off the reins to make sure the bow stayed put.

The salty wind buffeted us from the ocean, fluttering through my hair and whipping my curls out from underneath my helmet. I closed my eyes, tilting my face back so the warm sun could beat down on me and inhaling the good beach smells.

His stride changed when we reached the deeper sand on the beach and he automatically sat back on his haunches and went from a trot to a smooth walk. I sighed and opened my eyes to see that the water was boiling today, full of white caps and waves that crashed heavily onto the shore. It suited the way I felt perfectly.

"No playing in the water today, buddy. You'd get swept out to sea."

Red snorted as we picked our way carefully across the top of the beach, eyeing the waves suspiciously as they smashed against the shore and rushed up the sand toward us with greedy outstretched fingers. Each time they reached their limit they slid back out again with a sucking, hissing noise. None of them came anywhere close to us, but it was still intimidating to see our friendly beach turned into such an inhospitable landscape.

Mr. Ahlberg's boat rocked and bucked unhappily beside the dock, the buoys tied to its sides squeaking in protest with every wave that pushed it into the wood pilings. I didn't know much about boats, but I was pretty sure it wasn't supposed to be moving around quite that much.

It was a relief to head back up the hill out of the wind. The noise of ocean dropped away abruptly as soon as we reached the woods, and I rubbed my arms to get rid of the goosebumps. I loved the sea on a good day when it was calm, but I'd never liked rough weather. I knew some people loved it best that way, but churning sea always made me nervous. I guessed I was a creature of the land at heart.

Red pricked his ears when he saw the sandy trail stretching out in front of him, so nice for cantering.

"Hang on, buddy, we're going to try an experiment this time."

I made sure he was in a steady walk before I dropped the reins on his neck and then carefully unshouldered my bow and lifted it slowly to the side, pretending I was about to shoot. Red flicked an ear back and stopped dead in his tracks, swiveling his head around to look at the strange thing in my hand.

"See, it's okay, you silly horse, it won't hurt you." But I could tell he wasn't convinced. He started walking again when I asked but his back was tense and hollow underneath me and his ears stayed glued backward, one eye rolling my way.

What's wrong with him? I've never seen him act like this.

I shouldered the bow again in frustration and immediately felt him relax. "It's okay, buddy, that's just our first practice. You'll get used to it."

I thought of my quiver full of arrows and my new foam target already tucked safely in the guest room…now *my* room…at the Ahlberg's house, which reminded me again of the whole reason I had been crying out here in the woods, alone. This was supposed to be my home for the entire summer, so I had to make a decision.

I didn't think I could forgive Hilary so easily, but I also wasn't going to ruin this opportunity that had fallen into my lap. I was used to living with people who were unpredictable and untrustworthy; I was perfectly capable of living next to Hilary, of sharing a barn, a house, and meals with her while still keeping my distance from her. Wasn't I?

When I got back to the barn, Hilary was nowhere in sight; instead, her place at the picnic table had been replaced by Rob, who held Artimax's lead casually in one hand, letting the big horse graze.

My face prickled hot with embarrassment when I saw him, although I didn't know what I had to be ashamed about. Red flicked an ear back at me uncertainly and stopped, wondering why I'd stopped breathing and turned to stone on his back.

"Good boy," I murmured and swung lightly to the ground, glad I was able to at least do that gracefully.

"Hey," Rob said gently, looking carefully at my face.

"Hey." I tried to sound casual, but my voice came out squeaky like a five-year-old struggling hard not to cry. Red bumped me with his nose and then dropped his head to graze. I let the reins slide through my fingers and stared at the picnic table.

I knew I had no logical reason to be mad at Rob. According

to Hilary's story, he'd done nothing wrong; he'd acted as a friend to her and she said that he'd only been interested in me.

But he didn't tell you what had happened, a voice inside whispered. *He kept it a secret because he felt sorry for you. And now that he's kissed perfect Hilary, how could he possibly be interested in you?*

"So, Hilary texted me that she told you what happened. Astrid, I'm sorry. It was a mistake."

A mistake. Emotions roiled through me, crashing together in waves so violent I could hardly stop myself from screaming or running or exploding. Instead of doing any of those things I just stood there, frozen into place with my fingers and toes numb but my heart feeling like it was being sliced open wider and wider every second.

To my mortification, tears stung my eyes, but I couldn't even pull myself together enough to wipe them away. I sniffled, feeling ugly and stupid. I leaned into Red, feeling his warm, solid bulk supporting me, making me feel stronger.

"I should have told you," Rob said, staring anxiously into my face. "But Hilary was so upset; she apologized a million times and begged me not to tell you. I didn't think it was my secret to keep. I'm really sorry."

He stood and moved toward me, but I jerked away, not ready to let him get near me. I knew I was being ridiculous, that I had no right to be jealous when a) he hadn't done anything wrong, and b) we weren't actually a real couple. Sure we liked each other, but no promises had been made. He was free to do whatever he liked.

"I have to put Red away," I said, my voice shaky. I wanted

time to pull myself together, so I didn't sound like an emotional, unstable idiot.

"Sure," he said easily. "Take all the time you need. I'll be here."

Great, I thought, *he's not going away. And I'm going to cry in front of him and make a fool of myself sounding like a jealous, clingy girlfriend when really, I have no right to say who he does and doesn't kiss.*

My hands were trembling as I untacked Red, pulling off his bridle too fast so that I banged the bit against his teeth. He winced and lifted his head and I felt tears well in my eyes. Why couldn't I do anything right?

"I'm so sorry," I whispered to him and laid my hand on his big, round cheek.

He shook his head and then dropped his nose to his hay pile, any discomfort hopefully forgotten. I put his tack away and brushed him carefully until he shone, delaying the inevitable.

Finally, I took a deep breath and headed outside to where Rob was still sitting quietly at the picnic table. He'd put Artimax away and was now doing something with his phone.

He's probably texting her right now, I thought uncharitably and slid onto the bench beside him, sitting way down at the far end and putting my hands flat on the picnic table for support, not meeting his gaze.

But, that overwhelming emotion I'd felt before hadn't gone anywhere, it was still lurking inside of me, waiting to come out in all sorts of irrational ways. I was afraid that if I opened my mouth I would say something awful that couldn't be taken back.

"Why?" I said, finally, breaking the silence since it didn't seem like he was about to.

"Astrid, I told you." He sighed. "It was unexpected. I didn't see her coming until it was too late."

"No." I sniffled. "I mean, why *don't* you like her?"

He was silent again and I didn't think he'd answer.

"I do like her," he said finally. "Hilary's a great friend; she's just not my type, that's all."

"But...but she's perfect."

He laughed and shifted closer down the bench toward me, closing the distance between us. "She's a great person, Astrid, I'm not arguing that. But, I already like someone else."

"Oh," I said quietly. It had been inevitable. Rob was too perfect to stay single the whole time I was away up north. I'd been right not to get my hopes up that we had a chance.

"Dude," he said, nudging my arm, "it's you."

I just shook my head and refused to look up.

"Come on. Why is this so hard for you to understand?"

I took a deep breath and looked up, meeting his sincere gaze tentatively. "Because...well, because I'm just average...at best. There are so many girls out there who are flashier, and more fun and...who don't freak out just because you kissed someone *last* winter. Most girls wouldn't care."

"Astrid, I like you because you *do* care. You're smart and kind, and you care about not hurting people so much that you hurt yourself instead. And besides that, you're beautiful and funny and honest and, well...perfect."

"No," I said in disbelief, but in spite of the fact that nothing he said could possibly apply to me, I felt a spark light up inside me.

He looked down and gently reached out to wipe a stray tear

from my cheek with the tip of his finger.

"Yes," he said, "you are. Astrid, I've known you were special from the moment you stepped on that rope swing at that party at the Ling's lake house. You were so brave and, well, different from everyone else. I knew then that I wanted you in my life."

"You're kidding," I said, looking at him incredulously. "I broke their rope swing; I nearly drowned. I looked like a beached whale when they pulled me out."

"But, *before* that," he said, sliding closer until his leg was pressed up against mine. "Before that, you were spectacular."

My heart thundered in my chest at his proximity, and I'm pretty sure I forgot to breathe. He leaned over and touched my face again, smoothed my hair back behind my ear. And then he turned my head and kissed me, so gently, lightly brushing my lips with his so that it was just like being touched with the softest velvet. If velvet also was alive with this sort of electric current that lit me up like a Christmas tree. He pulled back and we just sat there, both staring and grinning at each other like idiots. In that moment, something inside me shifted, something in the universe shifted, and I had this overwhelming, cosmic feeling that every moment of my life so far had been leading up to this point.

The feeling passed as soon as it came, and it was just me and my best friend Rob still grinning at each other, and he'd now taken both my hands in his and was playing with my fingers as if they were his own in a way that made shivers run down my spine. And I didn't mind, I didn't mind at all. I had never felt so alive.

"Come on," he said finally, pulling me to my feet, "let's get these ponies exercised."

***

There must have been something in the air because Artimax, and even sullen Maverick, just wanted to run.

The wind had picked up even more since my earlier ride on Red, and it made both horses extra prancy and excited. We didn't disappoint them. Every time the footing looked decent enough Rob would turn to me with that look in his eye and we'd let them go, not just cantering but full out gallops that left all of us gasping for breath. Maverick looked truly happy for once.

We stopped for a few minutes on the rise overlooking the ocean to where the sea was now breaking with earnest against the shore. We didn't even dare to go down to the beach with the waves slamming into it like a million sledgehammers. Mr. Ahlberg's poor boat bucked and strained against its ropes, the hull groaning with every impact; it was going to need some serious fiberglass repairs if it kept getting smashed into the dock much longer.

We cut across in front of the house and headed up the usual trail to where the invisible archery range stood.

"We should make some targets tomorrow," Rob said. "It's the horse's day off so I'm free to help."

"Really? That would be great." The sudden thought that I was going to be able to spend the entire summer with Rob made me glow with happiness. "My dad bought me a 3-D foam target we can start with, too, and I ordered my horse bow, so it should be here in a few weeks."

"How did it go with Red today?"

"Not great, actually, I accidentally hit him with the bow. I think it scared him."

"Oh, I'm sure he'll get over it. You just need to take your time with him and build his confidence. He'll come around."

"Yeah, I want him to be happy. I'm hoping Darius can come over one day and give me some tips, too."

Chapter Thirteen

I stayed down at the barn for a long time after Rob left. I tidied up the tack room, making sure all the bridles were hung properly, the saddle pads folded perfectly, and then organized my locker. I fed the horses lunch and then an early supper, swept the aisle, and raked the area outside the entrance into intricate patterns. But finally, my growling stomach told me that it was time to head back up to the house and face the music.

Still, I couldn't force myself to hurry. I dragged my feet up the long driveway and stopped to look at the fallen fencing that still needed repair, and I paused to visit with the sheep who crowded to the edge of their pasture as soon as they saw me, and cleaned my pockets for the last crumbs of horse treats.

Finally, I trudged up to the house.

"Astrid." Hilary's mom was standing on the porch looking concerned. "You must be famished. Come on inside and get some dinner. We're roughing it tonight and having pizza."

"Sounds good," I said shyly, not sure how she'd feel about me after I'd fought with Hilary. They'd asked me stay here this summer so I could keep Hilary company, after all. Maybe they wouldn't want me now if we were fighting.

Mrs. Ahlberg wrapped an arm around my shoulder and gave me a squeeze. "Hilary's set up on the couch in the living room. Why don't you take your pizza and eat in there? She's feeling pretty miserable."

"Um, okay," I said reluctantly, secretly glad that Hilary was miserable.

It wasn't delivered pizza in a box, of course; Mr. Ahlberg had been testing out his new brick pizza oven and had made five different types with hand pulled crusts and fresh toppings.

I'm sure my eyes lit up when I saw them all spread out across the table.

"Wow, he is such a good cook," I said appreciatively.

"He loves working with food. I just hope he still loves it next year once it's his full-time job." She winked and handed me a plate. "Load up, Astrid, there's plenty."

I filled my plate with one of each type and reluctantly headed to the living room where I could hear the TV playing softly.

Hilary was stretched out on one of the couches, her foot propped up on a stack of pillows and a box of Kleenex beside her. She looked completely miserable.

I sat down in the cushy easy chair closest to the TV, furthest away from Hilary, balancing my plate on my lap carefully.

Hilary was watching old dressage freestyle footage from the Summer Olympics in Brazil, and pretty soon, I was completely immersed in the world of powerful horses dancing to powerful music.

"I love Valegro," she sighed when it was over.

"Yeah, me, too," I said, forgetting for a second that I was mad at her.

"Astrid," she said after a long, painful silence. "I am so, so sorry. This has been making me sick for months. I can't stand it that you hate me. You're my best friend in the whole world."

I sighed and set my empty plate down on the floor then turned to look at her, taking in her swollen eyes and tear-stained, puffy face.

"I know you are," I said finally, "and I don't hate you, Hilary, not really. It's just...well, maybe I don't trust people that easily. You've always been perfect and so nice, and I just assumed that you weren't even capable of being mean."

"Oh my gosh, Astrid, I'm far from perfect. I do stupid stuff all the time."

"Well, I guess I've always looked up to you then; you've never hurt me before now, Hilary. You've never teased me about my weight or when I messed up with Folly; you've always been there for me. I guess that's why it hurts so much."

We fell into silence again, only broken by Hilary's sniffles. But I thought over what I'd said. Hilary had been there for me so many times when I'd messed up. Maybe it was my turn to stick by *her*. Even though she'd hurt me and acted stupidly, she was clearly miserable about it. Maybe it wouldn't be the worst thing in the world to give her a second chance. Just one.

"Your dad is an amazing cook," I said, picking up my plate. "I think there was dessert in the kitchen, too. Do you want me to bring you some?"

Hilary looked up at me tearfully. "Is there pie?"

"I'll go check," I said and retreated quickly back to the kitchen.

There *was* pie; lots of it. There was no sign of Hilary's parents, so I loaded our plates with huge slices of blueberry, and apple rhubarb, and headed back toward Hilary.

"Oh wow, thanks so much, Astrid." She pulled herself awkwardly into a sitting position, wincing as her leg dragged across the pillow.

"Does it hurt a lot?"

She nodded. "And the pain meds make me sick. The doctor said that a sprain is often worse than a break in a way because of how long it takes to heal. I can't believe I was so stupid as to land wrong. I was just fooling around, too; our director is so mad. He lectured me the whole ride to the hospital."

"That's awful. So, you're completely out of the play?"

She nodded and bit her lip. "I could probably help with scenery, but I doubt I'd be much use. I can't even *ride* until the swelling goes down."

"Oh, Hilary, I'm so sorry."

"Yeah, me, too. Astrid, can I tell you something?"

"I guess so," I said warily, wondering what else she was going to spring on me. I didn't think I could handle any more surprises.

"Okay, don't tell my parents, but I am completely overwhelmed with this farm thing. When our family bought this place, I agreed that the horse part was going to be my business, my contribution. I thought it would be fun; I thought it would be like spending all day at Claudia's like we used to do. But it's different when it's your own business."

"What do you mean? The place looks great. Or, at least it will once it's finished."

"Thanks, but I honestly don't know what I'm doing, and I feel like I'm letting Sadie and Pender down by taking such crappy care of their horses."

"You take good care of them," I protested, "the only thing they need is pasture and a ring, and then it will be perfect. I think you're doing a great job here, Hilary. Claudia would be so proud."

She looked up, eyes shining again with tears.

"Claudia and Liza and Rob made it look so easy. Rob is all on his own at his place and he seems to manage perfectly well. I have no idea how he does it. I feel like I'm drowning sometimes, and my parents are so busy already that I hate to bother them. It was supposed to be *my* project."

"Yeah, but Hilary, it's okay to need a bit of help. It's not like they're going to think you're a failure. They love you."

She chewed her lip, lost in thought, and then sighed. "I guess you're right."

"And, as for money, did you call those people about the horse board? They pretty much wanted to move in right away."

"No, I wasn't sure if they'd be the right fit for the farm. I didn't plan on having little kids here. And besides, I wanted to make sure there's a space for Ally to bring Severus, too. It was supposed to be exactly like it was at Claudia's."

We fell silent for a minute, both probably thinking about how what we'd had at Claudia's was never going to be duplicated again. It was she herself who made the place magic. Without her, it just wasn't the same.

"But you need money coming in, right? And you never know, maybe they'll just want to stay for the summer."

"You're probably right. I should just call them. I can't be so picky, I guess. I was hoping to put it off until Liza gets here; I wanted to ask her opinion."

We fell silent for a few more minutes, both lost in our own thoughts.

"I'll make the call about the pasture," Hilary said quietly. "You're right, the horses are going nuts without turnout and I certainly won't be able to exercise mine enough now that I'm hurt."

"Oh, that's great," I said, feeling a weight slip off my shoulders. I hadn't realized how much the pasture thing bothered me until then. "Rabbit's going to be so happy."

"Sorry I didn't do it sooner," Hilary said softly. "I just didn't want to make a mistake spending the money. I was just overwhelmed."

"It's okay, Hilary," I said, "you're doing a great job here. The farm's going to look great."

"Thanks, Astrid. Now that I'll have nothing else to do, I'm going to sit down with my parents and go over my business plan again. I need to make sure I'm on the right track. And then I need to get the indoor up and running before Pender and Sadie get back."

Chapter Fourteen

The next week practically flew by. Marion and my dad ran around packing the motor home and getting last minute supplies. I did my best to stay out of the way as much as possible and spent as much time at the farm as I could. My dad and I did manage to get a few more bike rides in and they weren't completely awful. I still didn't trust him not to change back to his old self on a moment's notice, but there were short periods of time when I maybe actually enjoyed his company. At least he was trying and it helped that we wouldn't have to spend the entire summer together.

Changes were happening at the farm, too. The morning after our conversation, Hilary woke up on her made-up couch-bed in the living room with a fiery look of determination in her eyes. After breakfast, she hobbled down the hall to the library, dragging her dad in there with her to have a meeting. After about an hour she was back to the living room, propped up on the couch with a stack of books on the floor beside her. She went over them one by one, taking notes in a spiral-bound notebook, her forehead wrinkled in concentration.

How to Run your Own Business for Profit; How to make Friends and Influence people; How to be a Dolphin in a Sea of Sharks. I flipped through the stack incredulously. They were all on business, networking, and making money.... This wasn't Hilary's usual style at all.

"Hilary, are you actually enjoying these?" I asked when I came in from feeding lunch to find her in the exact same spot on the couch.

"Shh," she said, not looking up. "I'm at a good part. I'm learning so much stuff, Astrid. I should have really read these before I started building."

I left her to it, and two days later she shut the last book with a bang and struggled to her feet.

"I know what I'm doing now," she announced, a glint of religious fervor in her eyes. "Now I have to get to work."

I didn't know what exactly was in those books, but the very next day a crew of workers in matching green trucks showed up towing trailers loaded with supplies. They swarmed over the property from bottom to top, ripping out the fencing that couldn't be saved, pounding in new fence posts to replace the ones that were rotten, and replacing all the damaged wood with new stuff. In no time at all, we had lower pastures, and then the upper one was torn down completely and made into two smaller fields with our riding path kept intact around the outside. We had enough pasture to house dozens of horses if we wanted to.

"Now all we have to do is paint," Hilary said proudly from the seat of the new, shiny green golf cart she'd somehow acquired since it was too far for her to hobble on crutches to the barn. "But we have all summer to do that."

As a present, her parents had replaced our battered old wooden picnic table at the barn with one of those fancy patio sets. So now we had a covered table and matching chairs and two wooden lounging chairs complete with side tables. Hilary had commandeered one of the lounge chairs, propping her sore foot up on a stack of pillows and keeping her clipboard in hand so she could cross off her list of projects.

Now that she had nothing else to do, she'd thrown herself into her farm project with the fierce energy that bordered on scary. She was so full of ideas that she had to write stuff down on her clipboard every other minute. Her bossiness took on a whole new level.

"Astrid, you'll have to take over my Ellie project; no, don't look at me like that. She's easy to ride and we need to get her sold fast so I have space for paying boarders. Rob, if you can take on one more horse, I'm going to pay you for some rides on Jerry. Don't bother arguing; I'm not expecting you to do that for free and you're the only one I trust to ride him until Liza gets here. I can't have him sitting around and losing his mind completely."

As soon as the fencing was done, she had me and Rob lead Rabbit and Riverdance out to the closest pasture to stretch their legs. Back at Claudia's, I wouldn't have been afraid to handle Rabbit; he was a bit silly, but he'd always been harmless. But ever since I'd gotten to the farm, he'd been so different; high-strung and unhappy all the time. I was relieved that it was Rob dealing with him on his first day out and not me.

It was a good decision. Rabbit spent the first part of his walk down the driveway on his hind legs, his eyes bulging with excitement and trumpeting neighs every two seconds like he was reliving his days at the racetrack.

I probably would have dropped his lead rope and ran, but Rob acted like nothing at all unusual was happening. He waited for the horse to drop to the ground and then he walked along casually, the lead slack in his hand. He spoke softly to the big horse under his breath and stroked his shoulder reassuringly whenever Rabbit stopped acting crazy for two seconds.

Whatever he was doing seemed to work because finally Rabbit stopped rearing and dropped to a steady, bright-eyed march, his tail arched and his nostrils flaring.

Riverdance didn't bat an eye at his crazy friend. He followed along beside me peacefully, only lifting his head with more interest when we reached the pasture gate. He pricked his ears as Rob led Rabbit inside but waited patiently beside me.

"Hang on, Astrid, I'm going to let this guy go. Just wait outside there."

He turned Rabbit around to face the gate, and then slipped the halter off and stepped back through the gate smoothly.

Rabbit spun around, his hind feet plowing deep into the soft soil as he launched himself into the air like a rocket, grunting and squealing as he bucked his way across the pasture in a series of mighty leaps.

"Will he hurt himself?" I asked, biting my lip.

"I hope not," Rob said, "we'll just stay here with Riverdance until he calms down, they can't think straight when they're like that."

We watched as Rabbit blazed through the young spring grass, his hooves flinging up great clods of dirt behind him as he ran. I could truly imagine what he must have looked like when he was a real racehorse on the track. I was glad Rob had strapped the leather boots on Rabbit's legs before he went out, though. At least it gave him a tiny bit of protection from his own flailing legs.

We lost sight of him as he disappeared down the hill to the lower, marshy, part of the field only to reappear a few seconds later, charging up the far fence-line, his legs and chest spattered with mud.

He didn't stop when he reached us; it took four laps of the entire pasture before he slowed from a terrifying gallop to a slightly less terrifying canter. And it took another two laps before he broke into a trot and then dropped his nose down to the ground to check out what little grass he hadn't destroyed with his hooves of fury. His sides heaved, and his fur was damp with sweat, but he looked happy for the first time since I'd arrived here.

"Okay," Rob said, "bring Riverdance in."

Riverdance stood politely while I slipped off his halter, and then turned and trotted over to his buddy, nickering under his breath. Rabbit arched his neck while they sniffed noses, both of them squealing like they were meeting for the first time, and then they wheeled around and took off together.

It didn't last long this time, though. Rabbit had tired himself out already and Riverdance just wanted to eat, so pretty soon they dropped their heads again to graze.

Once we were sure they'd be okay, we went back for Red and Ellie. We'd decided that putting one high-energy horse outside at a time was the best idea for the first few days. So Jerry would have to hang out with Artimax and Ferdi in the barn while his friends went out to play. He'd get his turn tomorrow.

Red and Ellie were easy to handle, of course. We put them out in the pasture across from the other horses and watched as they had their own short gallop.

Finally, everyone was settled, and I took a deep breath in relief.

"I'm glad that's over; it's so stressful to put them out the first time."

"It can be," Rob said, slinging an arm casually over my shoulder, "but they're not stupid. Nine times out of ten they won't hurt themselves."

"Hmm," I said, a bit overwhelmed by him being so close to me. It felt nice but also weird and I didn't know how to react. Was I supposed to snuggle up to him or put my arm over *his* shoulder? I had no idea what couples were supposed to do so, as usual, I froze and did nothing. After a couple of strides Rob dropped his arm and poked me in the side instead, making me laugh.

"Do you want to go to a movie tonight?" he said, turning to walk backward so he could face me.

"Yes," I said honestly, "but I can't."

"Oh." His face fell. "Why not?"

"I have to wait until my parents go away. No, wait," I said, seeing his expression darken. "It's not what you think, Rob. I just…I don't want to give them an excuse to pay attention to me. You know? I need them to go away and not think about me at all."

"What?" he said, his brown eyes widening. "What are you talking about?"

I could see why he'd be confused. His dad did everything for him; you could always see how proud he was of Rob and how much he loved him; it practically shone out of his eyes every time he looked at his son. I'd bet they had long, philosophical conversations every night over dinner and talked about life and their feelings and stuff. How did I explain to him what it was like to live at my house?

"Rob," I said haltingly, "I'm not free like you are."

"Sure you are," he interrupted, "we live in a democracy…"

"Well, that doesn't apply to my life right now," I said, "at least, not all the time. Look, you'll have to trust me on this; just wait a few more days until they're gone and then we can go to all the movies you like."

He stared at me quietly, his eyes crinkling with worry. "Is it really that bad at home? Marion seems nice."

"She is," I said, shrugging, "and my dad's getting a bit better. He's in therapy now so at least he's trying. But it's still not safe."

"Not *safe*? Astrid, do they…does your dad *hit* you?"

"No," I said quickly, my face flushing with embarrassment. I could not believe I was having this conversation. I hated telling anyone about my home life, let alone someone who was becoming so important to me. I didn't want him feeling sorry for me or anything.

"There's, um, just some yelling I guess—" I stopped, not sure how to explain the tension in my house, the sharp comments, constantly having my every move monitored: the awful feeling of suffocating under that intense scrutiny. Was there even a word for all that?

Rob stared at me solemnly and then gave a sigh. "Why did you come home?" he asked finally. "You were so happy at the ranch."

"It seemed like a good idea at the time." I laughed wryly. "I don't know; I was homesick and I missed archery lessons with Earl. I spent my whole life dreaming of going to the Olympics; it's the only thing that kept me going sometimes. It felt like that just got sidetracked somehow and I wanted it back. And I missed you guys, the people up there were nice, but it wasn't the same."

We walked along in silence for a while and then Rob reached out and took my hand in his farm-callused one, holding it gently.

"Okay, movie date next week, whether you like it or not."

"Sure." I laughed. "That sounds great. As soon as they leave on their trip."

Chapter Fifteen

"You'll be fine, Astrid," Hilary said, huffing impatiently. "She's just another horse."

"But I'll wreck her," I said stubbornly, standing rooted beside the mounting block beside Ellie. I wished Rob was there; I always felt calmer and braver when he was around, but he was off schooling cross-country somewhere and Hilary had insisted that Ellie needed to be ridden right that second.

"Don't be silly. How could you possibly wreck her? You're just going to walk her up and down the driveway and get a feel for her. Then, if you're comfortable, you can trot her around in the pasture."

I wasn't comfortable; I was scared. I'd just gotten used to riding Artimax and Riverdance, who were solid, dependable horses like Red. I didn't think that it should be *me* riding a young, inexperienced horse. I didn't have the skills for this.

"Astrid, come on," Hilary said, sounding more patient. "Just walk her around one time and if it's awful then you can jump off. I promise she's really fun."

I looked over at Ellie who was standing there patiently,

watching our argument with interest.

"I'm going to ruin her," I said again, half-heartedly, but I stepped reluctantly up on the mounting block and then, before I could change my mind, climbed onto her back.

I sat there just patting her until the butterflies in my stomach stopped fluttering so hard. Then I gathered my reins gently and asked her to walk. She strode out confidently without hesitation, her stride very similar to Red's. Which made sense because they *were* related somehow.

"Good girl, Ellie," I whispered, walking her straight up to the pasture. I wasn't confident enough to do the entire looping trail ride, but I rode her around the outskirts of the field, gaining more trust in her by the second.

"Should we trot?" I asked her tentatively. She flicked an ear back, not sure if I was really asking her to pick up speed, and I added seat and a little leg to help her spring forward into a nice, active trot.

It only took a minute to adjust to her gait; it was a little faster and more upright than Red's, but soon, I was smiling from ear to ear. She was comfortable, and she felt completely safe underneath me.

I brought her down to a walk, circled the pasture one more time, and then headed back down the driveway, content to end our ride on a good note. Tomorrow I would take her on a real trail ride with Rob.

"See, I told you that you'd love her," Hilary said as soon as we got back, judging by the smile on my face that everything had gone well. "The more she gets ridden, the sooner we can get her sold."

"Oh." I frowned, not liking the note of impatience in her voice. I didn't want to rush Ellie's training just because Hilary needed to rent out her stall. Aunt Lillian was counting on us to find the mare a good home.

"We'll make sure that Liza gives you lots of lessons on her whenever she finally decides to visit us. For now, maybe just trail ride her until the ring's ready. Rob probably knows the most about conditioning."

"Yeah, that was my plan," I said. "I don't want to push her too hard."

"Oh, she'll be fine," Hilary said breezily. "I bet we can find a buyer for her by the end of summer. It would really help if you or Rob could take her to a few shows, get her out in public so people can see how pretty she is."

"Um, maybe," I said doubtfully, certain it wasn't going to happen in a million years but not wanting to argue. I'd let Liza handle Hilary when she came to visit; Hilary was bound to listen to her.

***

The next day Rob watched carefully as I walked, trotted, and cantered Ellie beside him and Artimax, and when we reached the path leading to the ocean, he stopped and laid a hand on my arm.

"You're a natural with her, Astrid," he said, "just keep doing what you're doing and you'll be fine."

"I don't think I can mess up too badly if we're just trail riding," I said, laughing, "Hilary has a crazy idea that I should show her, though."

"Stop being so hard on yourself." He frowned. "Going to a couple of schooling shows at the end of the summer is a good idea. We should find something that all the young horses can go to. And you can take Red, too. You'd ace it."

"We'll see what Liza says." I was confident that Liza would back me up and let us all stay home in our comfort zone forever.

***

As the days ticked along, I was more and more sure that Darius would never come and give me my lesson. I hadn't gone out and tried again on my own, but sometimes when I brushed Red I brought the bow into his stall so he could sniff it and not be afraid. He didn't *seem* scared of it, but I hoped that he would learn to associate it with food and brushing; all the things he liked.

Finally, with just two days before their departure Marion drove up one sunny afternoon and Darius was with her. Rob had just unloaded the two horses he'd brought that day and was hanging around waiting for me while I finished tidying the barn.

"Oh, look, Rob, there he is," I whispered excitedly, setting down the corn-broom I'd been using to sweep the aisle.

"I've brought a visitor," Marion called. "I hope you don't mind."

"No, not at all," I said, "we were just getting ready to ride."

Darius walked along beside Marion without smiling, but when I said the word 'ride' his eyes lit up. Then they dimmed again. I glanced at Rob, wondering if he'd noticed.

"Would you two want to come with us?" Rob asked, glancing back at me briefly. "I brought the calm horses today so you can have your pick."

"Well, *I* certainly can't." Marion laughed. "I have errands to do in town, but Darius might like to spend a few hours here."

"That's not necessary, thank you," Darius said quietly, but the yearning look in his eyes made it obvious he wanted to stay.

"Marion, come brush Ellie while we get ready," I said, knowing that she liked spending time with the little mare.

"Well, I did bring my gloves, just in case," Marion said. She'd been much less tense since she'd made the decision to go on the road trip.

While Rob and Darius chatted in front of Maverick's stall, I got Ellie's halter and gave Marion the box of brushes. I left her dreamily currying Ellie's golden coat in perfect circles, a pleased smile on her face.

"Astrid, you should grab your bow," Rob said as soon as I came out. "Darius said he'll give you some tips. We can just go on a quiet trail ride ahead of time."

I brushed Red and tacked him up quickly and then grabbed my belt quiver, my bow with the new shoulder sling I'd bought, and a handful of arrows from the tack room.

"This bow is too long," Darius said as soon as he saw me, taking the bow out of my hand and giving it a once over. "And it has a shelf." He ran his fingers over the narrow ledge where my arrows usually rested. "You can't shoot off a shelf. You need a bow without one so you can shoot from both sides."

"I know," I said patiently, "but it's all I have right now. I ordered a horse bow online but it will take a while to get here."

"Hmm," he handed my bow back to me abruptly as if it offended him. "Mounted archery is not like traditional archery. You don't have hours to focus on your target and set up a perfect shot. You shoot instinctively, without thinking. This is not something that can be taught."

Obviously it can be taught, I thought, *or they wouldn't have competitions all over the world; those people didn't pull their skills out of thin air. It can't be this complicated.*

"I have to start somewhere," I said out loud. "I just want to try. Can't you help me?"

He looked like he would still say no and then his shoulders slumped and he nodded. "Fine. Fine. Just this once."

Well, it was better than nothing.

He raised an eyebrow when Rob and I used the mounting block but wordlessly followed our lead; he probably thought it was some bizarre Canadian custom.

I didn't know if Maverick was exactly a treat to ride for Darius. He was probably used to horses that looked more…well, *pleased* to be trail riding, but he didn't seem to mind. Or, at least, he was too polite to say anything.

The afternoon was sunny, but the wind had picked up on the ocean and the breeze buffeted gently around us, smelling salty and fresh. The horses were content to just walk, Artimax leading and me and Red at the back of the line, Maverick sandwiched in the middle just in case Darius didn't know as much about riding as he let on.

He sat rigidly in the saddle, his back stiff and his face void of all expression. But he let Maverick have his head, which suited the horse just fine. When we dipped down into the rainforest section, though, he looked around in wonder as if he'd woken up from a deep sleep.

"What is this place?" he whispered, looking at the big trees in astonishment.

"They're old-growth trees, mostly fir," I explained, "they're hundreds of years old."

"It smells...different," he said, frowning in concentration. "and it's colder."

"I know, it's like these woods are more alive, isn't it? I'm not sure why that is."

It must be so different than the desert he grew up in, I thought, remembering the hot, dusty landscape in the videos. I didn't dare say anything, though; I wasn't going to ask a single thing about his past again.

"We have beautiful woods where I grew up in Syria," he said softly, "but I suppose those trees were younger; not like this."

A million questions sat poised on the edge of my tongue, but I shut my mouth firmly.

"My cousins..." he said and then fell silent again, reaching down to stroke Maverick's neck thoughtfully. "They were incredible with the horses; those animals were like children to them, they could train them to do anything."

He's speaking about them all in the past, I thought with a sinking heart. *Like they don't exist anymore.*

There was a long silence and finally, I couldn't stand it anymore.

"Is the whole ranch gone?" I asked helplessly. "Even the horses?"

Darius sighed and shrugged wearily. "Impossible to tell; when the war came, it was bad, very bad. I was away at boarding school when it began, and my parents told me not to come home. And then they were just gone.

"So little information gets out of the country...and you never know if what you're told is the truth. But I heard things. I know the first wave of bombs killed many of the horses, wiping out parts of a breeding program that began long before my great, great, great grandfather's time.

"My uncle was alive and still at the ranch last I heard, and my youngest cousin lost both his legs, but he was alive. The others, I don't know. Some stayed to help my uncle. Maybe some escaped, some are dead or were forced to fight. We probably won't know for sure until the war is over. If it's ever over."

"Couldn't they have escaped?" I asked, choking on sorrow. "Couldn't they have just taken the horses across the border to a safer country?"

He sighed and shrugged helplessly. "Probably not. There are aide teams that sometimes sneak in to bring food and medicine to both the humans and horses. So maybe there's hope."

He didn't sound very hopeful, though; he sounded like he was trying to cheer me up.

I felt sick and I wondered about all the things that he *hadn't* said. He was just a few years older than us and now an orphan. He didn't even know if any of his friends or family had survived.

I reached down to stroke Red's neck, barely able to imagine living in a place where everyone you loved could be ripped away instantly by forces outside your control. You could just be living your life going to school and shopping and riding your horses and, *boom*, it was all destroyed.

We're so lucky to live here, Red, I thought, *we're alive and we have enough food, and nobody is shooting at us.* It made my own problems seem pretty insignificant.

Rob had been silently listening all this time, riding in front of us, his head slightly tilted to catch our conversation. Now he gently reined Artimax in until he sat side by side with Darius.

"I'm sorry you had to go through that, man," he said quietly, looking Darius in the eyes. "I hope things get better from here on in."

Darius's eyes filled with tears, and then he shook his head and clapped Rob on the shoulder.

"Thanks. I know how lucky I am to have escaped and to have so many people helping me. One of my coaches at school worked night and day until he found a country that would take me. My mother's brother lives here and offered to sponsor me right away, but it took years to get it approved. Despite all the horror I've seen, there were always people helping, too. That's the thing I try to remember."

"You can ride with us any time," Rob said. "We should canter this section. The horses love it."

Now that he'd loosened up, Darius sat Maverick easily. He had a different style of riding; he wasn't so elegant in the saddle as Rob, but he sat his horse lightly and didn't interfere with his mouth. We cantered halfway to the ocean and then stopped to take in the view.

"Fantastic," Darius said, "I would never get tired of this view."

The wind buffeted around us, pulling at the horses' manes and tails, and whipping my hair out from under my helmet. It was exhilarating, and we cantered another stretch, staying above the beach until we reached the path to the woods.

"This is the place we'll be able to practice," I said, pointing out the berm where my three foam targets sat.

"This is a good place," Darius said approvingly. "This way you won't shoot anyone."

"Why does everyone keep saying that?" I said, laughing.

We stopped, and Darius slid down and walked the space on foot, measuring distances and muttering something under his breath.

"Okay," he said finally, "jump down and I'll show you how to begin."

I hopped off Red and let him drop his head to graze at the tender blades of grass lining the trail.

"Hand me your bow and watch closely."

I pulled my bow off over my shoulder and unclipped my quiver, handing them both over to him.

He took them gently and held them out to Maverick who looked at them with the barest of interest.

"This bow is too long," Darius muttered critically, as if he hadn't already told me that. "It's the wrong shape completely. But I suppose we'll work with what we have. So, first of all, the foundation work starts on the ground. Your horse must be a hundred percent confident. The sound of the arrow leaving the bow and the sound of it hitting your target is not natural to him, and he must be taught to understand it. It would be dangerous if he even so much as flinched underneath you, you see."

"Okay," I said, when he stared pointedly at me, clearly expecting a response.

"Watch," he said, and pulled an arrow out of the quiver, rolling it in his fingers a few times before he lifted the bow in one quick motion, shooting so fast I barely saw him move. At least, I saw with some satisfaction, the arrow landed well outside of the bullseye.

Maverick, who'd been barely paying attention up until that point, snorted loudly and rocked backward, ears flicked forward at the target and eyes wide with surprise. He snorted again and stamped a front hoof, peering into the woods as if he expected a cougar to appear.

"See, he can't know that it's my arrow making that noise in the woods, his first instinct is that it's a predator creeping up on him, and that he must prepare to run. That's not an unusual reaction, Astrid, and you should be prepared for it. If you do your groundwork, then your horse will begin to understand."

"Oh," I said in surprise. I hadn't thought of the horses reacting like that. I didn't think they'd care at all.

Darius spoke to Maverick quietly and stroked his neck until the horse looked less alarmed. Then he shot the rest of the arrows one by one.

Maverick flinched every time an arrow hit the target, but he didn't pull back again.

"So, here is your homework. Every day you will ride out here, dismount, make sure your horse is standing motionless *behind* your shoulder so he is well out of the way. He must stand calmly, no pulling, no fidgeting, no trying to graze"—he narrowed his eyes at Red—"he must be like a statue. Understand?"

He waited until I nodded before going on. "Shoot your arrows carefully one at a time and pay close attention to his reactions. If you can do this daily for two weeks then you will be ready for stage two."

"What's stage two?" I asked.

"Never mind about that," he said sternly, "focus on stage one and I'll help you when it's time to move on."

"But you won't be here," I said, "you'll be on tour."

"I have to fly back for my uncle's wedding. I'll make sure I stop in and see how you're progressing. Promise me you'll stick to the plan, and I'll make sure that you're the best horseback archer on the island."

"Um, I think I'll be the *only* horse archer on the Island." I laughed. "But, I get your point. I want the horses to be confident. We won't rush them."

"Good, okay. I'd better get back then. I still have to pack."

I was mostly lost in my own thoughts on the way back, thinking about my new training program for Red and maybe Ellie. I didn't feel comfortable training a horse in the ring, but Ellie already loved the trails and she was smart; I was sure she'd love archery once she got used to it.

Chapter Sixteen

Finally, the day came when my dad and Marion, with Caprice sitting proudly with her paws on the front dash, actually pulled their giant motorhome from in front of our condo and went off on their adventure, leaving me deliciously, gloriously on my own for two whole months. As soon as they were gone, I did an ecstatic dance of happiness right there on the street, not caring who saw me.

And with that milestone crossed, two other good things happened almost at once.

The first was that, the next morning before I'd even had time to feed the horses, a swarm of workers descended on the barn and began to work on the indoor at Mach speed. The noise of hammers, saws, drills, and shouting echoed through the early spring air.

The horses bugled and snorted and charged in and out of their stalls in excitement.

I threw them all hay as fast as I could, hoping it would calm them down, and then carefully rolled back the big door at the arena-end of the aisle a few inches so I could see what was happening.

"Good morning!" someone called from high up in the rafters and I waved back shyly, blushing at being caught spying.

They had worked fast; part of the roof was already on and the back wall was up, just the sides needed to be finished. Now that it was partially transformed I could see how big it really was; Hilary had been modest when she said that it was just a small ring. It looked huge to me.

On the far side, there was what looked like a small building being added to the outside wall. Was it more hay storage or an equipment shed? There was nobody near enough to ask so I slid the door back shut and turned back to the horses.

"Okay, guys, eat your breakfast and I'll put you all out on pasture as soon as I can so you don't have to listen to that all day."

I glanced over at Rabbit and bit my lip. It wasn't Rob's day to be there today, so I was on my own to handle all the horses. I didn't have much faith that the silly horse would walk calmly past dozens of people wielding power tools. I would have to come up with a plan to keep him calm.

Red had settled down as soon as his hay arrived but even he, the calmest horse there, kept swiveling around and dragging mouthfuls to the doorway of his stall so he could watch the action over the fence.

There was no point cleaning their stalls while they were eating, someone was bound to run me over in their excitement. So instead I tidied the tack room, cleaned my saddle and bridle, and swept the aisle until it practically sparkled.

Finally, I couldn't put it off any longer.

"All right, you guys. Now how are we going to do this?"

I looked up and down the aisle thoughtfully. Back at the ranch there were so many horses that they were often led two, or sometimes even three, at a time out to pasture. If I could just pair the excitable horses up with a calm one then maybe I could get them all out in one piece.

"Okay, Red, let's see if we can make this work."

I led him out of his stall and carefully tied him to one of the cross-ties at the entrance of the barn, patting him and telling him firmly to stay and not go anywhere before I headed back to Rabbit.

I might as well get the worst one over with first, I thought grimly, looking up at Rabbit's worried, rolling eyes and flared nostrils. And this way, if he got away from me he would probably just run back to the barn to be with his friends. Probably.

I took a deep breath, gathered his halter and his boots in one hand, and slid the door open slowly.

"No, get back," I said firmly as he barged toward the door, pressing his big chest against the narrow opening. I pushed hard on the base of his neck, and to my surprise, he reluctantly stepped backward out of my space. I shut the door carefully behind me and approached him with the halter.

He snorted and backed away, looking at me skeptically, his big ears swiveling in all directions.

Talk to him, I told myself firmly, *he's not being awful on purpose; he's actually scared. He's probably more scared than you are.*

"It's okay, Rabbit," I crooned, reaching my fingers out to rest them gently against his shoulder. His skin quivered at the touch, but he didn't move. I ran my hand over his velvety, soft skin and was surprised when he sighed and leaned ever so slightly into my touch. I moved my hand up his neck and gently scratched the place behind his ear, the place where Red liked to be scratched best.

He's so tense, I thought, *his muscles are like rocks. It must be exhausting to be so keyed up all the time.*

I pressed the upper part of his neck carefully. *I think this is the splenius muscle*, I thought, trying to remember the points on my muscle chart. I kneaded the spot just below his mane, working gently at the knotted muscles.

Rabbit sighed heavily and dropped his head, leaning into my hand, his mouth opening in a huge yawn.

"It's okay, buddy," I said, working my way down to his withers and then along his shoulder. I'd always been interested in horse massage, ever since Claudia had suggested that I should learn about it. Muscles were like interesting interlocking puzzles to be unraveled.

I'll have to get out my books again. I've forgotten almost everything I learned.

After a couple minutes, Rabbit looked much less tense and I felt comfortable enough to put on his halter and boots, and lead him out to where Red was still patiently waiting.

It wasn't the easiest thing to lead two horses, but it went better than I expected. Rabbit danced and nipped at Red and snorted at nothing every few steps, but we made it to the pasture without anyone escaping or me being trampled.

I let Rabbit go and do his usual five laps of full out galloping around the pasture before I let Red in with him and was relieved to see them finally just calmly eating grass together.

After that, things went smoothly; Riverdance and Ellie were

saints, of course. I'd been worried about Jerry, but he behaved pretty well, only stopping to stare at the workers climbing all over the indoor with large, anxious eyes. He stood rooted to the ground like a statue for about five minutes before I could convince him to keep moving. But when he did move, he walked obediently beside me, taking big careful steps as if the gravel might have changed to lava and looking over his shoulder the whole time as if the indoor might creep up closer and pounce on him if he didn't keep an eye on it.

With my biggest worry of the day safely behind me, I was free to clean the paddocks and stalls at my leisure, and I took my time, raking each paddock spotlessly clean and making sure the beds were deep, fluffy, and even.

I stopped in the middle of Red's paddock to lean on the fence and watch the army of workers put the finishing touches on our building. It was amazing that in such a short time a beautiful arena could be created out of that ugly wooden skeleton.

My gaze drifted to the shed-like structure that had been tacked on to the outside of the building. It looked less like an equipment shed and more like...stalls.

Oh, Hilary, so this is what you've been up to, I thought, laughing under my breath. I'd known she had a new plan of some sort brewing. For someone who didn't want to focus her whole life on horses, she sure seemed to be attracting more of them to the property.

One, two, three, four, five... I counted the unfinished stalls and groaned under my breath. Five more horses to feed and clean up after, plus the empty stalls still in our barn that were sure to be filled soon. I sure hoped she was planning on hiring someone to help with the chores. What would happen when school started back up again, and I wasn't living here anymore, and she'd be on her own? Knowing Hilary, though, she probably had some grand vision playing out in her head. And I knew firsthand that she, usually, got what she wanted.

The day was warm and sweet, and the horses were so happy out in the pasture that I didn't have the heart to bring Red in to ride him. I would ride him that night once the workers went home. Which left me with the whole day to myself with nobody around and nothing planned; something I'd very rarely experienced in my entire life.

Read a book? Practice archery? Go for a hike?

I settled on reading. I went back up to the house to root through my stack of horse books and settled on two on horse massage and anatomy, and a couple on training the young horse. Even though I was only trail riding Ellie right now, there would soon come a time where I would have to take her to the next level in her education; it would help if I knew what I was doing.

I couldn't wait until Liza got here; Rob's advice was always good, but Liza would have all the answers to the many questions churning around in my brain.

Just one more week, I told myself. Until then, I'd just be content to trail ride and build up their fitness.

Chapter Seventeen

With the new arena complete, I wasn't surprised when Hilary announced that the Andersons were coming to board with us.

I had mixed feelings. The mom was nice, and I knew Hilary needed the money, and I always liked meeting new horses, but the kids seemed like a bit of a handful. Callie was loud and annoying, and her sister seemed pretty bitter and high maintenance. I wasn't sure what it would be like to have them around full-time.

It wasn't more than a few days that a big, fancy horse trailer pulled up the driveway with a large, amiable warmblood and a fat, chestnut pony with high white socks in tow.

The horses barely looked around when they stepped off the trailer. I guessed they'd been showing their whole lives, so they probably thought it was just one more event. I wondered if they had friends at home that they'd miss. Did they even get to say goodbye?

"Don't be silly," Hilary said when I mentioned it to her, "horses don't think like that."

But secretly I wondered. It seemed to me that the bonds and

friendships they formed could be pretty strong; look at Folly and Figaro, for example. She wasn't even his real mom, but you could tell how much she loved him just by watching her. She followed him around and hovered over him anxiously to make sure he didn't get hurt, just like Callie's mom did to her. Or Doc and Fox; they had spent all sorts of time hanging out, and you could tell that they were best friends.

Either way, the new horses settled in without a fuss. The pony, Mister Sox, was probably the cutest thing I'd ever seen. He had a thick mane that stood straight up like a ridge along his neck and a puffy forelock that covered both eyes. When he wanted to see something, he'd toss his head to the side so that his forelock lifted in the air like a cloud of cotton candy and landed somewhere behind his ears like a furry hat.

Callie told me proudly that he was a Section C Welsh Cob, and when I looked confused, Annie launched into the complete history of Welsh ponies and Cobs. Most of it was over my head, but the upshot was that being a section C meant that Sox was stockier and more solid than other, finer ponies. He was super safe, though, and was broad enough that tiny Callie would be able to keep him a long time as she grew.

Annie's own horse was a sweet, wise-looking bay Hanoverian named Norman with a thick white blaze and wide, kind eyes. She said she'd done hunters on him for the last few years, but that he loved trail rides, too. I fell in love with him right away. He had impeccable manners and didn't look like he'd be any trouble at all.

While her mom and sister fussed over the horses and got them settled, Nori stood in the middle of the barn doorway, her arms crossed over her chest and a sour expression on her face. She said a few sullen words to her mother, but other than that, she just generally stood in the way and avoided being helpful.

She was clearly *not* coming with a horse. Apparently, Hilary had told me, her mother had tried to tempt her with all sorts of fancy prospects, but Nori was having none of it. She'd made up her mind to stay horseless and that was final.

"That works best for me, too, though," Hilary said. "I want to save a spot for Ally's horse Severus. I want it to be like it was before at Claudia's."

I leaned over and squeezed her hand quickly in sympathy, but secretly, I knew that no matter how nice or popular this barn became it would never be the same as at Claudia's. *She* was what had made the place extra special. This farm would have to find its own way to be special.

With the pastures finished and the arena built, Hilary started immediately on the next stage of her plan. A big area was cleared out beyond the indoor and a hole dug, dump trucks full of sand and gravel were brought in, and it took them three days to fill in the area and smooth it out. Then a fence was built around it, and when it was done, it was a huge outside sand ring that Hilary said was big enough to set up jumps.

"But aren't we a dressage barn?" I asked tentatively.

"Well, yes. I mean, we don't *have* to put jumps up...but having a big ring like this will attract all sorts of lucrative clients. I need to fill all the stalls next to the arena, too, in order to pay for all this. Don't worry, this place will be amazing when it's finished."

I had no doubt that it would look amazing. It already did.

But who would be taking care of all these horses?

Once the construction crew was finally gone, and everything was quiet again, I got up early one morning eager to be the first one to try out the rings.

I let Red eat most of his breakfast, and then slipped his halter on and led him down to the end of the aisle, into the attached indoor arena. I didn't turn the lights on, there was enough filtering through the skylights to see by, and it was peaceful in there in the semi-dark. Like being in a familiar, homey cave.

Red pricked his ears and snorted quietly when I led him in and rolled the big door shut behind us. We walked together through the thick footing, some type of dark imported mixture of sand or peat. Whatever it was it was springy under my feet and I couldn't wait to ride in it.

"Do you remember when we used to do this all the time, Red?" I said, kissing him on the neck and then slipping off his halter. "Do you want to play?"

Red dropped his nose to the footing, making that weird drawn out *whooshing* sound through his nose that meant he was about to play. I stepped back to give him space, and that was the only signal he needed to paw the ground, turning around in a tight circle like a dog after a flea, his tail swishing back and forth rapidly. Then his knees buckled and he collapsed heavily to the ground and flipped on his back with all four hooves waving in the air, groaning in pleasure as he scratched his back and neck in the footing.

"Oh, Red." I laughed. "You're filthy."

But he wasn't done, he gave a good lurch and heaved himself over to his other side to repeat the process, and then he leapt to his feet and gave a mighty buck before tearing off around the arena.

I let him gallop and buck for a couple minutes and then, when he looked like he was ready, I stepped a bit closer to him, focusing on his hind end, tightening my core to keep him moving forward.

He flicked an ear toward me to show me he was listening, and we fell into that familiar dance routine of transitions and yielding that we'd developed back at the ranch. It was so nice to be communicating like this again. I loved our trail rides, but there was something so special about playing with him at liberty. Even though Justin had told me it was all about reading subtle body language, it always felt to me like we were communicating telepathically somehow. That was probably a pretty unscientific way to think about it, but I couldn't shake the thought.

When we were done playing, I slipped his halter back on and led him to the mounting block Hilary had had delivered last night along with a truck load of other supplies.

I futilely brushed at the dirt on his back and then swung up on him, letting my legs hang loose and leaving him to wander around the ring at his own pace. It felt so good to being hanging out with him on our own like this.

I should make time to do this at least once a week, I thought, *even when things get busy. This is just for me and Red.*

***

It wasn't until Rob came over a few days later that I thought to try Red with his tack on in the ring and that's when his weird quirk came rushing back for the very first time since we'd been home. I'd mostly forgotten about it, but as soon as I swung up into the saddle, I could feel the difference. Instead of a lively, interested horse, he seemed half-asleep, ears drooping to the side, and his nose sinking slowly downward until it hovered a few inches off the ground.

"Oh boy." Rob laughed and shook his head. "Well, you do know it's not his saddle, since he's perfectly happy in it out on the trail and he's completely sound."

"Yeah, he was fine the other day when I rode him bareback in here," I said, feeling miserable. I didn't want to torture the guy if he truly hated ring work, but what was it about the situation that made him seem so depressed?

"I think we just have to show him that it's fun again," Rob said thoughtfully. "Did you ever do gymkhanas when you were a kid?"

"Jim-what?" I asked, looking at him blankly.

"Gymkhanas, like mounted games in pony club. Oh, right, I always forget that you didn't ride as a kid. It's just games that are supposed to help with your control and coordination when you're a young rider. Really, they're just about going fast and winning prizes, but they were fun, and it's not like we're little kids who are going to yank on the ponies' mouths. We should set up something like that; it would be a good spook-proofing exercise for the young horses, too."

"O-kay," I said slowly, still not sure what he was talking about or how it would help Red.

"Come on, let's just ride on the trails today, since he looks so unhappy. Tonight, I'll send you a list of supplies and we can play with them tomorrow. It will be fun."

"Sure," I said, not sure what I'd just agreed to, but happy to be out of the ring.

Red's ears perked again as soon as we were back out in the sunlight, and he heaved a huge sigh and then shook himself like a dog. Whatever it was that was bothering him about the situation was real; I just had to find a way to help him through it.

That night, Rob sent me a text that read: *three dozen eggs, six spoons, and a sense of humour. I'll bring the rope.*

It wasn't hard to find the eggs; the Ahlbergs had bought dozens of chickens in anticipation of the restaurant opening, and they were laying so many eggs a day we could hardly keep up with them; most of them went to the food bank.

I fed and took my time cleaning the paddocks and sweeping. Taking care of two more horses wasn't too much extra work, but it did take more time. I wasn't sure how I was going to keep doing this once summer was over and I was back in school. Hopefully Hilary was healed by then and could do some of the chores herself.

Rob's trailer pulled in; he had Artimax and Maverick in tow, and to my surprise, Annie's dark car was right behind him. Rarely had I seen them out at the barn so early; usually Annie and Callie rode in the afternoons.

"Hello!" Annie called excitedly, marching toward us with her kids in tow. She was wearing a sleeveless polo shirt and breeches, and I stared at the rippling muscles in her arms in astonishment. I didn't even know that women could get muscle like that.

She caught me staring and sent me her usual winning smile. "Weightlifting," she said by way of explanation. "I was in heavy training for this competition I just finished so I'm pretty ripped right now."

"Mama won," Callie said proudly. "She got a trophy and everything. She's the best."

"Congratulations," I said, trying, and failing, to picture what a weightlifting competition might look like.

"Oh, this was just a small one," Annie said, still looking pleased at the compliments. "Astrid, you should look into it, I bet you'd have quite a talent for it. I could show you some exercises to get started."

"Um, thanks," I said, blushing, not sure how to take it. Did she say that because she thought I was more stocky and thick then someone like Hilary was?

Of course she's not saying that, I chastised myself, *Annie's beautiful; she's thin, but she's powerful, too, and full of energy; she looks like an athlete. I would kill to look like her.*

"Thanks," I said again, afraid I'd seemed rude. "Maybe I will."

"So, Rob said you might need us to help you?" Annie said hopefully, looking for an invitation.

"Oh, he's helping me with this weird quirk that Red has. I'm not sure what he has in mind, though."

"Ooh." Annie's eyes flickered with interest. "A project. How fun."

"What's his quirk?" Nori had come up behind us, a bag of pastries clutched in hand and an iced drink in the other. She was watching me with narrowed eyes.

"Oh, well, he doesn't like to go forward in the ring when he's wearing his saddle. But he's fine on the trails with a saddle or when I ride him bareback. We're going to try—"

"Don't you ride with a crop?" Nori said scathingly. "Just give him a good whack with that. He'll shape up quick."

Be patient, I told myself, *she's just a kid…an annoying, know-it-all kid.*

"Actually, they tried that before at the ranch. It didn't help. Liza and Justin think it's in his head now. Rob has some plan to get him to associate saddles in the ring with fun."

"Fun?" Nori stared at me blankly, looking genuinely confused at the concept. "Like, for the horse?"

"Um, yeah?" I said. "It's a fifty-fifty partnership. Both partners should be having fun, right?"

Now all three of them, even little Callie were staring at me like I was crazy.

"Well," Annie said finally. "I've never thought of it like that but, yes, I suppose it should be fun for the horse, too."

They trailed off to the barn, leaving me staring after them in amazement. All the horses I'd known in my short riding career had been hard-working but, with the exception of Folly and maybe Maverick, they'd always seemed to be having fun during their riding sessions. What would be the point of forcing them to do something they didn't want to do? I thought it was a horse person's job to figure out what their horse liked. That's the way I'd always been taught, anyway.

Rob had brought Artimax and Maverick, and I helped him to unload.

"Did you bring the eggs?" he said, winking at me.

"Yes," I sighed, "and the spoons. But you know Hilary's going to kill us if we get egg in her new indoor, right?"

"Yeah, I thought about that. We'd better start in the outdoor ring first. That might be better for Red, too."

"Sure, do you want to fill me in on what we're doing, though?"

"Nope. Hey, Callie, are you and Sox ready to have some fun?"

"Yes!" Callie squealed and spun around in a circle.

"What about you, Nori? Do you want to give us a hand?"

"Um, I suppose so," Nori said skeptically. "As long as I don't have to ride."

She helped Callie tack up since the little girl was too small to reach the top of Sox's back, and I was surprised at how gentle she was with her little sister. I would have thought she'd be awful to her, but it seemed she saved her nasty side for her mom.

Just as we were headed to the ring, Hilary showed up in her golf cart. "What are you all doing?" she asked, wistfully.

"Come help us," I said impulsively, "Rob says we need a judge."

"O-kay," she said dubiously, looking at the bag of spoons and the cartons of eggs I'd stolen from their kitchen.

***

In the end, it was the most ridiculous, funniest day I'd had in my life.

The first race was something called egg and spoon, and it involved us lining up at one end holding spoons with an egg balanced on them in one hand and the reins in the other. The goal was just to get your horse from one end of the ring to the other without dropping the egg. If you lost your egg then you had to start over.

The horses were already excited by all the activity. Sox kept nipping the horses on either side of him, and Artimax had his tail flagged up and his eyes fixed on the finish line like he was ready for a real race.

Red's ears pricked, and I felt his muscles bunching in excitement. At that moment, he didn't even care that he was in a ring with a saddle on. He just wanted to play with his friends.

Hilary stood at the far end at the finish line to judge who won, and Nori stood at the start line with a carton of replacement eggs in one hand and her pastries in the other. We hadn't even started yet and she was already shouting instructions and advice to us like a drill sergeant.

"Come on, do you call that a straight line? Callie control your pony. I can't believe I'm helping you lot with this."

It was also her job to hang on to Maverick while Rob was on Artimax, and that's how she made the discovery of how much he liked pastries.

"Robert," she bellowed, "your stupid horse ate my food!"

That started us all laughing and gave Mister Sox the opportunity he needed to drag Callie halfway around the ring at a brisk trot, smashing her fallen egg under his hooves.

"No fair," Annie called, "you started without us, Callie."

"No, I didn't. Sox did. He's a cheater." She somehow managed to turn him by sawing her inside rein right back to her knee and thumping him as hard as she could in the sides with both legs, landing random blows with her sparkly crop on whatever part of the pony was in her reach.

The tiny crop probably didn't hurt Sox, but I winced when he gaped his mouth open wide, his eyes tense with pain. I hoped

Callie could take some lessons with Liza when she came. It wasn't fun to see her struggling so much.

Finally, Nori took pity on them and retrieved Sox back into line.

"You know, Nori, Maverick wouldn't be able to eat your food if you were riding him," Rob said, sending her a wink.

Nori stuck out her tongue and then looked at Maverick skeptically. "Yeah? He's a little short. I don't usually ride Quarter Horses."

"Well, give it a try," Rob said, "unless, of course, you're just afraid you'll lose."

And that clinched it. Nori swung easily onto Maverick's back, even though he wasn't wearing a saddle, and gave Rob a superior look with one eyebrow arched.

"Easy on his mouth, though," he said, his face serious. "He's just a baby and he's more sensitive than he looks, okay?"

"Okay," she said, and nodded like she meant it. "Egg me up."

Hilary had to be the egg person after that and finally, we were actually sort of racing to the finish line. If what we did could be called racing. Some trotted, some cantered, some walked, and Sox went around greedily eating as many fallen eggs as he could while Callie pummeled his fat sides with her heels.

Red had launched himself into a rocking horse canter which, of course, sent my egg flying, so I circled him back to Hilary and picked up another one and tried again. This time, I held my spoon higher and concentrated on balance, and if Maverick hadn't shoulder-checked me, I probably would have made it.

"I'm so sorry," Nori said, looking genuinely upset. "I was concentrating on my egg."

"It's okay." I laughed and cantered back for another. But by that time, Annie had crossed the finish line at a walk on gentle Norman, and that was the end of that. I allowed Red to canter all the way to the end and then let him walk on a loose rein. He was puffing, and his ears were pricked, and he looked like he was having a great time.

"Okay," Rob said approvingly. "That went well. Any sluggishness at all, Astrid?"

"None," I said, "he was totally forward and happy."

"Good, let's do the next game inside then."

"Oh no," Hilary protested, "no eggs in my new indoor."

"No eggs, I promise." Rob laughed. "Come on, everyone, keep up the energy so Red doesn't lose his enthusiasm."

Annie and Nori might have thought we were crazy, but that didn't stop them from forming a line with Red and trotting in formation back to the indoor. Red trotted along easily, keeping step without a care in the world.

Hilary rolled back the big back door, and we all trotted inside without stopping. In fact, the horses loved the springy, new footing and they rocketed along like they were war horses going to battle. Mister Sox was practically doing a flying extended trot with Callie bouncing along on his back laughing hysterically.

Everyone was laughing and gasping for air by the time we stopped.

"Okay, I'll judge this one," Rob said, riding Artimax back to where Hilary stood in the doorway. "Nori and Astrid, you're on one team, and Callie, you're with your mom. I'm going to give each team a piece of rope. You have to hold onto it between you two and get from one end of the ring to the other, while weaving through the cones I set up. Whoever makes it back first will be the winning team. If you drop your rope, you need to start again."

I noticed the double lines of cones for the first time and laughed. This should be a piece of cake.

Nori and I trotted side by side to the first cone but then, of course, the horse on the outside would get way behind of the horse on the inside and I had to stretch way forward in my saddle, practically lying down on Red's back to hang on to the rope.

Callie and Annie had it much worse since Sox was so short and Norman so tall, but they trotted through steadily and in the end, they were the winners.

We switched up so Rob could have a turn and then played a game of freeze tag where, if you were touched by the one who was "it" on your arm or leg, then you couldn't use that aide anymore. You'd have to drop that rein or hold your leg off the saddle. It was ridiculous but fun. When we were exhausted, we did one last group canter around the ring before calling it a day.

"What do you think, Astrid? Is he cured?" Rob said, coming up alongside me.

"Well, at least for today." I laughed. "I'm not sure if I can do this every time I ride in the ring, though."

"In a way you can," Rob said seriously. "You can ride him into the ring from the outside at a trot and canter. You can make sure there's another horse with you and trot side by side for a few laps. You just have to keep thinking outside of the box with him."

Nori had sidled up beside us on Maverick and was staring at

Rob thoughtfully. "You people are really different," she said, and I couldn't tell if it was an insult or a compliment. "But I had fun today."

She paused and then reached down to scratch Maverick's mane with her fingernails. "This is a decent horse," she said finally. "I could ride him for you sometimes. I mean…if you like."

Rob looked at her and frowned. "He needs steady, consistent work," he said. "You would have to follow his conditioning program exactly. Slow and steady and no jumping this summer."

"I can do that," Nori said quickly. "I don't need to jump right now. Maybe not ever."

"And you have to work on his archery skills sometimes. He's getting pretty brave."

"Sorry, his *what* skills?" Nori turned to me for explanation.

"Well, we're working on getting them confident with us shooting the bows around them so we can do mounted archery."

"Would I get to shoot an actual bow?" Nori asked, wide-eyed, looking impressed and maybe a bit excited for the first time.

"Sure." I shrugged. "Why not? I can teach you."

"Awesome," she said and then pinched her lips together, irritated at her own moment of enthusiasm.

Rob and I looked at each other and then burst into laughter, and in another second Nori did, too.

Chapter Eighteen

Every day, I rode Red out to the woods, past the ocean, dismounted, and faithfully practiced the way Darius had shown me on the archery range. Now when I swiftly drew an arrow and launched it at the target, Red didn't even flinch. He just stood obediently behind my shoulder looking bored. He'd been pretty disappointed in the beginning that I wouldn't let him graze when I shot, but since I always gave him a small cookie for being patient, he'd become content to stand around and wait.

My bow had finally arrived in the mail, and even though it was much different than my other bows, I still loved it. As Earl had suggested, I'd picked what was basically the equivalent of a kid's bow with a twenty-pound pull. It was made of dark polished wood and had beautiful curved lines that made it look like it had stepped out of the pages of a history book. I could completely imagine ancient horse archers bearing down on their enemies with a bow like this.

There was no shelf or arrow rest, just a piece of leather wrapped around the middle. It felt strange at first, but after a few days I was in love; the smaller length sure made slinging it over my shoulder when I rode that much easier.

I was dying to move Red along to the next stage, but I'd made a promise to Darius, and I didn't want to ruin the slim chance of him showing up to teach me again.

Ellie, on the other hand, I was content to go as slowly as possible with. I still wasn't confident enough to ride her on my own without someone else around; less afraid that she'd do something silly and more afraid that I'd make a mistake and ruin her by accident. So, I rode her when Rob came to exercise his horses, and on the other days, I just brushed her and took her for walks or played with her at liberty in the indoor.

Despite her easy-going personality, she was not as confident as Red when it came to some things. She wasn't afraid of my bow or the arrows when I showed them to her, but she hated the sound of the arrow hitting the target. She'd stopped flinching after the first few days, but she would still get that pinched, nervous expression on her face and flick her ears around uncertainly as I drew back my bow.

It was getting better every day, but I still had to be much more patient and give her more encouragement than I did with Red. She was very sensitive to her surroundings and would stare wide-eyed at the woods behind the target, and then duck behind me as if for protection. She was adorable, and if it wasn't for the fact that I was petrified of messing up her education, I'd enjoy spending more time with her.

***

It was another full week before Darius showed up, driving a red sports car that he said belonged to his uncle.

He got out of the car and stopped dead when he saw Hilary balanced expertly on one crutch with a broom in the other hand sweeping the aisle.

It had been her idea. She was sick of watching me, Annie, and sometimes Rob, do everything, so she pitched in where she could. She could sweep, sort of, and feed the horses, though it took her twice as long as it did the rest of us.

But Darius didn't know that, and he marched straight up to her and took the broom from her hand without asking.

"You should be resting," he said sternly, escorting her firmly to the patio set. "Please let me do that for you since your *friends*"—he shot a pointed glance at me—"will not help you."

"Hey," I protested, "I actually do most of the work around here, you know."

"Are you in pain?" he asked her, ignoring me completely.

"No, but I am thirsty," Hilary said in a small voice, opening her eyes wide, "there are drinks in the tack room fridge. Maybe you could get us some?"

Darius was off like a shot, returning with a drink for each of them and none for me. "You shouldn't be working in this hot sun. Here drink this; you should keep your strength up."

Wow, I thought, leaving them sitting there staring at each other with lovestruck eyes, *I don't think I'm getting my archery lesson today.*

But, just as I was finishing paddocks, Hilary's mom pulled up in front of the barn.

"Oh, hello," I heard her say, "I don't believe we've met."

And a few minutes later, two car doors slammed and the car took off faster than necessary.

I heard him enter the barn, but I didn't look up from brushing Red.

"I don't think Hilary's mother approves of me," he said, sounding sad.

"Well," I said pointedly, "you are a lot older than her." I wasn't thrilled that these two were still interested in each other, either.

"Two years and a month," he said quickly, "that's not such a big gap."

"Except she's still a kid in high school and you're..." I paused thinking of how to describe him. A grown-up person with god-like beauty? "...a professional athlete."

"Not by choice, or at least, not forever. I would like to start my studies again someday; after I've fulfilled my obligations to my sponsors, of course. I want to make something of myself."

"Hmm," I said, thawing infinitesimally. "Couldn't you just be friends for now until she's old enough to date?"

"Oh, yes," he said earnestly, "I never expected anything else. She is who I will eventually marry. I would never dream of treating her without the upmost respect."

"Marriage?" I said in horror, but maybe I was biased. After years of watching my dad and Marion's tense married life, I'd vowed a long time ago that that was never happening to me.

"Of course. When she is eighteen and I am able to support her in the manner she's accustomed I will propose to her."

I wonder if Hilary knows about that part of the plan? I thought. I wondered if her *mother* knew? So far, I'd hardly seen them actually say more than ten words to one another, there was mostly just a lot of intense staring. How did one base a marriage partnership on that?

"Um, are we going to do an archery lesson today?" I asked hopefully.

"Oh, yes, of course. That's why I'm here."

I tacked up Red before Darius could change his mind and let him brush and tack up Ellie. He'd been fine riding Maverick so I couldn't imagine him damaging Ellie in just one ride.

"Let me see your new bow," Darius said when we reached the range. I jumped down off Red and unslung it from my shoulder, glad I'd polished the wood only the other day.

He turned it over in his hands, frowning. "It will do the job," he said finally, "but it's cheaply made. See if you can get a custom one at some point."

"Um, okay," I said, resisting an eye roll. He sure had expensive tastes for someone who had lost everything.

"So, show me your progress."

Nodding, I led Red parallel to the first target, took a deep breath and quickly launched an arrow into space. Red stayed tucked nicely behind me and didn't even acknowledge the *thwunking* sound of the arrow ploughing into the target. I repeated the action twice over, and then turned to smile triumphantly at Darius.

"Nice shooting," he said, raising his eyebrows, "very impressive. I did not have high expectations."

"Wow, thanks, Darius. I'll be sure to let Hilary know what a nice guy you are."

"I didn't mean any offense," he said quickly. "I just didn't realize that you were such a good shot."

"Well, thanks…I guess." I barely restrained myself from rolling my eyes. "Could you show me the next step, please?

There's nobody else on the Island who does this. It's either you or more online videos."

"Okay," he said seriously. "I'm sorry. I've acted rudely. Mounted archery has a very deep tradition in my family, so it's hard for me to even talk about it without thinking of everything we've lost. But I will help you. Get on your nice horse here and I will show you the next step."

I shouldered my bow again and swung up on Red.

"For the first few times, you will drop the reins, and I will hold his bridle. Just to make sure he's solid. If you go slow and steady at this point then he'll always be confident underneath you."

He led Ellie over and held the cheek piece of Red's bridle while I faced the target side-on. I took a deep breath, rolled my shoulders, and then launched the first arrow.

Red's ears flicked forward briefly when it hit the target. We moved to the next one, and the next.

"One more time," Darius said.

I went and retrieved my arrows, and then we did it again, but this time we didn't completely stop at the targets. He kept Red moving slowly as I hit one, then two, then three in quick succession.

He nodded approvingly and smacked me on the thigh. "Good job. I know this part seems like slow-going at first, but it's like building a foundation for a house. At first, it seems to take forever, but you build it up brick by brick and then, before you know it, construction is complete, and you have a home for you and your beautiful new wife to raise a family in."

What? I turned to look at him incredulously, but he was

staring up at the treetops with a small smile on his face.

"Darius?"

"Oh, right. So, switch horses and we'll do it again."

We went much slower with Ellie. She was still inclined to be nervous, but Darius was still happy with her progress.

"I will come back for the next two mornings to teach you, Astrid. I would love if you would let Hilary know that I will be here."

"Fine," I sighed, "thanks for helping me."

"It is not a problem. Thank you for letting me ride again."

Chapter Nineteen

Darius was good with his word, and Red and I progressed from being led to walking the short course by ourselves and shooting the arrows one by one. Ellie still had to be led, though, she wasn't quite as confident as Red.

"You do this for one week, and then you can progress to trotting on your red horse and walking without a leader on your little mare. Yes?"

"Yes." I nodded happily.

"You do this for two weeks, and then send me a message. I'll give you the next step, and in a month or so I'll come home and check your progress."

"Thanks again, Darius."

I texted Hilary as soon as we were done so she could drive her golf cart at top speed down to the barn to have her picnic and stare session with Darius at the little patio table.

He'd brought some delicious, strange Middle Eastern pastries and coffee, so I helped myself and took my snack into the barn to give them some privacy.

***

I didn't see Hilary again until later that afternoon when I wandered into the kitchen to find a snack and found her in the middle of an argument.

"Ask Astrid," Hilary demanded, "she'll tell you how wonderful he is."

"Hilary," her mom said, sounding exasperated, "it's just not appropriate. He's older than you and he has much more life experience. We know nothing about his background and his family."

Finally, I thought, *someone's going to talk some sense into her.* I had actually started to like Darius, but I still thought he was too old for Hilary and honestly, I wasn't sure he was good enough for her; she was my friend and it was my duty to protect her. And his talk of marriage creeped me out.

"Mom, you can't blame him for being an orphan. How is that his fault?"

"I didn't say it was his *fault,* but his experiences were very traumatic; he's going to have some baggage that comes with that. How could he not?"

"So. Doesn't everyone come with some sort of baggage? It's not like *we're* perfect."

"Yes, of course but—"

"And you can't be judging him because he doesn't have any money. Dad built his company up from nothing and you're proud of him. Plus Darius is an athlete with sponsors and everything. And, anyway, his uncle here has sort of adopted him and he's doing well enough. It's not like Darius is living on the street."

"I know," said her mother, "but the point is, Hilary, that you don't even know this boy and you're already planning a future with him based on nothing but a fantasy. You need to take time to figure out what sort of person he really is without letting your emotions take over."

I thought this sounded like excellent advice but Hilary set her jaw in a determined line.

"I *know* what type of person he is," she said stubbornly, "I know it in my heart."

"Hilary." Mrs. Ahlberg pinched the bridge of her nose. "Right now, you see what you want to see. I'm not saying that you're wrong. I don't know him, either. I'm saying to take your time, get to know him, use your head and not just your heart."

"So, you're saying I can't see him?" Hilary was not budging an inch.

"Honey. You're sixteen years old and it's my job to protect you. Look, I know I can't completely forbid you to see this boy. So, I'm going to set some limits. You can meet him, in public, with supervision—"

"Mom, come on. That's so demeaning. I'm old enough to make my own decisions."

"I know," her mom said, "you are. And most of the time you are the most mature, responsible person I know. You're running a whole stable with minimal help from your father and me. But, like everyone, you are capable of making mistakes. We all are, right?"

"I guess so," Hilary said grudgingly.

"I'm not going to lie to you, Hilary, this situation makes me afraid. I don't want you getting hurt; not physically and not emotionally. I feel like things could go so wrong. We know nothing about him and it's not like I can go meet his parents."

"That's not his fault."

"No, it isn't. But it's the reality of the situation. I don't want to lose you, Hilary."

"Okay, fine," Hilary said, biting her lip. "I'm sorry I worried you. But I know this is the right thing."

"Maybe it is. And if you still feel this way in a few years then I'll back you up a hundred percent. Right now, you're still too young to make these big decisions."

A flash of anger lit up Hilary's face, but this time she didn't argue. "Fine," she said, gritting her teeth. "But you'll find out you're wrong."

"I hope so," her mom said, wrapping Hilary in a tight hug. "Nothing would make me happier."

Chapter Twenty

"She's here," Hilary said excitedly, hobbling in her air cast to the front door. She'd been waiting by the window expectantly, and now her face was lit up with excitement like a kid at Christmas.

I followed her to the door, dancing on her heels, and we were both on the porch waiting when Liza and Justin got out of a big white truck.

"They're *both* here," I squealed and ran down the porch steps to give them both a hug.

"Justin, I didn't know you were coming. Just wait until you see Red; Rob figured out how to get him to go forward in the ring, and he's so fit, and he's learning to tolerate the bow, and I'm riding Ellie now, but I haven't ruined her yet. I hope."

The words just poured out of me and I talked so fast that probably neither of them understood a thing.

"It's so good to see you, too," Liza said, laughing and letting me go so she could turn to hug Hilary, who had hobbled down the porch steps in my wake.

We dragged them inside for lunch and showed them their rooms and then, ignoring how exhausted they must be after their drive, we dragged them out to the barn to show them the horses.

Both Liza and Justin were impressed with all of Hilary's renovations on the farm, and they were happy how nice and fit Red and Ellie were. Excitedly I explained to them about Rob's conditioning program, and about the trails that surrounded the property.

"That's perfect," Liza said, "you're obviously doing a good job with them. All the horses look great."

That night we all had a fabulous feast in the half-constructed restaurant and Liza filled us all in on what was happening back at the ranch.

I had to know how every single horse was doing, and how big Figaro was getting, and whether Folly was any more sound.

"She's definitely improving," Liza said, "we're doing light stretching and suppling work in the ring, and trail riding the rest of the time. She's getting stronger every week."

"I hope she heals," I said, feeling that old familiar stab of guilt. It was my fault Folly had been hurt. There was still no way around that fact, though I'd done my best to make amends.

"Well, at the very least, she's sound enough to live a normal, happy life, Astrid. Time will tell if she'll ever compete again, but if not, I'll just have to breed her to that trouble-maker, Fox."

She grinned to show me that she was joking about calling him names. Fox was a bit pushy, but he was kind, and I knew she'd taken over riding him when Kade left. It wouldn't have taken long for her to fall in love with him.

"I have some news for you two," she said to Hilary and me, "but I'm not sure what you'll think about it."

"Tell us," Hilary said excitedly.

"Well, my friend Oona has been riding in Belgium for the last few years. She wants to come back to Canada, and she's looking for a place to start teaching again."

"Oh," Hilary said with interest. "She wants to come to the Island?"

"Yes, she has family here. I know you couldn't pay her a salary, Hilary, but she's looking for a place to live and to build up her business as a coach. It might work great for her to start here. Even if it's for a year or so."

"There's the suite above the barn," Hilary said, glancing at her parents quickly to gauge their reaction, "it's not finished yet, but it wouldn't take long to get it set up. It's not very big, though."

"That's okay, it would just have to be a place she could call home for a while. You should know, though…she's a little what you might call eccentric sometimes."

"Oh, like how?"

"Well, in some ways she's completely old school, so she likes all her students to be dressed properly and the horses have to be groomed within an inch of their lives before she'll give you a lesson."

"That doesn't sound too bad," Hilary said hopefully. "That's like Claudia."

"Hmm," Liza said, "well, she's also a painter. She's sold her works in galleries, so she has this artistic side to her. You know, I think you should just meet her and decide for yourself. Maybe do a trial for a few months at the end of summer."

"Yes!" Hilary said excitedly, "that would be great. I'm dying to be in real lessons again."

***

Even though Liza had only planned to give Hilary and me a couple lessons over her vacation, it didn't take long for both she and Justin to be fully booked.

After watching Rob's lesson on the magnificent Ferdi, Annie decided overnight that she and Norman were switching to dressage, and she went out and bought him all new tack and about ten new saddle pads in a variety of colours and trims.

"I'm sorry, you'll have to take it back," Liza said when Annie held up her new double bridle. "Just plain snaffle work for now."

She loosened Norman's noseband two holes and pulled off the flash that Annie had wrapped snuggly around his face. "Rider's should earn their double bridle. You'll thank me later. Always start simple; it's easy to add more if we need it."

"Okay," Annie said, looking at Liza intensely like she was waiting for mysterious dressage secrets to just fall out of her mouth.

Nori refused to have anything to do with Liza and Justin, but Callie and Mister Sox went into full boot camp with two lessons a day. Justin did some groundwork with him and Liza made sure to ride Sox herself before each lesson to make sure he was ready to listen.

Callie's spurs and sparkly crop were banished to a hidden cupboard in the tack room and, by the end of the visit, she and Sox were able to make their way around the ring with a reasonable amount of success.

"I can steer just with my legs now," she bragged to her sister, "and I know how to count his steps. Sox listens to me now...sometimes."

"Good for you," Nori said darkly and skulked around the barn like a dark shadow, avoiding talking to Liza or Justin at all.

In the middle of all this, Pender and Sadie arrived home from their European tour, fresh from a week of riding Lusitano stallions in Portugal and dying to practice what they'd learned on their own horses.

Luckily, Rob had put a bunch of rides in on Rabbit because Pender insisted on having lessons every day that Liza was home. Luckily, she'd been keeping up her skills on their multi-country riding holiday because Rabbit tested her in a dozen different ways before he finally settled down to work. It was a good thing she hadn't seen him a few months ago.

It was an exhausting week, but I loved every second of it. Justin rode Ellie for me every day and gave me some exercises to work on in the ring, some basic leg yields and serpentines; things I hadn't wanted to attempt on my own.

"She moves forward nicely, Astrid, and she's confident and well-conditioned. She just needs miles under her belt. I like your plan so far. A couple days a week of ring work, and the rest just conditioning rides, and the archery is a great idea. We just want to widen her experience."

My lessons with Justin and Ellie were nothing compared to my exhausting lessons with Liza and Red.

The first time I snuck out to the ring ten minutes early so I could give him a long, careful warmup at the walk. He always performed much better once he'd had a chance to loosen up first and I wanted Liza to be impressed.

I timed it perfectly and I had Red moving at a brisk trot by the time she walked into the arena. I changed directions in sitting trot and circled around her, Red moving quickly over the springy footing, his head in the air and his ears pricked. He was excited, and I was glad that Liza would get to see him moving forward instead of how sluggish he used to be.

She watched us closely with her arms crossed over her chest, her head tilted to one side.

"Good," she said slowly, "now change direction again."

Red slowed in the corner for a second and his nose came down and I felt him gently mouth the bit. Then his head popped up again and he was off at that trundling trot.

"Okay, bring him over here, Astrid."

She frowned as we approached and for a second I was worried about what she'd say.

"First of all, great job at getting him moving forward; he's like a different horse. You've really tapped into a new gear with him. But," she said, "in doing that, you've lost some of the refinement that you had before. He's developing some muscle underneath his neck from travelling a bit inverted with his nose in the air and sometimes he's a little disconnected in his hind end. You must have felt this?"

I nodded and sighed. "I did but I didn't want to wreck his forward motion. We worked so hard to get him moving in the first place and I didn't want to ruin it."

My face must have fallen because she came over and patted me on the knee. "Don't worry, it's nothing that can't be fixed and, you're right, this summer it was more important for you to get him thinking forward. Now, our mission is going to be to harness this new power you've created without interfering with his momentum. Did you feel the difference when you rode that corner right there? He was tracking up from behind and propelling himself along rather than just rushing."

"Definitely," I said, thinking of how much easier it had been to sit his trot for those few beats in the corner.

"Right, so now it's your job to recreate that moment for as much of your ride as you can. We're not going to force him into a frame…instead, we'll help him find his natural balance and rhythm again, which will be so much easier now that you've got him moving forward so nicely. You've built a really nice foundation on him, Astrid."

After that, she made us get to work. I had to drop my stirrups and stay at the sitting trot, weaving serpentines and small circles and squares and half circles around the arena until I was dripping with sweat. Red was hardly winded at all and seemed much more supple and responsive at the end of our ride than he had at the beginning. I could feel his back come up underneath me, arching like a cat, as his powerful hindquarters propelled him across the ring.

"Thank you so much," I said as soon as we were finished. "That made such a difference."

"You're a quick student," Liza said, smiling at me fondly. "I'm lucky to have you. Work like that every day and you'll soon find he's a new horse. He's already miles different from the horse you showed me back at the ranch."

I leaned down and wrapped my arms gratefully around Red's neck, so happy to have him in my life.

***

The days passed too quickly and soon, it was time for Liza and Justin to go. Everyone showed up to see them off and Pender burst into tears as she hugged Liza goodbye.

"What will we do without you?" she wailed. "Rabbit needs structure; he needs a routine. He needs lessons. How can we convince you to stay?"

"Oh, you'll be fine," Liza reassured her. "We'll be back next month and in the meantime, you can practice on your own and do some trail and conditioning rides, it would do him some good."

"Oh no." Pender paled and bit her lip. "I will just stay in the ring, thank you. No trail rides for this old girl."

"Oh, for heaven's sake," Sadie said, "you're the same age as me. That's it, next week you, me, and Annie are going on an adventure. We're perfectly capable."

"Right," Annie said, "Norman and I are in."

"Goodbye," Liza and Justin called as they pulled away and just like that, we were on our own again.

Chapter Twenty-one

Nori was the only one thrilled that our guests had gone. She'd taken to appearing out of nowhere with a small bag of Maverick's favourite pastries in hand whenever Rob's trailer pulled up.

"Is it still okay if I ride him today?" she'd ask awkwardly every single time, blushing, as if she'd grown out of practice of being polite.

There wasn't enough room in the main barn anymore for Rob to put his horses, so his dad now pulled up to the far end of the arena and he'd put them in the paddock areas with the new shelters.

It wasn't as much fun for me because I missed chatting back and forth between stalls while we groomed and tacked up. That pre-ride ritual where we hung out and talked about nothing in particular had become something I looked forward to almost more than the riding itself.

***

Nori had taken to archery enthusiastically, if not accurately. Her natural competitive nature had taken a back seat to learning a new skill, and she practically killed herself with laughter every time her arrows shot off into space, ploughing into the dirt bank nowhere near her targets.

"Oh my gosh, Astrid, this is so hard. How do you make it look easy?"

"Years of practice," I said. "Come on, let's fix your stance, try again." Maverick had graduated from ground-shooting to mounted-shooting with someone standing on the ground beside him, just like Darius had suggested. Even though Nori couldn't hit a target to save her life, she was a fearless rider and didn't see why she had to have a handler.

"What if he spooked, Nori?" I said patiently. "Your instinct might be to grab the reins, and what if you'd already drawn back the bow to shoot? You might react so fast you wouldn't have time to think about safety; you might accidentally shoot Maverick instead. You need to practice everything slowly first so your body and mind can work together. That's what we learn at the range; form and technique first, and then everything else will fall into place. Getting shot with an arrow can kill you…or at least hurt a ton."

I gave her arm a squeeze and smiled up at her. "You're doing great, though. Let's do it again at a walk."

***

Annie was beside herself with joy that Nori was not only taking an interest in horses again, but was happier, and much less sullen, than before.

"Thank you so much, Astrid," she said, pulling me aside one day when Nori was off helping Rob clean the paddocks he'd used. "I can't thank you enough for what you've both done for Nori. She's almost back to her old self again."

"Oh," I said, blushing, "it's nothing. She's doing great. She gets along with Maverick, and he actually seems to like her; he doesn't like that many people."

"Well, I want to thank you anyway; I've been wracking my brain to think of how to best show my appreciation. And I think I know how."

She stared at me with her eyes lit up and her hands clasped together at her chest in an expectant way that made me slightly nervous. She'd been plotting something.

"Rider fitness classes."

"Oh," I said.

"Now hear me out," Annie said, laughing at the unenthusiastic expression on my face. "You look like Nori when she's already set her mind against something. You know I own a few of the gyms in town, right?"

"No, I didn't," I said in surprise.

"Well, I don't expect you to keep up with local news, but we were voted best local business on the island last year. Anyway, one of our specialties is helping athletes with cross-training. What often happens is that you train so hard for your specific sport and you forget the other aspects of your fitness."

"Oh, right," I said, remembering how hard my ex-friend Miranda had trained at the gym when we were in archery together. She was always driving herself toward some internal level of perfection that she'd never seemed to reach.

"I've had an idea in my head that I'd like to tailor a program specifically for riders; a program that combines strength training, cardio, and nutrition."

"Okay," I said. That didn't sound so bad, except the nutrition part maybe. "I think my stepmother hates food," I said without thinking. Instantly, I regretted it. Why had I said *that*?

"Oh dear." Annie frowned. "Sometimes that happens. But you need nutrients to build muscle and be strong. You're an athlete, so you probably know all about that."

"Me?" I said quickly. "Oh no, I'm not athletic at all."

"Astrid." Annie looked at me incredulously. "Every time I see you, you're either riding a horse or doing barn work; I don't think I've ever see you sitting around just hanging out. And Nori said that you were pretty competitive in archery. That sounds pretty athletic to me."

"Oh, but I don't run or go to the gym or anything…"

"Never mind that," Annie said, shrugging off my protest. "We can fine-tune the cross-training to target any weak areas. But, my dear, you are very much an athlete, whether or not you admit it."

She stared at me expectantly, waiting for an answer.

"Um, okay," I said tentatively, not sure what I'd just agreed to.

"Excellent. Give me some time to work out a program for you. You won't regret this Astrid, you're going to love it."

Love what, exactly? I thought, watching her stride back to the car, a satisfied smile on her face. I really hoped she wasn't going to try to put me into some sort of fitness boot camp. My dad had sent me to the Windy Shores "health spa" often enough that I was heartily sick of any sort of fat busting experiments. Besides, I was already up to my eyeballs in work; cleaning up after a barn full of horses was exercise enough.

Chapter Twenty-two

"Oh my gosh, that was so much fun," I said, patting Red on the neck enthusiastically. "I never knew jumping would be like that."

We'd set up a few logs alongside our trails, and Red had finally been convinced to hop over them rather than stopping and stepping over each one carefully.

"Ha, I knew I could convert you," Rob said with a laugh. "It was only a matter of time."

We walked the horses back to the barn side by side, chatting away happily, and we were so caught up in our conversation that we didn't notice the black SUV parked in the driveway.

"You're fantastic, you know," Rob said and leaned over to plant the gentlest of kisses on my lips. I melted into him, feeling that electricity build that we always seemed to generate these days until I could feel it in my toes.

"Hey!" someone shouted, and I jerked backward, staring at my father's thunderous face in horror, my stomach twisting sharply as he marched toward us, his hands balled into fists.

"Get your filthy hands off her, you little..." his last words were garbled with rage. "Astrid, get off that horse," he barked,

"I'm not paying a fortune in board for you to waste your time here fooling around with every boy in the neighbourhood. You should be ashamed of yourself."

I work off Red's board, was my first thought, *you have nothing to do with him. And I'm not ashamed of Rob; he's the best person I know.*

But I didn't say anything; I sat there numbly, my limbs turned to ice.

"I said get down," my father bellowed, "you're going home. You can say goodbye to your little boyfriend. You won't be seeing him again."

My legs shook as I hit the ground, and I leaned against Red to keep myself upright. Rob landed smoothly beside Possum and moved over beside me, putting his arm around my shoulders. When I glanced up he had a furious expression on his face.

"You can't talk to her like that," he said. "Astrid hasn't done anything wrong."

My father laughed, but it wasn't a nice laugh; his face was dark with anger.

Rob's arm tightened protectively around me. I wished I could stay there like that, tucked in safe beside him forever. I wished that he had the power to somehow be a buffer between me and my father's rage, but I knew that that was an illusion.

"Astrid, get in the car," my dad said, his voice deceptively calm but the vein in his head bulged, the way it did when there was a storm of anger coming my way.

"I've got to go," I said, slipping reluctantly out from under Rob's arm and pressing Red's reins into his hand. "Please take care of him for me."

"Astrid," Rob protested, looking concerned and furious at the same time.

"Take care of Red, please," I repeated, looking into his eyes, trying to channel all the things I felt about him and Red into that one glance. "I'll be back later."

Without looking back, I went to the car and slid into the passenger seat, my hands shaking so badly I had to sit on them to make them be still. My stomach churned and I hoped I wouldn't throw up.

The yelling started as soon as we were halfway down the driveway.

"How could you be so stupid," he ranted, slapping his palm against the wheel. "We trusted you to make good decisions. You will never go near that boy again. I will be calling the Ahlbergs to let them know what I think…." It went on and on, some of the words sunk in, making me feel small and terrified, but most of them rained down on me in a confusing hail of anger. I just hunkered down in my seat and waited for it to be over.

"Get up to your room and stay there," he barked when we reached the underground garage. "That horse will be going back to Lillian as soon as we can arrange transport. You're lucky I don't own it or it would be going to the packing plant."

A stab of pain slammed through my belly, and I doubled in half before scrambling out of the car and breaking into a run.

I reached the elevator way before my dad and jumped inside, pressing the button frantically until the door closed. I crouched in the corner, gasping for air, consumed by the wild panic slamming around inside my chest like a trapped bird.

"Astrid," Marion said in astonishment as I barged into the

condo and rushed past her. Choking back sobs, I fled to the safety of my room, slamming the door and throwing myself onto my bed to cry and cry. It was one thing to threaten me, but to threaten *Red*, who was so sweet and innocent and kind; that was the worst kind of awful.

But he'll be okay, I reminded myself over and over, *he's Aunt Lillian's horse and she will always take care of him. He has a home at the ranch. He's safe; nobody can touch him. Nothing can happen to him; he'll be okay.*

But what would I do without Red around to keep me sane and happy? He was the very best part of my day. I loved taking care of him and hanging out with him, he brought me so much joy. I couldn't imagine life without him.

Nobody came to check on me. I stayed huddled in my room well into the night, well past dinner, shivering and shaking and imagining what my new life would look like.

No Red, no Rob or Hilary, or the barn. Probably not even archery. How would I survive two more years until I was legally able to move out of this house on my own?

You could run away, a tiny voice whispered, *you could hide somewhere until they stopped looking and then sneak to Aunt Lillian's.*

The thought made me pause but, of course, it wouldn't work in real life. Aunt Lillian would have to tell my parents where I was, wouldn't she? She couldn't just hide me away in secret for two years.

Still, the thought gave me hope. I sat up in bed and wiped my tear-stained face on the duvet then reached under my bed to find my phone that had dropped there earlier when I'd flung into the room in a panic.

And that's when the yelling started.

I sat straight up in bed, my heart thundering, clutching the covers to my chest.

"Don't you dare threaten me, Marion," my dad's voice boomed, "she's my daughter and I make the decisions in this house."

I couldn't hear what Marion said, but I could hear her voice rising, high-pitched and sharp in a way that was very unlike her.

I slipped out of bed and moved to the door, opening it a crack so I could hear.

"You don't know anything about it, that boy was all over her. We have to stop this now before it's too late...."

More angry words from Marion that I couldn't hear, and then somewhere in the house, Caprice began to bark. Just a few yaps at first, and then a steady stream of high-pitched shrieks; her danger bark.

"You've always been on her side. I know you two plot against me," he bellowed, his voice rising up and mixing with Caprice's staccato yelps.

A door slammed somewhere, and then another. Thuds sounded somewhere around the kitchen. What was happening?

"Don't you dare walk away from me, Marion."

Caprice's hysterical barking ratcheted up a few notches, and then chaos erupted. There was a bellow from my dad and Marion's sudden scream, and then a series of sharp yelps followed by silence.

Not stopping to think, I flew out of my room and barrelled down the hall.

I skidded to a stop in the kitchen, staring in horror at the drops of blood on the floor and the sight of Marion clutching a shivering Caprice to her chest.

My dad stood at the sink running cold water over his hand, an indecipherable expression on his face. And everything was completely, horribly silent. Nobody made a sound, not even the dog.

I stood frozen in the doorway, looking at the scene like it was something playing in a movie.

"Marion?" I said, my voice coming out a rasp.

She looked up and met my eyes, but still said nothing.

I took a few steps into the kitchen, looking uncertainly between her and my dad. He was staring down at his hand, still dripping blood under the running water into the sink.

"Marion, are you okay?"

She nodded woodenly and then her face crumbled, and to my surprise she began to laugh and cry hysterically at the same time. I reached her, wrapping her and Caprice in a tight hug, all three of our bodies shaking.

"Come on," I whispered, tugging on her arm, trying to get her to follow me. All I could think of is that we needed to get out of here now. This wasn't a safe place to be anymore. We could go to Hilary's place…they had all those extra rooms. Or Aunt Lillian's. Or anywhere; Marion had lots of money of her own, she was free to go anywhere in the world.

"She bit me," my dad said from his place at the sink, still looking shocked, and then he began to laugh.

"Come on, Marion," I whispered, giving her arm an extra tug, but instead of following me she slowed to a stop.

"It's okay, Astrid," she said softly, taking a deep breath and wiping her eyes with one hand, "everything's fine. Caprice thought she was protecting me and she bit your dad. I think he might need stitches. It was just a misunderstanding."

I stared at her incredulously and stepped back, seeing her as if for the first time. She was still the Marion who loved me and tried hard to protect me in her own way, but she was also the one who let my dad walk all over us, who put her own needs last all the time, and who could say that an *awful* scene like this was just a misunderstanding.

I felt the tight bond I'd always shared with her rip away thread by thread until we were just two strangers staring at each other across a bloodied kitchen floor. And suddenly, I knew I couldn't stay here anymore.

"No, Marion," I said, giving her one last chance, even if it was probably pointless. "Everything is *not* okay. Your dog shouldn't think it has to protect you from your husband. That's not normal, no matter how hard you pretend that it is."

There was a long silence with only the sound of our rapid breathing, and the running water splashing into the kitchen sink.

"How about we talk about this in the morning," Marion said finally, pulling herself upright. "I'm going to run your dad down to emergency to get that hand stitched up. The bite was pretty deep. I can't believe Caprice did something like that; we'll have to talk to the trainer."

"Give her to me," I said woodenly, reaching out to take Caprice's shivering body into my arms.

"Astrid, it was just a misunderstanding," Marion said again, handing Caprice over reluctantly. Her voice quavered, a note of uncertainty in it, but I didn't look back. I marched down the hall to my room and sat on my bed with Caprice nestled in my arms, shaking with a mixture of leftover fear and outrage. I held on to that feeling, letting it fuel me.

I waited until the second the front door shut behind them, and then scrambled for my phone. I'd had the volume off like I always did when I rode the horses and I hadn't checked it since that mortifying scene with my dad at Hilary's place. I hadn't wanted to answer any questions or face anyone's pity right then. It was too embarrassing.

But now I saw that that had been selfish. There were multiple missed texts and calls from both Hilary and Rob, and also from the Ahlbergs; everyone wanted to know if I was okay.

There are lots of people looking out for me, I thought, my hands shaking, *I'm not alone.*

"Hilary," I said, when she answered on the first ring. "I need your help."

"Astrid, where are you?" Hilary said, her voice rising up in a wail, "we were so worried. We left so many messages."

"I'm coming over. I've got to go before they get back. I'll see you soon."

I hung up, took a deep breath and with shaking fingers, I called a taxi.

"Yeah, it will be fifteen minutes," said the dispatcher in a bored voice when I asked him to hurry. "It's a busy night."

"Thank you," I whispered. I didn't have time to grab much. Most of my stuff was still at Hilary's and I'd come away without my wallet or even a change of clothes.

I grabbed Caprice's dog bed and her favourite toy and set them by the front door. Caprice curled up in her bed, whimpering. She didn't look good; her tail was tucked and she wouldn't stop shaking.

Please be okay, I thought, *please don't be hurt.*

I rummaged around Marion's office until I found the small stash of money that she kept stuffed away for emergencies. I counted it frantically; surely, it should be enough to pay the taxi to Hilary's. It couldn't be that expensive, could it?

I took one last look around, standing poised in the doorway to our condo.

There's nothing left for me to take, I thought, feeling a pang of sadness so keen it was like a knife cut, *it's like I left a long time ago.* Then I lifted Caprice in her dog bed and ran for the elevator.

"Come on, come on," I said out loud, pressing the downward button over and over. I was suddenly, irrationally afraid that when the elevator door opened, they'd be inside. Maybe the emergency room had been full, maybe they'd changed their minds and come home.

When the door finally opened, my palms were slick with fear. But the elevator was empty, and I stumbled inside and pressed the button for the lobby, my heart clubbing away in my chest. It took ages for the door to creak shut again and finally, we were lurching slowly down to the lobby.

"Everything okay?" the night desk clerk said in concern, staring at my blotchy, tear-stained face. He wasn't one I knew well, but I thought he might be a cousin of Dom. He watched me with a kind look on his face.

"Yep," I said, staring out the front window, wondering if he would attempt to stop me from leaving.

I glanced over to find him watching me, his kind eyes full of concern.

"Actually, no," I said. I was done with hiding stuff now. I was done protecting people who hurt me. I took a deep breath. "I'm going to stay at my friend's house because my dad flew into one of his rages and threatened my stepmom, and our dog attacked him. He needs stitches in his hand and I'm glad. I wish she'd gone for this throat instead."

"Oh," the clerk said and then he riffled through his desk. "Should I call the police? Do you need money for the taxi?"

"No! I mean, no thanks," I said, my heart stuttering at the word *police*. Surely, they'd tell me to turn around and just go back home to my family.

"You sure you have a safe place to go?" he asked. And a wave of gratitude washed over me. He wasn't going to turn me in. He genuinely wanted to help.

"Yeah," I said firmly. "I do. I've got this."

"Okay," he said, pointing to the door, "your taxi's here, but if you ever need help, don't hesitate to ask. That man has been a self-centered obnoxious bully since the day he moved in and I don't mind telling you that. We've always tried to look out for you. You deserve a much better home."

I turned to him, startled, but he'd already turned back to his desk.

"Go on," he said, "your taxi's waiting. Good luck."

Wow, maybe I should have confided in them sooner. I'd grown up here and they'd always been encouraging about my archery wins, or giving me compliments when I passed through the lobby. And they'd kept my secret when I was sneaking to practice at the range last summer. It was strange to think that people I didn't even know very well were looking out for me.

The taxi driver wasn't thrilled to have Caprice in his car, but I ignored him, slid into the back seat, and shut the door, feeling a wave of relief wash over me.

I've done it, I thought, *I'm free.*

We drove to Hilary's mostly in silence and my mood shifted back to fear. I stared out the window and caught myself watching for glimpses of my dad and Marion on the darkened streets. Of course, they wouldn't be there, but I couldn't help looking anyway.

A siren started up somewhere in the night and I flinched, catching the taxi driver's glance in the rear-view mirror. I smiled at him nervously and fixed my gaze back outside the window.

When we reached the barn, I gave the taxi driver a handful of cash, told him to keep the change and stepped out into the darkness. I stood there, waiting for him to leave, not sure if this was really happening. If I stepped into that barn then there was no going back. I would have made my choice for better or worse.

But of course, I'd made that choice the second I stepped away from Marion in our kitchen.

The sky was blanketed with a thick network of stars, and I tilted my head back and took a deep breath, closing my eyes and letting all those tiny pin-pricks of light shine down on me as if they could give me courage.

One of the horses made a questioning little *huh, huh, huh* noise from inside the barn, and there was the sound of hooves rustling through deep shavings. They knew I was here.

I rolled the big barn door back just enough to get inside and went to Red's stall instinctively, not needing to turn on the barn lights.

"Good girl, you stay," I whispered, setting Caprice down in her bed just outside in the aisle. I didn't want her getting stepped on in the dark. I slid the door back and slipped inside, searching with my outstretched hands until I found his comforting bulk, already moving toward me, his soft muzzle gently searching my pockets.

"Oh, Red," I said, the last remains of the anger that had fueled my escape leaking out and leaving me feeling hollow and fragile as an empty shell. I wrapped my arms around him and twined my fingers in his mane.

"I don't know what I'd do without you," I whispered, wiping my tears with his mane.

He just stood there patiently, not moving a muscle, not trying to get to his hay or push me away. There was a noise outside and he lifted his head, his ears swivelling toward the front door. From outside the stall door, Caprice growled low under her breath; a warning.

I froze, my fingers anchored in Red's mane, my heart thudding a million miles a minute. I'd been stupid, of course they'd look for me first. Why hadn't I thought of that?

"Astrid?" Hilary's voice was uncertain in the darkness, and then the overhead lights flicked on, and I blinked painfully in the sudden glare.

"Astrid," she said again, limping toward me in her air cast. Her eyes were huge in her pale face and she looked like she'd been crying.

I gave Red one last kiss and slipped out of his stall. Bracing myself for a storm of sympathy and questions that I didn't think I could handle right then.

She must have sensed it somehow. Because she came up quietly and just squeezed my hand once, tightly, before kneeling down and picking up Caprice.

"Come on," she said to the little dog, "let's get you home. You never have to go back there again."

I only hoped that by some miracle she was right.

Hilary's parents didn't say much, just a quick hug and a few questions to make sure I was okay. I couldn't tell by their expressions whether they were angry with me for dragging them into this or if they would send me right back home the next day.

I was so tired that I fell into bed with Caprice curled up under the covers beside me in the curve of my stomach, her little body completely motionless.

Please don't be hurt, I thought again, *please be okay.*

And somehow, I fell asleep.

Chapter Twenty-three

The next morning, I opened my eyes and sat bolt upright in bed, my heart beating so loud it thundered in my ears.

What have I done? I thought, panic lodged in my chest like a trapped bird. *He's going to hunt me down today. I have to get out of here.*

The events of last night came flooding back, and I remembered their fight and Caprice's yelps, and the drops of blood on the floor, and the fact that I'd run away. Last night, I'd been fueled by anger, but in the cold light of the morning, I could hardly believe that I'd been that brave, or that stupid.

I could still sneak home, I thought desperately, *maybe they haven't noticed I'm gone yet.*

But that was laid to rest when I heard Mr. Ahlberg's raised voice from downstairs.

"Stay," I whispered to Caprice, who lay burrowed under the covers with only her little nose sticking out; she didn't look like she planned on moving anytime soon. I tiptoed out into the hall, leaning carefully over the stairwell so I could hear everything.

"Really? You want to threaten me?" he said, and there was a

cold, ruthlessness in his voice that I'd never heard before.

"Let me lay the situation out for you so it's plain and simple. I have a child here who was too terrified to stay at home with her own family last night. I have a dog who wouldn't stop shaking and will most likely need veterinary care this morning. You are lucky Astrid had a safe place to run to, Bruce. What if she'd had to sleep on the street last night? Plenty of kids do and they're lucky if they survive. We've watched you put that child through hell for years, and I'm ashamed that we didn't step in before today."

There was a long silence, and then Mr. Ahlberg spoke again, his voice lowered so that I had to lean far over the railing to hear.

"I'm done listening. If you step foot on my property again, I'm calling the police, children's services, and the SPCA, and laying every charge at your doorstep that I can. I have an excellent lawyer, Bruce, and I'm not afraid to use him. Astrid can stay here as long as she wants to, and I'm afraid you just don't have a say in the matter, unless you'd like add assault and battery to your current list of criminal offenses."

I had my hand clamped over my mouth already, so I didn't squeak too much when Hilary came up beside me and wrapped an arm around my shoulder, leaning her head against mine. She must have been standing there listening for a while because her eyes were glistening.

"Astrid, you can stay with us forever and ever," she whispered. "You don't ever have to go back there again."

"But I'm not eighteen," I whispered back. "They can come take me back any time they like."

"No, they can't. Not if you're afraid to go home. You can lay

285

charges against him if you have to, but I don't think you'll need to. We see street kids at the church shelter all the time. Lots of them have run away from bad homes. My parents do their best to help them get on their feet. They don't have to go back if it's not safe."

"Really?" I asked in astonishment. "Why didn't you tell me this before?"

"Well, you never asked," Hilary said slowly, "and I never wanted to bring it up. You hated talking about home so much that I kind of avoided it, but maybe I should have pushed you more."

"Huh," I said, my thoughts tumbling over each other in my head. "Maybe I should have looked into it for myself. I never even thought to try."

That's a good lesson, I thought, feeling like I'd stumbled on an important truth, *I guess there's always an answer to everything if you look hard enough. I won't forget that again.*

So, for that morning anyway, I was allowed to stay. It was a quiet, subdued breakfast, even though the Ahlbergs did their best to cheer me up. Part of me felt so guilty for leaving Marion. I couldn't stop thinking of her standing there in the middle of the kitchen clutching Caprice. She'd looked so scared and lost.

But she had the chance to go, I reminded myself. *She chose to stay.*

My guilt was quickly replaced by anger when we drove into town to take Caprice to the vet.

"She won't stop shaking," I told the vet in a quavering voice, "and she's limping on her bad leg again. She hasn't stopped all night. Is she going to be okay?"

"She's in a lot of discomfort," the vet said, after he'd run his hands over her whole body, pressing gently on her sides and on each limb. "There's a large, painful area here on her side, I can even see some bruising through the fur. What did you say happened to her again?"

"I'm not sure," I said quietly, "she bit my dad, though, and maybe he kicked her or something afterward? I didn't see it happen."

"Oh." The vet frowned, colour flooding into his face. He tapped his pen nervously on the desk a few times and shuffled some papers around. "Does this type of thing happen often?"

"It's okay," Hilary's mom interrupted, and she reached out to squeeze my shoulder. "Astrid is living with us now and so is the dog. So there won't be a repeat of this."

"Great," the vet said, blowing out a relieved breath. "Good. I hate dealing with these, er, situations." He glanced at me and blushed even deeper. "Would you be okay if we ran some x-rays? We should make sure none of her ribs are broken."

"Okay," I squeaked and when he carried her away, I wiped the tears furiously from my cheeks.

"She'll be fine, Astrid," Hilary said, handing me a box of Kleenex from the counter. "They'll take good care of her."

I nodded but couldn't say anything else; I was too miserable. It felt like ages before the vet came back with a wagging Caprice clamped under one arm.

"She did great, Astrid." He smiled at me reassuringly and set Caprice down on the exam-room table. "My staff gave her lots of cookies and made a big fuss over her. And, good news, no bones broken, just a lot of bruising. I've given her an injection of pain control that will last twenty-four hours. And I'll send some medication home with you. She's a nice little dog. You take care of her...and yourself."

"Thanks," I said, clutching Caprice to my chest and smiling shyly up at him.

When I'd left home so quickly I'd completely forgotten to bring her dog food and bowls, so I bought some supplies for her and I cringed when I saw what the bill came to.

"Astrid, don't worry about paying for things right now," Hilary's mom said. "You just let us treat you and Caprice as our guests."

"Oh no," I said quickly, "it's okay. You don't have to do that." But secretly I wondered if my card would even work. Had my dad cancelled it as soon as he knew I wasn't coming home? That sounded like something he'd do. Maybe I could get a summer job to pay for all the extra things I needed.

"Nonsense. You're doing all of Hilary's work at the barn; don't think we don't know how bossy she is, even before she was on crutches." She looked over at Hilary lovingly. "It's a pleasure for us to have you safe with us, Astrid, you have no idea how much I've worried about you over the years. You just let us take care of you and Red and Caprice right now, and we'll sort out the details later."

"Okay," I said, gratitude overwhelming my embarrassment. "Thank you."

***

Rob was waiting at the barn when we got back, and as soon as I stepped out of the car he strode over wrapped me in a tight hug and clung on to me like he'd never let go.

"Don't ever do that again," he growled. "I was so worried. Anything could have happened to you."

"I'm sorry," I whispered, pressing my face into his chest, "I should have called."

"Astrid," he said, "you have no idea…."

He stopped and tightened his hold on me another inch before letting go. Then he kissed me solidly on the forehead and leaned down to pet Caprice who'd planted herself on his foot and was leaning her head against his knee.

"Hey, Caprice," he said gently, then glanced back at me. "Is she going to be okay?"

"I think so. She looks better already. The vet thinks it's just bruising, but we have to keep an eye on her."

Rob's hand stilled on Caprice's head, and he reached out and took my hand carefully in his. "Can you promise me something?"

"I hope so," I said hesitantly.

"You have to promise me that you'll never go back to live with them again. No matter what happens. Stay with your aunt or with Hilary…or with me. Just don't go back there."

"I won't go back," I said quietly, hoping it was the truth. I didn't feel strong today, I felt weak in the way that you do when you're recovering from a long illness and just want to stay in bed and sleep forever.

"No, I mean, *really* promise me," Rob said firmly. "I've seen stuff like this before, Astrid. My auntie was with a horrible man; he could be sweet and charming, and then it would be like flicking a light switch and he'd be coming at her with both fists swinging. We tried to help her so many times, but as soon as he apologized and begged her forgiveness, she'd go back to him. It happened more times than I can remember, and it ended with her in the hospital and him in jail."

"Oh," I said quietly. "I'm so sorry."

"Don't be sorry; just promise me you won't make the same mistake."

"Okay. I promise. I won't go back."

"Good," he said, squeezing my hand again and then linking his fingers with mine.

Chapter Twenty-four

I had a whole week of peace before the inevitable phone call came from Marion that they wanted to see me. They hadn't sent texts or called ever since that first morning. I wasn't sure whether that was because they were both still angry with me, or if Mr. Ahlberg had warned them off.

"You can say no, Astrid," Hilary's mom said firmly, putting her hand over the phone. "You're in charge here, and you don't have to do anything you don't want."

I bit my lip and stared at the floor, not sure what to do. The truth was that I *didn't* want to talk to them. I wanted to pretend that they didn't exist at all and that the Ahlbergs had always been my parents.

But, another part of me missed them and wanted things to just be the way they had been before that awful night. It hadn't been so bad, had it?

I glanced down at Caprice, still limping and clingy ever since that night, and I had my answer. I wasn't going back to live with them and neither was she. Things had gone too far for that.

I need to see them one last time, I thought, *I need to tell them that I'm not ever going back.*

"Okay," I said finally. "But can you be there, too?"

"Absolutely. I won't leave you alone for a single second. We'll do it right here, you don't have to go anywhere."

We booked a time for noon, and to keep himself occupied, Mr. Ahlberg made five different types of cookies, and tea, and set up the library as a meeting room.

When my parents arrived, both looking pale and serious, it was the Ahlbergs who met them at the door and shepherded them inside.

"Oh, Astrid," Marion said, stepping forward. But she stopped when I shrank back from her touch, and she stood in the middle of the room with her hands hanging uselessly at her sides, her eyes wide and her lower lip trembling.

I felt awful just looking at her. Marion had been on my side for my whole life, and it felt like such a betrayal to treat her like this. Part of me wanted to go to her, but I just couldn't. I couldn't even look at my dad.

The awkward moment was interrupted by high-pitched barking as Caprice scrambled into the room, her claws sliding on the wooden floor, and threw herself at Marion.

"Oh, Caprice." Marion knelt down beside the little dog. "I am so, so sorry. Are you all right?"

Caprice bounced around her, hysterical and yelping, squirming her body in a dozen different directions.

"She's okay?" she said, looking up at me for confirmation.

"Yes," I said, my voice coming out a squeak. "She will be. Nothing was broken."

My dad had gone to the far side of the room and was staring out the window with his back to us. It was impossible to tell what he was thinking.

"Let's sit down," Mrs. Ahlberg said pleasantly once Caprice was quietly nestled in Marion's arms again. I gulped, wondering if I'd done the right thing by taking her away that night, she'd clearly missed Marion a lot.

I sat down on one of the leather chairs and looked down at the ground.

"Astrid." My dad cleared his throat, and I glanced up hesitantly. He looked extremely pale and uncomfortable. "I want to apologize for my behaviour last week. I'm sorry I scared you."

There was a long silence, and I realized that I was expected to say something.

"Okay." I pressed my palms together in my lap to stop my hands from shaking.

"So, your stepmother and I have been doing a lot of soul searching the last few days. My therapist has been helping us through this rough patch."

He paused, and I glanced up again and then looked away quickly so I didn't see the struggle on his face.

"Astrid, I want you to know that I know my behaviour was wrong. That it's almost always been wrong. I've known this for a long time, but I've had difficulty changing."

He put his elbows on his knees and rested his chin on his hand.

"I know we haven't always been the best parents to you. At least"—he glanced over at Marion—"I haven't been the best father I could be." He paused. "It's not easy for me to admit this to you or to anyone. When I was growing up, it was a rule in our house that you never admitted that you were wrong."

"Oh," I said, interested despite myself. My dad hardly ever talked about his past.

"And here's the thing I've learned this week, Astrid; you don't flourish when you live with us. I'm a big enough person that I can admit that now. When you came home from your Aunt's ranch, you looked like you were a completely different person; you looked brave and confident, and I was so proud of you."

"You were?" I couldn't help but ask, since this was news for me.

"Very proud. But, in the first few weeks you were home with us, I could see you changing again. You got quieter and had that worried look back in your eyes that always drove me crazy."

"Oh," I said, twisting my fingers together on my lap.

He put his head in his hands and then rubbed his temples as if he were warding off an oncoming headache. "Astrid, I'm selling the condo."

"What?" I said, astonished. That wasn't what I'd expected at all. "Are you buying a house then instead?"

"No, it's time for a fresh start. After the squash tour is over then Marion and I are going to travel. There's more of Canada and the States to see; we're thinking of going up to Alaska next. I've always wanted to see a polar bear. We'll stay in the RV mostly. We need time to work on ourselves and our relationship."

"I'm not going with you," I said quickly, just so it was clear.

"No, I don't expect you to. Ahlbergs have agreed to keep you on over the winter. That, or your Aunt Lillian would love to take you. It's up to you."

"I'll stay here," I said firmly, already decided. "And I want to keep Caprice. Oh, and I'm dating Rob," I said, feeling my face flame with heat. "And I'm keeping Red."

There, I'd said everything I wanted to say.

My dad made a choking sound and then his shoulders slumped and he sighed. "I don't get to make those decisions for you anymore, Astrid. You'll just have to make the right choices for yourself now."

"Astrid always makes good choices," Linea said firmly, which was sweet, if not exactly accurate.

He didn't answer, just nodded in agreement.

"Astrid, I want you to know that your mother would have been so proud of you; I don't believe in an afterlife…I guess I don't believe in much of anything. But if there was a way then I know she'd be watching over you all the time; she loved you so much. And she would have been so upset with the failure I've been at raising you, and loving you, like I should have."

I stared at him, astonished, but then the whole situation just became overwhelming and I had to get out. I turned and bolted up the stairs to the safety of my room.

A few minutes later, the front door clicked shut and a car started outside. There was a clicking sound on the stairs, and then Caprice pushed inside and leapt onto the bed, licking my face before curling up happily beside me like she never wanted to leave.

Chapter Twenty-five

"Come on, Astrid, catch up," Nori called impatiently, turning around in her saddle as she urged Maverick up the trail from the beach. "I want to shoot. I have to practice before camp."

"We're coming." I laughed. When Nori had found out I was helping Earl with summer archery camp, she'd convinced her mother to let her sign up for not just one week but two, and she'd been practicing hard in anticipation. She'd somehow gotten it into her head that we were going to the Olympics together. All I could say is that she'd better start improving her aim if she wanted to win anything. At least she was stubborn and hard-working; that was probably half the battle.

I turned to grin at Rob, who had sidled Artimax right up to Red, so close that our knees brushed together. He gazed out over the ocean, his chiselled profile looking more beautiful in the early evening light than a person had a right to be. It still blew me away that he was in my life.

I inhaled deeply and, overwhelmed by my good fortune, I reached out and linked Rob's fingers in mine, holding on tightly. He glanced over, surprised, then looked down at our entwined hands and smiled quietly to himself.

"I'm glad you're here," he said.

"I'm glad I'm here, too. That was close, though. Things could have ended much differently."

"No." He shook his head. "I always had faith in you."

I sat there quietly, thinking. "You always believe in me, don't you?" I said finally, "even with that mess with Folly."

He smiled and shrugged, not looking at me, as if the answer was obvious.

We sat there silently for a long time, staring out over the wide blue ocean. I shivered, not because it was cold, but because suddenly, I had one of those weird feelings again that I was stepping out of one phase of my life and into another.

So much had changed in the short time that I'd been back to the island, but it felt like it had been ages ago that I first stepped foot on Hilary's farm. Now it was my new home, maybe it was only temporary…with my family anything could happen…but I still felt at peace.

The rest of the summer stretched on endlessly in front of me, now full of wonderful possibilities. I had two horses now to work with, a new instructor arriving soon, archery camp to teach, and a student of my own with Nori. Maybe I would even find my courage again and take Ellie and Red to a show.

And for some reason, there was a boy who cared about me more than anyone else, even though I still secretly had no idea why.

"Come on," I said, "let's go shoot some targets."

And that's what we did.

The End

Resources

Are you interested in learning more about Classical Dressage? Visit Sylvia Loch's Classical Riding Club (www.classicalriding.co.uk) for links, videos, articles and books to help you improve your position, connection and relationship with your horse. It's free to join and anyone is welcome no matter what their riding level; it's all about learning. There are even online tests and lessons you can do from the comfort of home.

Some of my favourite non-fiction horse books are; The Classical Rider by Sylvia Loch, Centered Riding by Sally Swift, That Winning Feeling by Jane Savoie, The Complete Training of Horse and Rider by Alois Podhajsky and Dressage for the New Age by Dominique Barbier. There are so many more. Do you have a favourite training book to recommend?

Are you interested in learning more about Horseback Archery? The International Horseback Archery Alliance has links to organizations in various countries as well as postal matches where you can compete from home and send in your scores. https://www.horsebackarchery.info/links

If you enjoyed Defining Gravity, Flight, Freefall or any of my other books, I'd love if you'd take a moment to write a review on any of the platforms where they are sold.

Astrid's Series

Defining Gravity
Flight
Freefall
Crosswind (Coming Winter 2018)

Short Stories

The Horses of Winter

The Strange Adventures of Carolina Brown

The Opposite of Living
An Aching in the Bone
Wayfarer's End

Visit my website at www.genevievemckay.com
Follow on Twitter @Geners_Mckay
Or join my Facebook author page:
www.facebook.com/authorgenevievemckay

Acknowledgments

Huge thanks to my fabulous editor Jinxie Gervasio who always laughs and cries in the right places and is full of good advice.

Massive appreciation, in no particular order, to Heather Stewart of Sweet Water Stables, Helen Yeo, Helen Cartwright, Jules Kirby, Mariko Brown, Jennifer Warburton and the rest of the beta reading team. Your help was invaluable!

Fabulous cover design credit goes to *Cover Design by James, GoOnWrite.com*

Interior design credit goes to the wonderful folks at Polgarus Studio.

And last, but not least, many thanks to Messenger and Champers who are the kindest, most generous of teachers.

Genevieve Mckay is a seven-time novelist and horse enthusiast living with her family on the wet and wonderful West Coast. She has two fantastic horses and an assortment of other farm critters. She is an enthusiastic, if not very accurate, archer.

Made in the USA
Middletown, DE
10 December 2018